continued . . .

A Gala
Event

Sheila Connolly

BERKLEY PRIME CRIME, NEW YORK

BERKLEY
PRIME
CRIME

An imprint of Penguin Random House LLC
375 Hudson Street, New York, New York 10014

A GALA EVENT

A Berkley Prime Crime Book / published by arrangement with the author

ISBN: 978-0-425-27581-8

PUBLISHING HISTORY
Berkley Prime Crime mass-market edition / October 2015

PRINTED IN THE UNITED STATES OF AMERICA

10 9 8 7 6 5 4 3 2 1

Cover illustration by Mary Ann Lasher.
Interior text design by Laura K. Corless.

Penguin
Random
House

Acknowledgments

One of the characteristics of old New England towns is that the past is always present. But the towns keep changing. My characters in the fictional Granford keep finding that out, especially when old crimes resurface—and can be solved now. (The real town on which Granford is based is much luckier: they've had only two murders in the past decade. I've apologized to the police chief there for increasing his homicide rate.)

Life in Granford moves on, and so do my characters Meg and Seth. Two years after they met, they're finally getting married. Some people say that marriage spoils the romantic tension of a series. I disagree: I think these two people belong together. I hope you'll feel the same way.

I want to thank Norm Abram of *This Old House* and a trustee for Old Sturbridge Village, for giving Seth (and me—yes, I asked) permission to install a Victorian-style bathroom in a house that dates from 1760. The reality is, there wouldn't have been a bathroom at all until the nineteenth century, so that's the earliest option. And, yes, Massachusetts requires official inspections for just about everything in a house.

The town of Granford would not continue to exist without

the ongoing help and support of my agent, Jessica Faust of BookEnds, and my editor, Tom Colgan of Berkley Prime Crime, and I am grateful. And the series would never have happened or gone forward without the guidance of Sisters in Crime and the warm enthusiasm of the Guppies.

1

"Hey, ladies, how're you doing?" Meg Corey leaned on the fence that surrounded the goat pen outside her house and watched her two goats, Dorcas and Isabel, munching on their hay. They stared back with their weird eyes, then returned to pulling out clumps of hay from the bale.

"I know, food is more interesting than I am," Meg said. Still, she kept watching, mostly because she could: for the first time in the past few months, she had the leisure to pursue unimportant things, like goat-watching. The harvest from her orchard was almost complete, with only a few apples lingering on the trees now in November. She'd put in plenty of hours picking apples alongside her hired pickers and her orchard manager, Bree, and now she gave herself the right to take a break. She was management, wasn't she? Not that the goats seemed to care, as long as their food showed up on time.

But after a few more minutes, she was feeling the chill

in the autumn air. A cup of coffee sounded good. Meg turned around to head for her kitchen door—and came face-to-face with an unfamiliar creature. Its head was about five feet off the ground, and it was covered with fuzzy wool. Not a sheep—she would recognize that, and besides, its neck was too long. Short ears, doe-like eyes. It regarded her steadily, checking her out much as she was checking it out.

"Seth?" she called out. The last time she'd seen her fiancé, Seth Chapin, he'd gone up the stairs to his office over the shed at the back end of the driveway. Of course, if the windows were shut he probably couldn't hear her. At the sound of her voice, the animal had taken a startled step backward, but it was still staring at her. "Seth?" she called a bit more loudly.

She heard a window opening, and Seth stuck his head out. "You want something?"

"Uh, we have company?" she told him, waving her hand at Large Fuzzy Creature. Creature had turned its head toward Seth at the sound of his voice, but now returned to its steady contemplation of Meg.

She could have sworn that Seth smiled, but all he said was, "Be right down." She heard the window shut again. The goats had come over to the fence line and were now doing their own checking out of the newcomer, who showed no particular interest in them. He—or she?—seemed to prefer Meg. She thought briefly about trying to shoo it away, but it didn't look hostile, or seem afraid of humans, and she wasn't sure where it belonged or which way it would go.

Seth came up behind her, now definitely smiling. "Oh, I forgot to tell you—we have new neighbors. This is one of them."

"Yes, you did forget to mention that. First of all, what is it?"

"It's an alpaca."

"What I know about alpacas might fill an index card. Don't they produce yarn?"

"So I'm told. I can't speak from experience."

"Okay, Alpaca, nice to meet you," Meg said, in the interest of interspecies friendship. "I assume the alpaca didn't sign a lease or take out a mortgage?"

"No, that would be the Gardners. They retired from city jobs and decided to find a place in the country and raise alpacas. They bought a chunk of land up toward Amherst—it's too steep for most farmers to bother with, but apparently alpacas like hills, at least sometimes. I think they originated in Peru—that's where the Andes are, if you recall."

"Should we tell the Gardners that one of their, uh, flock is here?"

"Probably—and I think it's called a herd. They aren't supposed to roam around. I'm pretty sure there's a town ordinance about livestock getting loose, although I can't remember if it says anything specific about alpacas."

"A phone number for the Gardners would help, Seth, unless you want to make friends with this fine specimen of alpaca here. Although I think it likes me better than you, but I wouldn't want Dorcas and Isabel to get jealous."

"I've probably got it in my office—I'll be just a sec." With that he turned and walked quickly toward the stairs to his office, leaving Meg face-to-face with the alpaca, who did not seem at all disconcerted. At least it wasn't a bull or something large and hostile. "I wish I knew your name. How'd you get loose, anyway? I bet your people miss you. And your friends." How many alpacas were there in the herd? Meg wondered.

The alpaca appeared to become bored with Meg, and wandered over to the goat pen, where the animals exchanged tentative sniffs across the fence. At least they weren't fighting.

Seth reappeared quickly. "Someone is on the way. Their place is only a couple of miles from here, as the crow flies. Or, in this case, as the alpaca . . . what? Lopes? Trots? Shambles?"

"Take your pick. I'd offer you some coffee or something, but I don't want this lovely creature to get into any trouble or wander off. I don't know anything about their habits, and I'd hate to see it end up in front of a car on the road. It seems kind of trusting." Meg eyed the animal's shaggy fur. "I'd like to pet it, but I'm not sure it would be happy about that."

"Better not to, for now. We can ask its owner if it's friendly. Although I see what you mean—you kind of want to bury your fingers in the fur."

Only a few minutes had passed when a battered car towing a small animal trailer crept into Meg's driveway. A large woman with short, silvery hair climbed out. "Sorry, sorry—I hope she didn't cause you any trouble. Lulu, get your hairy butt over here!" The alpaca just stared at her. "Well, it was worth a try—they seldom come when called, unless there's food involved. I've got a bridle. Mind opening the back gate on the carrier, Seth?"

"No problem, Patty." Seth walked over and opened the gate, while the woman sweet-talked Lulu the alpaca while slipping the bridle over her head. Meg almost giggled, because it looked like the alpaca gave a small sigh of regret at losing her short-lived freedom.

"Come on, baby, be a good girl," the older woman said, leading the animal to the carrier. It walked in peacefully enough, and the woman secured the gate behind it, checking it twice. Then she came back to where Seth and Meg were standing. "I'm really sorry about that. Oh, I'm Patty Gardner—I just moved in a couple of weeks ago, a mile or two north of here. You must be Meg—Seth's mentioned you. Our house is in pretty good shape, and there's some okay pasture, but the fences leave a lot to be desired, and we haven't had time to make the full circuit and patch them. But I didn't mean to barge in on you like this."

"Don't worry about it, please. Yes, I'm Meg Corey—I live here, and I have an orchard up the hill, as you can see. I haven't even been here two years myself. I'd ask you in for coffee or tea, but I'm guessing you want to get Lulu home again?"

Patty smiled. "Yes, I do, and I need to figure out where she broke through the fence and if any of her pals followed her—I could be chasing alpacas all night."

"How many do you have?"

"Fifteen at the moment. It's a small herd by most standards—what they call a foundation herd. We're pretty new at this, so we're starting small, but we'll be breeding them. We want to expand once we get the hang of it, and get some more of the pasture fenced in."

"Why alpacas, if you don't mind my asking?" Meg said. Seth had said the woman was retired, but she looked strong enough to handle an alpaca.

"Well, they're not too big—Lulu here is full-grown—and they're sociable, at least with each other. They can look after themselves. They're pretty quiet, except they hum now and then. They don't eat too much. And there's a market for their wool. And I should warn you—they spit, mostly at each other, but sometimes at people. It can be kind of nasty."

"Got it. So if I see another alpaca wander by, I should call you?"

"I'm the only herder around, as far as I know. Right, Seth?"

"At least within town limits. You're breaking new ground here, Patty."

"Beats wrangling government regulations—I've had my

fill of that." Patty turned to Meg. "Can I get a rain check on that coffee? I'd like to get to know my neighbors."

"Sure. My harvest is almost over, and now all I have to worry about is planning our wedding, which is less than a month away. Right, Seth?"

"You've got it." Seth smiled. Meg smiled back.

"Then I guess congratulations are in order. Look, I'd better get Lulu back and hope she doesn't tell all her herd buddies how much fun it is out here. Thanks for snagging her. See you later, I hope." Patty strode off to her car, carefully maneuvered the trailer behind until she was pointed toward the road, then pulled away. Meg and Seth watched them go.

"Well, that was fun," Meg said when they were out of sight. "Is it just me, or is an alpaca a supremely silly-looking creature?"

"What, you're judging solely on appearance?" Seth exclaimed in mock horror. "As Patty informed us, they're fairly nice animals. You've been lucky with Dorcas and Isabel, right?"

"I have, although I don't think goats and alpacas are related. But I stand corrected: I will reserve judgment about the nature of alpacas, especially since now I have to live with them as neighbors. Can we go inside now? I'm freezing."

"Shoot, I was hoping to get something done this afternoon. Never does seem to work out that way, does it?"

"Not often enough. But the alpaca invasion was not my fault. If anything, it's yours. Doesn't Granford have a fence-walker or something?"

"Not for the past couple of centuries. I vote for coffee—I think you're turning blue."

"Not my best color," Meg said, leading the way into the kitchen. Once inside, she shucked off her coat and set about boiling water. "Would you rather have tea?" she asked Seth.

"Coffee's good. Where's Bree?"

"Still up the hill, I think. But we're down to the last couple of varieties. Maybe she's hiding out just to avoid the paperwork. She owes me the year-end summary, or at least an estimate. Maybe it's bad news and she doesn't want to know."

"I can sympathize—I hate the paperwork part of my business, but if I don't send invoices, I don't get paid. Where are we on . . . well, everything else?"

"East of nowhere, I'm afraid." Meg poured water over coffee grounds. "We've asked Christopher to officiate, but I don't know if he's done anything about getting the special license, and I'm not sure how long that takes." Christopher was a professor at the nearby University of Massachusetts campus and had managed the orchard, mainly as a teaching tool, before she had shown up and decided to take it on. And he'd recommended Bree, for which she would be forever grateful to him. "I told Nicky and Brian to hold the date at the restaurant, but we haven't talked about food or drink or even set the time. You and I need to get our own paperwork in order, for the state. Have you decided what to do about a best man?"

"I figure it's got to be Art."

Meg filled two mugs with coffee and brought them to the kitchen table. She sat down with a sigh of relief. "That's fine with me, although of course it's your choice. And if anything goes wrong, we'll have the law on hand to handle it."

"Heaven forbid. What about you?" Seth asked.

"Maid of honor? Or matron? Normally I'd ask Rachel, but either she'll be about to pop with the baby, or she'll be exhausted from dealing with a newborn. Of course she and her family are invited, but I'll leave it up to her to decide whether she can face coming and how long to stay. So that kind of leaves Gail, who's the best friend I've got around here. Do you know, I've probably spent more time with her than almost anyone else in Granford? Except you, of course. But I haven't asked her yet."

"I like Gail. See? We've made a pair of decisions already: Art and Gail. You know, it's a wonder we ever managed to get invitations sent out."

"Don't remind me," Meg said fervently. "I cringe every time I go into town, worrying that I forgot to invite someone. But the restaurant holds only so many people safely. Anyway, it's your fault—you grew up here, and you know everybody in town. I think my own list had about ten names on it."

"They'll understand, I'm sure. If it turns out that the other half of the population of Granford is miffed at us, then we'll just have to throw another party. Maybe a solstice party."

"You can plan that one," Meg said. "But I guess we're making progress. I've alerted my parents, but we haven't pinned down when they're going to arrive. I'd really rather they didn't stay here. Oh, and we need rings, don't we? And I have no idea what I'm wearing."

"About them staying here . . ." Seth began slowly.

"You don't want them to? Or you do?" Meg protested before he could finish. She wasn't sure which answer she wanted to hear.

"No, I'm happy to have them. But I'm guessing that one reason you don't want to put them up is because of the bath-room situation."

"You'd be right. The one bath is barely adequate for the three of us, and I can't imagine adding two more people to the mix. Why do you bring that up?"

"I've been thinking . . . I want to give you something special as a wedding present, and I thought maybe an over-haul of the plumbing of this place would be good. Are you horrified?" Seth looked uncharacteristically uncertain.

Meg was momentarily speechless, and then she burst out

laughing. "I love it! Nothing says true love like plumbing."
Seth looked bewildered, as if unsure of what she was saying,
so she took pity on him. "Seriously, Seth, I think it's a terrific idea. What did you have in mind?" *And when will you
find the time?* Meg added to herself.

"I was thinking that I could carve out a smaller bath from
that niche in the master bedroom—shower only—without
taking anything away from the main bathroom. Although
all the pipes there definitely need to be replaced. And if I'm
going to have things opened up anyway, I thought I could
add a powder room directly beneath it at the same time."

"That would be amazing, Seth," Meg said, and meant it.
"But we will have one functional bathroom throughout the
whole construction process, right?"

"Of course. And everything that shows will be historically
accurate, at least on the surface. I figured you'd want some
say in picking out the fixtures. Whenever you have the time."

"I love the way you think, Seth Chapin. I think it's a
brilliant idea. And I have no idea how I'm going to match it."

He smiled, clearly pleased by the success of his suggestion. "Don't worry about it. This is kind of a shared gift
anyway—I'll be happy not to have to fight either you or Bree
for time at the mirror while I'm trying to shave."

"I haven't dared ask Bree what she wants to do about
living arrangements. I'm sure she'd rather not intrude in our
newlywed bliss, but I can't afford to pay her enough to rent
someplace nearby. Or at least, I don't think I can. I won't
know until after she's run the numbers for our sales and
expenses. Are we really supposed to figure all this out in
the next couple of weeks? Oh, and by the way, are we planning a honeymoon?"

Seth looked stricken. "Do you want one?" he said
anxiously.

Meg burst out laughing at the look on his face. "If you could see yourself! Sure, you know me—I'm pining for a week in the Bahamas, with well-oiled pool boys bringing me endless fruity drinks with umbrellas in them."

"Then you shouldn't be marrying a plumber," Seth responded.

"Excuse me, a specialist in period home renovations with a growing client list," Meg corrected him. "And don't worry about it. The idea of sitting here and catching up on the last six months' worth of . . . well, just about everything sounds like perfection to me."

"Amen," Seth said. "Although maybe we could try a restaurant or two."

"Or a weekend in Boston?"

"Don't get ahead of yourself, woman!" he said in mock anger. Then his tone softened. "Happy?"

Meg smiled. "I am. Very. It will all work out."

2

Meg's cell phone rang as they were finishing their coffee. She fished it out of her pocket to see the restaurant's number. "Hey, Nicky or Brian. What's up?"

"It's Nicky. Things are quiet at the moment, and we wondered if you wanted to come over and discuss wedding plans now?"

Meg checked her watch: just past three. "Sounds great—Seth and I were just talking about all the planning we still have to do. You want him there?" She looked up to see Seth shaking his head vigorously. "Or maybe we should rough out something and I can show it to him."

"Either way is fine. So we'll see you in a few?"

"I'll be there." Meg hung up and turned to Seth. "What, you don't want to talk about menus?"

"I trust you. And I eat just about anything, as you know. Just include something for the vegetarians and vegans and we'll be fine."

"I don't have to have carrot cake, do I? Because there's a lot about traditional weddings that I won't miss, but I want an indulgent, over-the-top cake."

"I'm not going to argue." Seth stood up. "Well, those invoices are calling my name. See you at dinner. Don't go too crazy—but I haven't had a bad dish at Gran's since it opened."

"I'll try to control myself, and I'll listen to Nicky's ideas. I agree—she's a great chef, and we're lucky to have her in town. Happy invoicing!"

"Yeah, right," Seth muttered as he went out the back door.

Meg was beginning to understand why people eloped: it was so simple. She had never been all that interested in weddings, and the few friends she'd kept in touch with from her pre-Granford days seemed to be avoiding marriage altogether, although most of them had a partner of some description. Meg had considered the idea of living with Seth—briefly— but rejected it. The reality was, Seth was spending about ninety percent of his time at her house, but that was not the same as standing up and declaring your intentions to spend your life together in front of your friends and your community. She and Seth hadn't explored the concept in much detail—after all, he'd been married once before, and that hadn't worked out. He was surprisingly unbitter about the end of that relationship, and would only go so far as to say that he and Nancy had discovered that they wanted different things from their lives, and had parted on reasonably good terms. But he wanted the public declaration of their joining now, maybe more than she did.

In an odd way, Meg felt like she was marrying the town by marrying Seth. His Chapin ancestors had helped settle the town of Granford over two centuries earlier. Of course, her Warrens hadn't been far behind, but Meg hadn't grown up in the town, the way Seth had. But Seth didn't just live in Granford—he helped run the place, as an elected select-man, which was an unpaid and occasionally thankless task.

But she'd never pored over *Brides* magazine, never oohed and aahed about dresses and table decorations. She hadn't talked any of this over with her mother, Elizabeth, but she had a sneaking feeling that Elizabeth was simply happy to see her getting married at all. Seth's mother, Lydia, who lived just over the hill, was equally laid-back about the whole thing. So it was up to Meg to make the myriad of decisions about what and where and how this was going to happen. She realized that in her mind she visualized one large happy party that happened to include a small element that would make Seth and her a legal entity in the eyes of the state and country. Whatever that meant. With a sigh, she stood up, pulled on her jacket, and went out to her car to drive the couple of miles to the restaurant.

The sight of Gran's, housed in a sturdy Victorian building perched on a low hill at the end of the town green, never failed to cheer her up. Meg was proud that she had played a role in creating it—not with the cooking (Nicky handled that brilliantly) but by figuring out a way to make it finan-cially possible in a highly competitive area by involving local providers as partners. It had worked well, and the res-taurant had been open a year now. It was even drawing visi-tors from the surrounding college-based communities like Amherst and Northampton, and that was high praise indeed from the local foodie community. She parked beside the building and walked up the front steps. Nicky opened the front door before Meg reached it.

"Welcome, blushing bride!" Nicky said, throwing her arms around Meg. "I'm so glad you chose us for this won-derful event."

Apparently Nicky was more excited about the wedding than Meg was. "The blushing part I've got down pat—it's the 'bride' part that still boggles me."

"Ha! You and Seth are made for each other. Any dummy could see that."

"Considering that I started my career in Granford with a murder in my backyard and by creating chaos at a town meeting, that's a small miracle. How've you been, Nicky? How's business?"

"Great, to both. Come in, sit down. I made some nibbles for us—this planning stuff is hungry work."

Meg complied. "Will Brian be joining us?"

"Nah. I'll tell him what the plan is, and he'll make it happen. Besides, he thinks this is girly stuff."

Meg smiled. "I have a sneaking suspicion that Seth feels the same way. He's more or less said, 'whatever you want.'"

"Well, what do you want?"

"I want a party where people have a good time."

Nicky eyed her. "Oh, sure, no problem. We'll just order up a bunch of good-time supplies. Okay, let's start with the basics. The date is December fourth—that's a Friday. Why not Saturday or Sunday?"

"It was my grandmother's birthday, and she was one of my favorite people. I see it as kind of an easygoing event, after work for some people. I haven't invited a lot of people from out of town, so it will be mostly the people Seth and I know around here."

"Well, since we're talking about Seth, that's the entire town. How did you narrow down the list?"

"It wasn't easy, believe me. I'm sure somebody's feelings will be hurt. Or I'll just blame it on you and Brian and those pesky fire regulations."

Nicky grinned. "Okay, I'll take the heat. And I wouldn't

expect Seth to bend the rules about capacity, even for his own wedding."

"Don't forget that the entire select board of Granford and the chief of police will be here, too," Meg added.

"Exactly. We can't just stuff people in willy-nilly. The place might collapse. How're the RSVPs going?"

"About fifty percent so far," Meg told her. "Not too many 'nos' either."

"Of course there aren't," Nicky replied quickly. "People have been betting on when you two would figure things out for the past year—they wouldn't miss it." Nicky got a faraway look in her eye. "Of course, we might be able to enclose the porch with removable panels and some portable heaters—that would give you some more capacity. But we'd have to be sure the porch can take the weight. I'll have to ask Brian about that." Nicky made a note on the pad of paper she had brought to the table. "Okay, next. Sit-down or buffet?"

"Shoot, I don't want a formal thing with fancy tablecloths and six forks and three-foot centerpieces on the tables. Buffet is fine. And no assigned seating—let people sit where they want and with whoever they want."

"Open bar? Champagne only?"

Meg sighed. "Rough me out some numbers on that, will you?" She knew that an open bar could get expensive, but it seemed stingy to offer guests only one option for liquid refreshment, and cash bars were kind of tacky for a personal event.

"What kind of food?" Nicky was as relentless as a drill sergeant.

"Buffet food?" Meg ventured.

"Hot or cold?" Nicky snapped.

Meg held up a hand. "Nicky, I love your food. Why don't you suggest a menu? And since this will be in December, I guess there had better be some hot food in there somewhere. But not too drippy."

"Got it." Nicky made another note. "I'll e-mail you some choices. Decorations?"

"Well, it's after Thanksgiving, but I don't want a Christmas theme. Greenery?"

"How about pine boughs with a few nice red apples thrown in? That would look back to your harvest, and forward to the winter season."

"Perfect. I'll supply the apples, if you'll tell me what you need."

"Maybe a few real candles with hurricane globes—exposed candles always make me nervous, especially with greenery around. Too easy to tip over."

"I hear you. Are we done yet?"

"Of course not. One big cake, or individual ones?"

"I told Seth I wanted an extravagant wedding cake. That's the one thing I remember from most of the weddings I've ever been to. Can you do that here?"

"Of course I can. Flavor?"

"Whatever you do best. And like to make."

"Red velvet cake? With white frosting and red sugar apples?" Now Nicky had a wicked gleam in her eye.

"Fine. Wonderful. How much is all of this going to cost us?" Meg said.

Nicky looked at her directly. "I wish I could say it's on the house, since we both owe you so much. But the business can't take that. How about I charge you what the ingredients cost us? Of course, additional waitstaff will be extra. And the liquor, of course. But our labor will be our gift to you two."

Meg was touched. "Nicky, that seems more than fair to me. Thank you."

Nicky grinned. "Don't thank me until you've seen the

bill. But I won't load things up with filet mignon and truffles. Call it the best of New England, locally raised."

"I love it. Is that all?"

"For now. I'll send you over a proposal, and we can fine-tune it. How's the harvest look?"

"Not bad, all things considered. We survived." Despite a drought and an insect invasion and a small forest fire. "I'm hoping we can afford a pump for the wellhead this year, which will make our lives a whole lot easier in case we get hit by another drought."

"And Seth's business?"

"Still kind of transitional, I guess. Plumbing jobs pay the bills, but his heart is in historic renovations, which are rarer. He's still getting his name out there. And then he gives time to things like the overhaul of the Historical Society, which he did pro bono. Have you been inside yet?"

"No time. But I have to say, I was impressed that it came in on time and on budget. That's unusual anywhere. And Seth must have had a hand in that."

"He has a hand in just about anything that goes on in Granford." Meg checked the time—nearly five. "Nicky, I must be keeping you from your own work. Don't you have to prep for tonight's meal?"

"I do, but I wanted to make sure I got things squared away with you. Like I said, we owe you big-time, and I'll do everything I can to make sure this event is something special."

Meg felt the prick of tears. "Thank you, Nicky. That means a lot to me."

Loud noises of clattering pans came from the kitchen, and Nicky stood up quickly. "Oops, gotta go. I'll get you that estimate later this week, okay?"

"That's fine. Thanks again."

Outside on the porch, Meg took a deep breath of the

autumn air. There was a hint of smoke—were people already using their fireplaces? Should she have hers cleaned? Did they have any firewood? *Stop it, Meg! Just enjoy the moment, all right?* The town green looked lovely. The light was already fading, now that it was past five. The steeple of the white church at the other end of the green soared into the deep blue twilight sky. Meg noticed that there were lights on at the Historical Society just down the hill from it. Was it still open? It shouldn't be, but maybe Gail Seldon was trying to catch up on cataloging, or setting up the new exhibits. Renovation had been completed only a month or so earlier, and then they'd had to wait to install new shelving in the newly dug basement, and then they'd had to paint, and so on. So while Gail had gleefully assembled the Society's collections from the buildings across the town, where they'd been "temporarily" stored, some for as long as a quarter century, she still hadn't had time to update the cataloging so she knew what they had. But she also wanted to make the place welcoming, by arranging new exhibits that showcased the local historical objects. And somehow she had to squeeze in time for her husband and their two school-age children.

Meg decided to walk over and say hi to Gail, if it was indeed her. It could be one or another of the Society's board members, but she knew most of them as well. If it was Gail and she was alone, maybe Meg would have the chance to ask her about being matron of honor. Meg walked down the porch steps, then crossed the road and the length of the green.

Only a few of the lights inside were on—saving electricity?—and the door stood partially open. Meg rapped on it. "Hello? Gail?" she called out. There was no answering voice from inside, but Meg could hear a peculiar mewling sound. Human? Animal? She pushed the door open and stepped inside, through the unlit foyer, into the single big room beyond. And stopped in her tracks.

Gail was at the far end of the room, leaning heavily on an old kitchen table—the corner was given over to a mock-up of a kitchen circa 1900. The strange noises were coming from her, and as Meg took in the scene she realized that Gail was covered with blood.

3

Meg rushed across the room and grabbed Gail gently by her arms. "Gail? What happened?" Even as she asked, she scanned Gail's body for any injuries—and didn't find any.

It took Gail a moment to stop hyperventilating and focus on Meg. "Meg?" she whispered. "What are you doing here?"

"I saw the lights on and I thought I'd stop by. Is all this blood yours?"

Gail looked down at herself. "Oh my God! No, it's not mine!"

Both she and Meg seemed to realize at the same moment that Gail was clutching an odd object in her hand, something that Meg couldn't immediately identify. But it was clear that it was completely covered with blood. "Gail, can you put that down, please?" Meg said softly.

Gail reacted with horror and dropped it suddenly. It clattered on the tabletop and spun for a moment. But Meg was distracted when Gail slumped against her, and she guided her to the nearest chair. If it was a priceless antique, she didn't care, because Gail's legs didn't seem to support her. "Are you sure you're not hurt?"

"No, I'm fine," she said, her voice stronger. She took a deep breath. "There was a man . . ."

Meg stopped her. "If all this blood is his, I think we need to call Art. Is that okay?"

"Wait! Check and see if he's anywhere in the building. He must be hurt, bleeding like this."

Gail had a point. The man could be dying in a dark corner in the building, or outside. Art could wait for two minutes while Meg took a brief look around. "Will you be okay if I go look, Gail?"

Gail nodded without speaking.

Meg took a quick scan of the room, then crossed to the door to the foyer and turned on the lights—all the lights. She looked around again, and immediately saw a trail of blood drops leading from the kitchen corner to the front door, where she had entered. She felt a surge of relief: the man wasn't in the building. He'd left. She thought for a moment: when she'd been standing on the porch at the restaurant, had she seen anybody on or near the green? She couldn't remember noticing any movement, apart from the cars on the main road. So he'd been gone for a few minutes, the time it had taken her to cross the green. But how far could he have gone, if he was losing that much blood?

She went back to the corner where Gail was sitting, At least her breathing had returned to normal, but she had her arms wrapped around herself. She looked up when Meg approached. "Anything?"

"No. Looks like he went out the front. Gail, I want to hear your story, but let me get Art over here so you don't have to repeat yourself. Is your family expecting you at home?"

"No, thank God. I told my husband I wanted to work late, and he said he'd pick up the kids and feed them and take them to a movie. I'd hate to have them see me like this." She looked down at the blood that covered her front, now darkening and stiffening.

"I'll call Art. Can I get you something first? A glass of water? A cup of tea?" Meg tried to recall what you were supposed to do for shock and came up blank. Sugar? "Are you warm enough?"

"Meg, just call, will you? The heat works fine," Gail snapped.

Meg stepped into the foyer to make the call. After five; would he still be in his office? Luckily he was, and Meg was put through quickly. "Hey, Meg. How're things going?" he said. "I don't see much of that guy of yours."

"Art, no time for small talk," Meg spoke quickly. "There's a problem at the Historical Society, and I think you'd better get over here."

"What's wrong?" Art's tone had changed quickly, and now he was the Granford chief of police instead of a friend.

"I came by and found the door open, and when I walked in, I found Gail Selden here, covered with blood. Not hers— somebody else's. But whoever it was isn't in the building now."

"I'm on my way." He hung up abruptly. Meg calculated it would take him no more than five minutes to get to the town green. Should she call Seth? She almost laughed: Why should she call Seth? What was he supposed to do? After she'd talked to Art, or watched Gail talk to Art, if he let her stay, then she could call to say she'd be late for dinner. She could explain then.

She went back to Gail's side. "He'll be right over. Are you sure you're all right?"

"I'm not hurt, if that's what you mean. I'm scared and rattled and pissed at the whole situation. What could anybody want here? It's not like we've got any money—maybe twenty bucks in singles for the souvenirs up front. And it's not like we've got scads of valuable antiques, either."

"Maybe a homeless guy looking for someplace to keep warm? It is getting cold out there," Meg suggested.

Gail just shrugged. They waited in silence until they heard a car pull up outside. Meg went to open the front door. When Art climbed out of his car, Meg said, "There's a blood trail on the front steps here. I didn't notice it when I came in, so I've already tramped through it."

"Nice to see you, too, Meg. Duly noted. Gail inside?" Art stepped carefully only on the edges of the massive granite slab that made up the front step.

"Yes. She seems to be holding up okay. I haven't asked her anything, once I was sure that she wasn't the one who was bleeding."

"Thanks, Meg." Art preceded her into the big main room and stopped in his tracks; apparently he hadn't expected to see quite so much blood. Meg suppressed a smile, which was wildly inappropriate: had he thought she was exaggerating?

"Gail, you okay?" he said, advancing cautiously, watching where he put his feet.

"Hi, Art. Physically, yes. Otherwise . . . I'll let you know later."

"What can you tell me?"

Apparently he wasn't going to throw her out, so Meg went to what she knew was a small storage closet at the back of the room and brought out two folding chairs. She gave one to Art, who nodded, then sat in the other, next to Gail.

Gail took a deep breath. "I was working on setting up the kitchen exhibit, unpacking some stuff I hadn't seen before. There was no one else here. It was just before five, but I hadn't locked up yet. I mean, why would I? There's nothing here worth stealing. So I'm pulling stuff out of the packing box, and I look up and there's this guy standing in the doorway. I say, 'We're closed,' or something like that, but he just keeps standing there. Finally he says, 'You run this place?' and I say, 'Yes, but you'll have to come back some other day.' I mean, if it was somebody I knew, I wouldn't mind chatting, but this guy was kind of weird."

"Can you describe him?" Art asked.

"Tall, maybe a bit over six feet—I'm just guessing. Skinny. Older than me. Dark hair with a lot of gray in it, short but badly cut. His clothes were kind of nondescript—I mean, there was nothing much to notice. He wore clothes. Jeans, shirt, jacket, running shoes. Nothing that stood out. But he acted odd—he just kept staring at me. Then he said, 'You keep all the stuff from Granford here?' And I told him again, 'You'll have to come back some other time.' But he just looked at me. So I came out from behind the table and said, 'I'm closing up now. You'll have to leave,' and he wouldn't go. And then he took a step closer, and I backed up. When I put my hand on the table behind me, it landed on that." Gail pointed toward the bloody object lying on the table.

"What the heck is that?" Art asked.

"It's a food chopper, circa 1880. It was part of the collection that I was unpacking."

"So you picked up the chopper. Then what?"

"The guy took another step closer, until he was about

two feet away from me. And I guess I panicked, and I just slashed out at him with that chopper. It has a really sharp blade."

"I'll bet it does. I'm guessing you connected with him?"

"I did. If you ask me where, I can't tell you. He was so startled, I don't think he even tried to defend himself. I may have shut my eyes and swung at him a couple of times. When I opened my eyes again, he was standing there, staring at his hands, which were covered with blood. And then he looked at me, and turned and ran out the front door."

"How'd you end up with all that blood on you?" Art asked carefully.

Gail looked down at herself and finally realized the implications. "Oh God, I must have hit something important! He could be out there bleeding to death, if he's not already dead. You've got to find him!"

"Gail, keep it together," Art said. "Yes, you might have hit an artery, but that doesn't mean he's dead. I'll call a couple of guys from the station and we'll look for him. Too bad it's getting dark out there."

"Find him! Please?"

"We will, Gail. Meg, you have anything to add?"

She shook her head. "No. I was up at Gran's, and I took a moment to look out at the green, and saw the lights on here. Then I walked over from there. I didn't see anyone. I stopped in here because I thought it was probably Gail inside. That was just after five. So this guy has to have left before that, though not by much. And he's been out there bleeding for over half an hour now." Unless he was already dead, in which case he would have stopped bleeding. No, Meg wasn't about to say that out loud.

"I'll call the station," Art said, then walked a few feet away.

"What if I killed him?" Gail whispered. "What possessed me? I mean, it wasn't like he was threatening me or anything. I didn't see anything in his hands. I was just so surprised to see anybody else in the building. He seemed kind of . . . lost. Confused. And all I could do was lash out at him. And when he left, I couldn't even get it together to call 911."

Meg put an arm around Gail's shoulders. "Don't beat yourself up over this, Gail. He frightened you. He was coming toward you, even after you'd warned him off. All you did was defend yourself. And we don't know that he's dead." Or who he is, or what he wanted here. "Art and his guys will find him."

Art returned quickly. "Gail, if you can't think of anything else I should know, why don't you go home now? Get cleaned up? Unless, of course, you don't want the kids to see you like that?"

"They're out at a movie with my husband," Gail said. "Thanks, Art—I'd feel a whole lot better if I could get out of these." She looked down at her clothes. "Should I save them? I mean, do you need them for evidence or something?"

"Might as well keep them, I guess."

"Art," Meg interrupted, "Maybe I should drive Gail home? I don't think she's in any shape to handle driving right now. Then I could bring the clothes back to you."

"I've got a better idea," Art countered. "Let me tell the guys what they're looking for, and then you drive Gail's car to her house. I'll follow you and collect the clothes there. Chain of evidence, you know. And I'll bring you back to your car here."

Evidence of what? Being bled on? But the clothes would certainly show how much blood had been spilled. "That works. Gail, you okay with that?"

"Sure. I want the clothes out of the house as soon as possible."

"Then it's a plan." Art went out the front to greet the arriving officers, and spent a couple of minutes explaining the situation. Then he sent them out to look around the grounds. Would there be a blood trail? The light outside was all but gone—could they even see it? Which way would this person have run?

Art came back in. "Sorry to bother you again, Gail, but did you hear any cars near the building? When the guy arrived, or after he left?"

Gail shrugged. "No, but I wasn't exactly paying attention. You think this guy drove away?"

"We can't eliminate that possibility. Meg, why don't we leave now? I'll come back and give 'em a hand once we've dropped Gail off."

"Can it wait until I've cleaned up a bit?" Gail asked. "I want to wash . . . this off." She held up her arms.

"Of course, Gail," Art said gently. "Take your time."

Gail disappeared into the bathroom that had recently been added—by Seth, of course—and they could hear running water. "Hell of a thing," Art said in a low voice. "I can't remember anything like this happening in Granford. At least Gail's all right, although I'm not so sure about the other guy."

"It seemed like a lot of blood. You think it was someone just passing through? Looking for some quick cash? No, that wouldn't be right. Gail said the man asked about Granford records, so he must know the town."

Gail emerged from the bathroom and retrieved her bag from somewhere in the back of the building, and wordlessly handed the car keys to Meg. At least Meg knew the way to Gail's house, so she didn't have to give directions. Mostly they were silent, until they neared the house. "What am I going to tell my husband?" Gail whispered.

"Wait until the kids are in bed, and tell him the truth. You can decide how to explain it to the kids in the morning."

"There's bound to be something in the news," Gail protested. "If Art doesn't find him tonight, they'll have to put out a bulletin, won't they?"

"Probably. But I don't think Art's in any hurry to call the press. Let's just take it one step at a time."

Meg pulled into Gail's driveway. Before she got out of the car, Gail laid a hand on her arm. "Thanks, Meg. I'm glad you were there."

"We'll talk tomorrow." Meg climbed out of the car and handed the keys back to Gail. She stood watching until Gail had let herself into the house, then turned and walked over to where Art was waiting in his car. Once she was settled, she asked, "Anything new?"

"Nope. So you just happened to walk into this scene?"

"Yes, Art, I did. Find the guy, will you? I know Gail doesn't want you to find him dead, and neither do I."

"I'll do my best, Meg."

Gail reappeared at the door, with a large brown paper bag. Art went to the door to take it from her, said something to her, then came back to the car to drive Meg back to the green.

4

Meg finally made it home close to seven. "You're late," Bree said. "I cooked."

Meg didn't want to discourage her orchard manager and housemate when she had made one of her rare efforts to cook. "Sorry. I meant to call, but things got a little complicated." She hung up her jacket and dropped heavily into a chair at the kitchen table.

Seth walked in through the outside door, took one look at her and said, "What's wrong?"

Bree turned around from the stove, startled by Seth's question. "What? What're you talking about?" She gave Meg a harder look. "Okay, what's going on?"

Am I really so easy to read? Meg wondered. "I went to Gran's this afternoon to talk with Nicky about plans for the wedding—I'll fill you in later, Seth. After we were done there, I noticed the lights were on at the Historical Society, and I thought Gail might be there, so I went over to say hi.

When I got there, she was there, but she was covered with blood, and it looked to me like she was in shock."

Seth sat down next to Meg and took her hand. "Is she all right?"

Meg nodded. "The weird thing is, it wasn't her blood. She said a man came in, and when he approached her and got too close, she grabbed the first thing she put her hand on, which happened to be a wickedly sharp antique chopper, and slashed at him. It looks like she connected, based on the blood all over her. She had to have hit something important, with that much spatter."

"Is the guy dead?" Bree asked.

"We don't know—he left the way he came. We called Art, of course, and he and some of his men were looking for him, but it was already getting dark."

"I'm so sorry, Meg," Seth said, and she gave him a grateful smile. "Did you see the man?"

She shook her head. "No. I must have come out of Gran's just after he left, because I didn't see anyone at all on the green."

"Did Gail know the man?" Seth asked.

"She said she didn't recognize him. Older than we are, with some gray in his hair. I wondered if he was just looking for a warm place, although since the lights were on and the door was unlocked, he must have known there was someone in the building. Gail didn't say he was armed or threatened her, but he sure scared her."

"Did Art have anything to say?" Seth asked.

"Not right then. He got Gail's story, and then we took her home so she could change before her family arrived. You haven't heard anything about a homeless guy around town, have you, Seth?"

"No, but I don't know everything that goes on. Especially since I've been so busy lately. Art would know more."

"He hasn't called?" Meg looked at Bree.

"Not while I've been here," she said.

"I don't know if that's good news or bad," Meg said. "I assume Art will call either way. Since I'm involved."

"Again," Bree said. Seth sent her a warning look, and she shot back, "What? It's true."

"She's right, you know," Meg told him.

Meg's cell phone rang, and when she pulled it from her pocket, she recognized Art's number. She glanced at Seth before answering it. "Speak of the devil." She pushed the button to connect. "Hey, Art. Any news?"

"Nope. We didn't find the guy. We lost the blood trail in the grass, and it was getting too dark to see it anyway. It's possible that either he drove away, or somebody picked him up, or he's still hiding out."

Meg noted that he didn't mention a final alternative: the man had bled out somewhere. Art surprised her by going on. "Jeez, I hate the idea of some kids stumbling over a body."

Seth gestured toward the phone, and Meg handed it to him. "Art, it's Seth. Anything we can do? Mount a wider search?" He listened intently, then ended the call before turning to Meg.

"He's alerted the area hospitals to be on the lookout for a wounded man, but he said Gail wasn't even sure what part of him she hit. You told me it bled a lot, and that much blood loss isn't good. If the hospitals don't turn up anything, Art says we may have to look more widely in the morning, when it's light. The guy can't have gone far, not in his shape."

"And of course you'll be there," Meg said.

Seth looked at her oddly. "Yes, I will. I know this town pretty well, including the best places to hide, because I grew up exploring them. Why? Did we have something planned for tomorrow?"

"Sorry, I'm in a lousy mood. No, we have no specific plans—just the buckets of usual ones. Plus wedding stuff."

"Did things go well with Nicky?" Seth asked.

"I think so. How many people do you think will come?"

"Everyone we asked?" Seth offered. "Seriously, are we okay for space?"

"So far, but a lot of people haven't responded. We were figuring a percentage wouldn't come, weren't we?"

"That place used to be a house, right?" Bree said. "Not many houses were planned to hold a hundred-plus people."

"True." Seth turned to her. "What do you suggest? Lottery? Time slots—some people come at four, others at five? You have a better idea?"

"Hey, I manage trees, not people. I'll think about it," Bree said. "Right now I've got to finish making dinner. You two need to keep your strength up for all this . . . wedding stuff."

"We could shift it all to summer and have a big tent," Meg said glumly.

"You know you don't mean that," Seth told her. "You wanted December. And I don't want to wait another six or eight months."

"I don't, either," Meg said softly.

"Cut the mushy stuff, you two—we're about ready to eat," Bree said from in front of the stove.

They ate quickly, talking about noncontroversial topics that didn't involve blood or violence—or weddings. When they had finished, Bree pushed her chair away from the table. "I cooked, so you clean up. I'm going upstairs. By the way, Michael and I have plans for tomorrow night, if you want some private whoopie time."

Meg managed to hold in a laugh until Bree had left. "Whoopie time?"

"Well, she got her message across, didn't she?"

"I guess. Problem is, either one or both of us is, er, are usually too tired for anything like whoopie."

"Maybe that's why she gave us twenty-four hours' notice."

"Could be. We still haven't talked to her about where she'll be living. You think she wants to live with Michael? Because I've gotten very mixed signals from her about that."

"One step at a time, lady. You've got a handle on the food end, even if we don't know how much or how many."

"I was going to talk to Gail about . . . you know."

"And I haven't talked to Art, either. Now we have a great opportunity. 'Hey, guys, if you can spare a minute from identifying that body there, would you two consider being in the wedding party?'"

"I don't want to laugh," Meg said. "Gail was upset, understandably. And I don't want her to feel guilty about someone else's death, even if she acted reasonably and in her own defense."

Seth's mood sobered. "I know. She doesn't deserve that. Keep your fingers crossed that the guy walked or rode away, and got whatever help he needed. Anyway, I'll take care of the dishes."

"I'll sit here and admire your efforts," Meg replied. "If I lie down now, I'll just go to sleep. No more stray alpacas?"

"Not that anyone has reported. I don't know how good they are at hiding. Lulu seemed pretty domesticated."

Meg thought for a moment. "Seth, why would anyone just walk into the Historical Society? The way that guy did? Normally it would have been closed. He must have seen the lights inside."

"I don't know. Probably not because he's fascinated by history. What other reasons would there be?"

Meg started counting on her fingers. "One we've already mentioned—a warm and quiet place, maybe just for the night.

Two, looking for cash, but Gail said they don't keep much there. Although he wouldn't have known that. But then, looking at the building, would anybody assume there's a nice drawer full of money? Three, looking to steal something. Although Gail also said that there's not much of particular financial value in the collections. Sentimental reasons? The guy had always coveted an 1870 vertical apple peeler? But how would he know there was one there?"

"Is there?"

"I don't know. Gail said she was interrupted during unpacking a collection of antique cooking implements. That's what the weapon she used was. Wicked-looking thing, I have to say. Does any one of those reasons make sense to you?"

"No. Or they all make equal sense. You know, a lot of homeless guys have psychological problems, like bipolar disorder. Maybe this man is one of those, and in that case, whatever he was thinking might not make sense to any of us, only to him. So motive won't necessarily help us to identify him."

Meg stood up. "My brain is turning to mush. I'm going upstairs. You coming?"

"Perfect timing," Seth said, as he hung up a dish towel. "Right behind you."

Once upstairs, though, Meg opted to stay vertical. "Walk me through this bathroom idea?"

"With pleasure. I don't want to lose any space in this bedroom, not that we spend a lot of time in it."

Meg leaned against him. "Quality time, not quantity. Go on."

"I'm guessing that there used to be a full room, if small, off this side—the nursery. When whoever it was built the existing bathroom, they used most of that, and left this kind of closet-slash-alcove here. Not that I'm running down closets—older houses seldom have enough for modern needs. We have too many clothes these days."

"You could take some off. Oops, not right now. So you think you can fit a bathroom in what is now a closet?"

"It's been done. It might be tight, if you actually want a door that opens and closes. But since the wall for the current bathroom is not original to the house, we can knock it down and move it if need be. And I told you, I'll have to replace the pipes in any case, so we don't lose anything by doing that."

"We will keep one bathtub, won't we?" Meg asked. "Because it's great to soak in after a long day of working in the orchard."

"Of course. But I thought you might like a real claw-foot model, if I can find an old one in good condition—they're nice and deep."

"That sounds good. And you said a powder room, too?"

"Yup. Right below the current bathroom—all the plumbing will run through the same wall space. Easy."

"If you say so. I promise I will stand by and applaud your efforts. How authentic do I have to be when I choose things?"

"Well, I think glass tiles and halogen lights might be pushing it, but I could live with a modern reinterpretation of Victorian."

"Good, because I like Victorian. With the right kind of tiles? Those hexagons?"

"Whatever you want, as long as it's not pink. I hate pink bathrooms."

"Deal." She leaned in to kiss him, and the kiss lasted. "I am a lucky woman."

"I won't argue with you. Bed?"

"Bed."

5

The distant ringing of a phone woke Meg. Her phone? Seth's? The land line? It took her foggy brain a moment to realize that Seth had climbed out of bed to retrieve his cell phone from his pants pocket, and had gone out into the hall to talk.

He was back in under a minute, and sat on the foot of the bed. "Meg?"

"Yeah, I'm awake," she mumbled into her pillow.

"That was Art. No sign of Gail's intruder, so he's bringing in some more people, including me. I'm going to go meet him at the station. I'll give you a call when we know anything more."

Meg rolled over reluctantly. "It's Saturday, right? So Art wants to get out there early before every Jane and Joe in town tramples over what evidence there might still be?"

"That's the general idea."

"Go. Find him. I may try to call Gail, but maybe she won't want to talk with anyone today, except her family. Otherwise I should be around, either in the orchard or muddling through the paperwork. Take care, will you? Even if he didn't attack Gail, we don't know that he isn't armed."

"Don't worry—I'll have half the police force of Granford to protect me."

"Don't forget, I know most of them—that's not really reassuring."

"Bye, Meg," Seth said impatiently, and leaned over to kiss her once he'd pulled on jeans and a shirt.

Meg shut her eyes after he was gone, and started making and revising her mental lists. She should call Rachel and see how she was doing. She couldn't imagine just sitting around waiting for a baby to happen. Rachel wasn't overdue yet, but she was within the normal range of her due date. And it was her third child: wouldn't it be a quick delivery? Oh, heck, Meg didn't know—her expertise was limited to a few articles she had read online.

Also on the list: call her mother. She'd been putting that off because she still wasn't sure she'd nailed down the details for The Big Event, and she didn't want to have to worry about entertaining her mother and father in the midst of the inevitable last-minute crises. Sometime soon she would have to sit down with Seth and Bree and figure out the housing situation. And she needed to ask him about a time line for his bathroom project. Did he hope to complete it before the wedding? That might be a tight schedule. She'd heard of early American barn raisings; could they hold a bath raising? The image of a bunch of men bumping into each other in a small space, working on different parts of the installation, brought a smile to her face. It would probably not speed anything up.

All right, Meg, start small with little tasks that you can accomplish. Like breakfast, for you and for Max and Lolly. That she could do, and the thought spurred her to get out of bed.

Dressed and with clean teeth, she made her way downstairs and set water to boiling for coffee, then fed Max, Seth's still-puppyish Golden Retriever, and Lolly, short for Lavinia, her rescue cat. She ground coffee, poured water over it, then took Max out the back door to do his business. While he sniffed around, choosing just the right spot, she scanned the area for any more wandering alpacas. She wondered what Max would make of an alpaca, if he met one, which would probably happen. He'd probably want to make friends, but she wasn't so sure how the alpaca would react. Did they kick? Front legs or hind legs? Luckily none wandered by, so she went back inside, poured herself a cup of coffee, and searched the refrigerator for food options.

Bree stumbled down the back stairs that led to her room over the kitchen. "God, you're up early."

"Not my idea. Art called Seth—they're calling in more people for the search."

"So the guy didn't show up at a hospital, or ask anyone for help?" Bree said. "He's either hiding or dead."

"Art didn't say, but it looks like it to me."

"I see Seth didn't take Max." Bree nodded toward the dog, now lying on the floor waiting for breakfast crumbs. "Isn't he a tracker?"

"I think the only person in the world he could find is Seth. Maybe me, if I was wearing a shirt of Seth's. I'm sure there are other dogs in town who are better prepared. Sorry, Max, but it's true," Meg said. Max wagged his tail at her. "Where are we on orchard stuff?"

"Between five and ten percent of the trees still need to be harvested. That'll run through the next week, and then I think we'll be done. And you can work on your fancy-pants wedding."

"Fancy? Ha!" Meg said. "So far what we've got is a bunch of people—number to be determined—hanging out in a local restaurant on a Friday night, presumably eating and drinking something."

"Hey, you've got a bride and groom. That's all you really need."

"Yes, but it also takes some legal paperwork, and somebody to perform the ceremony."

"I thought you asked Christopher."

"I did, but I have no idea whether he's submitted his paperwork to make it legal."

"I think you're worrying too much about the whole thing," Bree said bluntly. "I mean, you've got the guy. You're more or less living together already. What's the big fuss over some pieces of paper?"

Meg struggled to answer that. "It's not so much the paperwork, at least until there are children involved. It's more about celebrating a landmark in our lives, with our community and friends and relatives. Maybe I'm old-fashioned, but I think making a formal commitment, with witnesses, makes a psychological difference to everyone. Maybe your generation thinks differently."

"Meg, I'm only ten years younger than you—that's not a generation. But we're coming from different places, I guess—and I'm not talking about countries."

"I think I know what you mean." Meg sighed. "My mother's generation was all riled up about feminism and equality. I support those in principle, but I can't see that a whole lot has changed since her day. Women still make less money than men, in the same jobs. And men still get the better-paying, more important jobs."

"So what's the point of getting married?"

"Commitment, I guess. Believing in something—or someone—and standing up and working for it. Maybe it's not for everybody, but that's our choice. What about you and Michael?"

"Apples and oranges," Bree said tersely.

Meg was wondering whether this was the time to broach the subject of living arrangements, but then her phone rang: Gail. She answered quickly.

"Gail, are you all right? Have they found him?"

"I'm okay, I think. No, I haven't heard from Art or anyone else."

"Do you need something? I'd be happy to help out."

"What I could use is some company. My husband is treating me like I might break if he looks cross-eyed at me, and we still haven't said anything to the kids. He said he'd keep them busy today. Listen, Meg, I hate to ask this, but could you take me to the Historical Society and hang out with me for a bit?"

"You sure you want to go back there? So soon after . . . And it's still got to be a mess . . ." Meg fumbled for words.

"You mean all that blood? Meg, I'm not a fainting violet. Most of it ended up on me, anyway, and on that slicer, and Art took that away. But right now I figure it's like getting thrown from a horse—you've got to get right back on."

"Gail, have you ever ridden a horse?" Meg asked.

"No, but I subscribe to the theory. Will you come?"

"Of course I will. I'll pick you up and drive you over. And if you chicken out, I'll turn around and take you home. Or to lunch. Up to you."

"Thanks, Meg. I'll owe you one."

"See you in fifteen," Meg replied firmly, and hung up. She turned to Bree. "You heard all that?"

"Yeah. Good for Gail—it takes guts to face your demons.

I guess she must really care about the place. You go ahead—
I can handle stuff here. And I told you I'd be out tonight."

"Yeah, yeah, I know: whoopie. Along with crime solving
and wedding planning. My, aren't we busy people?"

"You got that right," Bree said. "I'll see you when I see you."

Meg ran upstairs, swapped her jeans for a better pair, and
set off to Gail's house. Gail was sitting on her front stoop
waiting, and she stood up when Meg arrived. Meg leaned
across the front and opened the door for her. "You look a heck
of a lot better than you did the last time I saw you," she said,
as Gail settled into her seat and fastened her seat belt.

"It's amazing what a long, hot shower will do for you. I
feel bad—I think I overreacted when I saw that guy. I mean,
he looked harmless enough. I never even gave him a chance
to talk—I just lashed out."

"Don't beat yourself up. It was late, and dark, and he
startled you. You defended yourself." Meg pulled out of the
driveway, then turned the car toward town.

"I wish they'd find him. I hate this not knowing."

Even if the worst case turns out to be true? Meg wondered, but didn't say to Gail. "Well, now that Seth has joined
the hunt, I'm sure they will," she said lightly.

"Seth sure does know this town," Gail commented. "I
don't know what Granford would do without him. You aren't
going to drag him away to the big city, are you?"

"No way," Meg said, laughing. "He'd probably wither
away and die. Can you imagine him getting up and putting
on a suit every morning? Besides, I like it here."

They arrived at the Historical Society building in five
minutes. No crime scene tape across the door, Meg noted.
But then, nobody was sure if there was a crime involved.
Maybe the poor guy had had a projectile nosebleed, if there
was such a thing. "Art says it's okay to go back in?"

"He told me he's collected whatever evidence there was, which wasn't much. And I don't think the guy ever touched anything, so there's no point in taking fingerprints." Gail took a deep breath. "Let's do this."

She climbed quickly out of the car, and Meg followed. When Gail reached the door and pulled out her key, Meg saw that her hand was trembling, but in the end Gail managed to get the door open. Inside it was surprisingly warm. "Drat," Gail said. "Usually I turn the heat down when I leave—no sense in wasting the power. I guess I was a little distracted last night."

"You might say that," Meg said. At least Gail could joke about this.

Gail squared her shoulders and marched into the main room, then stopped, her eyes roaming over the site. To Meg's eyes, nothing seemed out of place, or at least, nothing had been moved since the night before. The kitchen exhibit had borne the brunt of the . . . incident, and the well-worn wooden table was covered with blood spatter, as was the cardboard box Gail had been unpacking when she was interrupted. A few blood drops were visible, leading from the kitchen corner to the front door. There was no sign of damage.

"What we need now is some hot soapy water and sponges, I think," Gail said, her voice a little shaky. "We've got those in the storage closet, and thanks to Seth we now have hot water in the bathroom. Can you get me a bucket and fill it, while I clear away this stuff?"

"Sure, no problem." Meg found the items Gail had requested, and took the bucket into the small new bathroom to fill it. Despite the space limitations, it was well designed— kudos to Seth. It gave her hope for her own anticipated bathroom. She filled the bucket, added cleaner, found a couple of pairs of rubber gloves, and brought it all out to Gail. Gail had removed the box of kitchen utensils and the other articles that had been on the table—including, Meg was amused to see, the hypothetical vertical apple peeler she'd mentioned to Seth. Her subconscious mind must have noticed it the day before. For a moment she wondered how it might work, but Gail called her back to the task at hand. "Clean!" She held out a sponge, and Meg took it.

An hour later the room was sparkling, and cleaner than it had been before last night. Meg and Gail stood side by side and admired their work. "Looks good, Gail," Meg said.

"That it does. I think I'll finish unpacking that box and play around with the kitchen display—that's always popular. Shoot! I think we used up all the paper towels. We've got plenty more, but there isn't room to store them in this building, so we stuck them all in the shed behind the house across the street."

"That's right—you own that property."

"We do. It's rented out, to a really nice older couple, and we said they could use one parking space in the shed. But the Historical Society reserved the right to store some of our less-fragile collections at the far end, and at the moment that includes bulk cleaning supplies. Do you mind running out and retrieving a couple of rolls while I sort through this stuff?"

"Sure. I won't startle the residents, will I?"

"I'm not sure they're around this weekend—I didn't see any lights on there last night when I arrived. But they're used to us coming and going."

"Okay. Back in a sec." Meg retrieved her jacket and went out the door. It was a typical late fall day: the maples around the green had lost their colorful leaves, some of which were skittering around the grass. The general store across the green was doing a good business. Gran's parking lot was full with the lunch crowd. She turned and walked across the street and past the colonial house to the rambling shed behind, which ran parallel to the house. To her eye it looked as though it had started life as a barn, a century or more before, but had kind of grown in fits and starts with later additions. There was no car in the open end. Meg stepped into the low building and let her eyes adjust to the half-darkness, then spied some definitely modern shelves stacked with paper goods in plastic bins along the front side.

She was making her way toward the shelves when she happened to look down and see the blood.

6

Meg froze, listening. No sound of movement, other than the wind whistling through the cracks between the old boards. The sensible thing to do, Meg told herself, would be to pull her phone from her pocket and call Art and let him check this out. And risk looking like an idiot if it turned out to be nothing more than a stray cat? Surely Art or his men had examined this building last night. It was adjacent to the Historical Society. They would have seen the blood trail. Wouldn't they?

The trail led in a straight line toward the far end of the building, where a motley array of boxes and barrels were stacked. Meg wondered briefly what collections items could withstand the extremes of hot and cold in this drafty building, but that was not her problem. She took a tentative step forward: still no sound. And another, and another. And after a few more, she could see around the stacked boxes. And she could see the bloody man on the floor, his back propped up against one of the boxes.

She froze again. Dead or alive? His eyes were closed, and his skin looked kind of grayish, or so she thought in the dim light. He matched Gail's description: older, thin, graying, nondescript clothes. And blood, now dark and stiff on his thin jacket. She thought his chest was rising and falling slightly, but no way was she going to get any closer to find out. She pulled out her phone.

And nearly jumped out of her shoes when the man said, "Don't." And after a pause, "Please?"

Okay, not dead—yet. But too close for comfort. "You need help," Meg said, surprised that her voice wasn't quavering.

He tried to pull himself up straighter, and grimaced at the effort. "Maybe. But no cops."

"Get real, pal. Who'm I supposed to call? And I don't have a Band-Aid big enough to deal with that." Meg waved vaguely at his bloody arm. "Besides, the chief of police is a good guy, and a friend. You can talk to him."

The man slumped back against the boxes, and his eyes fell shut. But before Meg could make the call to Art, Gail came hurrying in. "Meg, did you find them? You've been gone awhile," she said nervously. But when she neared Meg, she stopped. "Oh my God, that's him. That's the man. Is he dead?"

"Not yet," Meg said. "I was about to call Art."

Gail was now staring at the man with a peculiar fascination. She took a step closer. "No, it can't be." She turned to Meg with an odd expression. "I think I recognize him," she said in a whisper.

"What?" Meg said, her eyes not leaving the unmoving man. "You didn't last night. Who do you think he is?"

"Last night I was in a panic. But now . . ." She shook her

head. "I don't understand. It looks like he's unconscious—better make that call now. I'll explain when Art gets here."

Meg wasn't about to argue. She hit her speed dial for Art's personal number.

"What?" he barked when he answered. "Oh, sorry, Meg. My wife told me I had to help clean up the yard, but whacking through brambles is not fun. What do you want?"

"You can stop whacking. We've found your man."

"What? You've got to be kidding. Where are you?"

"In the shed next door to the Historical Society. Gail's with me."

Art let loose a creative string of curses. "But we looked there last night. There was no blood trail."

"There is now," Meg informed him. "And the man that goes with it. He's passed out and he looks pretty rocky, so I think you should hurry."

"I'll call an ambulance. Be there in ten." Art ended the call.

"He's on his way," Meg told Gail. "You look pretty calm."

"Ha! Well, for a start I'm relieved he's not dead, and I hope he stays that way. But now I'm trying to put some pieces together, and it doesn't make sense."

"You know him from Granford?" Meg asked.

"Yes, but not personally. And it was a long time ago. Please, can we just wait for Art?"

Meg and Gail leaned against the shelves, keeping an eye on the man on the floor. He didn't move, didn't open an eye. At least Meg didn't see any fresh blood—was that a good sign? But there had been a lot yesterday. He probably hadn't had anything to eat or drink since last night, so he must be dehydrated, and weak from blood loss. As she studied him, she realized that he didn't exactly look homeless, or at least, not like the homeless men she had seen in Boston. His clothes were not new, but they were reasonably clean. There were no holes in his shoes. He was wearing a cheap watch. He might or might not have a wallet, but no way was she going to check his pockets; she was going to maintain a safe distance. Her responsibility stopped here: she had found him, she had reported it to the right people, and she was going to make sure he wouldn't disappear again, which at the moment looked highly unlikely.

Art pulled up outside the shed, without sirens, and Meg was glad to see Seth's car behind his—Art must have called him. Art stalked into the shed and came alongside Meg and Gail. "Where is he?"

Meg pointed. "He was conscious when I found him, barely. He hasn't spoken since I called you. Where's the ambulance?"

"On its way." He walked closer to the man and studied him. The man still didn't move.

Seth came up behind Meg. "You okay?"

"I'm fine. Just another ordinary day in Granford, yup." Meg realized she sounded too sarcastic, and softened her comments by adding, "I'm glad he's not dead."

"Art, Seth, I think I know who he is," Gail said tentatively.

Art turned to her. "You told me last night you didn't recognize him."

"Last night I didn't—it was dark, and he surprised me, and I was scared, uh, spitless. But now that I see him by daylight . . . I think it's Aaron Eastman."

Art stared at her for a long moment. "That's before your time," he said finally.

"There's a clipping on the wall inside the Historical Society."

"I thought he was in prison. Maybe his sentence was up," Art said, almost to himself. "What the hell is he doing here? And what was he doing at your place last night?"

"Hey," Meg interrupted, "will somebody explain to me what you're talking about? Who's Aaron Eastman?"

Before anyone could explain, the sound of an ambulance siren interrupted them. Art went out to talk to the EMTs who emerged from the vehicle then bustled in and set about their business. They had the man who was or was not Aaron Eastman hooked up to an IV and loaded onto a gurney and into the ambulance in less than two minutes, and then they pulled away, scattering gravel behind them.

"I'd better follow to the hospital," Art said without ceremony, and hurried to his car.

That left Meg, Seth, and Gail staring at each other. "Now will someone please explain?" Meg asked plaintively.

"I need food," Gail announced, "and Gran's looks crowded. Let's see if we can find a place where we can sit down, and I'll tell you what I know. Seth, I'll bet you can add something, too."

"How about sandwiches?" Meg suggested. "We can pick some up at the pizza place and take them back to our house. I'd really like to know what you think is going on. Since I found the man."

"Good idea," Seth said. "Meg, you take Gail over to the house. I'll pick up sandwiches on the way."

"And chips. And cookies. Lots. We need it," Gail said, with something approaching a smile.

They settled into their respective cars, but before Meg could leave, Gail said abruptly, "Wait! I need to get something." She was out of the car before Meg could ask any questions, and she ran quickly over to the front door of the Historical Society and unlocked it. She was inside only a minute, and emerged carrying a picture in a frame. She got back into the car and said, "Okay, all set. Don't worry—I'll explain when we all sit down together."

Meg had to bite her tongue to keep from asking questions, but Gail had a point: better to tell the story once, when they were together. At least Gail seemed to have rallied. Her reaction last night seemed out of character for the person Meg knew, but she had to admit that being startled in an empty building by a shabby figure looming out of the dark could unsettle anyone. She probably would have done the same thing. The fact that Gail had felt safe in the building, and had even left the door unlocked, said something about Granford, or at least how people saw Granford, as a safe, peaceful place. Not a place where escaped convicts lurked in the dark. If that's what he was—Gail's identification was not confirmed.

She pulled into her driveway, and waved at Bree up the hill as she climbed out of the car. Bree waved back but didn't approach, so Meg assumed everything was going fine. At least she and Seth would have time to hear whatever Gail had to say. "Come on in," Meg said, as she opened the kitchen door—which was unlocked. She'd adopted Granford ways, it seemed.

Gail followed her inside, still clutching her picture frame.

"Sit down, Gail. You want something to drink?"

"Coffee, if it's easy. Not that I need to be any more wired than I am already. God, I can't believe it. Aaron Eastman . . ."

"Are you doing this to drive me crazy?" Meg demanded, as she started making her second pot of coffee of the day. "Are you playing the mean kid who won't share secrets?"

"Heck, Meg, it's not a secret. Anyone who grew up in Granford knows the story—if they remember it. But I don't have a lot of time—I promised the kids I'd be home in a couple of hours—so I only want to say this once. Well, to you guys, at least. I'll probably have to run through it all again with Art."

"Well, we don't know how long he'll be tied up, so you and Seth can give me the short version over lunch. And here's Seth," Meg said, watching him pull into the driveway and emerge with a few grease-stained paper bags. Seeing them, Meg realized she was hungry—apparently finding bodies had that effect on her. She waited until Seth had come in and dumped the bags on the kitchen table, then said, "Okay, grab your sandwiches and tell me about this Aaron Eastman."

After they'd all settled themselves with sandwiches and chips, and Meg had made and distributed coffee, Gail slid the framed item across the table to her. "Read this—it might save time. Just don't get mayo on it, please! It's the property of the Historical Society."

"I'll try not to," Meg said, wiping her hands on a napkin. She picked up the frame and looked at what it held: a reproduction of a newspaper clipping dating from 1990, with the headline "Tragic Fire Destroys Historic Granford Home." Meg quickly scanned the details. Stately Colonial home of Eastman family . . . three dead . . . fire burned quickly . . . no chance of escape.

She looked up at Gail. "So this was Aaron Eastman's home? His family?"

Gail nodded. "Yes. His parents and his grandmother died in the fire. The place was completely in flames before the fire trucks even got there."

"Where was the house?" Meg asked.

"On the west side of town, toward the river," Seth answered promptly.

"So where does Aaron fit into the story?"

Seth answered first. "Aaron was found unconscious on the lawn outside the building, but from drugs, not the fire. The Eastmans were the proverbial pillars of the community. They had two older kids, in college and prep school, but Aaron was the bad seed of the family. He'd been kicked out of the prep school that his brother still attended and was going to the local high school. He'd been arrested for possession of small

amounts of pot, but his parents got him off—they had clout
with the police chief before Art. The fire looked suspicious—
the place went up awfully fast—but our fire department was
mostly volunteers then, and they didn't have an arson inves-
tigator. They got one in from Worcester, I think, or maybe
Boston, kind of after the fact."

"So Aaron was arrested for arson? And the deaths of
three people?" Meg asked. "On what evidence?"

"Enough to convict him," Seth said. "People around here
knew and liked the Eastmans, but nobody trusted Aaron—
he was a loose cannon, even at seventeen. Maybe he was
the scapegoat, but the public wanted somebody to pay. Not
Granford's proudest moment, I'll admit."

Meg sat back and thought for a moment. "Why do both
of you know so many of the details? This happened when
you were a kid, Seth."

"It was a major fire, which made it a big deal back then.
I remember riding my bike over there while the rubble was
still smoking. Maybe I hoped to catch a glimpse of a couple
of charred corpses, although of course they were long gone
by then. It still ranks as the biggest—and deadliest—fire in
Granford. It became part of the local mythology. Beautiful
house, too—wish I could have seen the inside of it, not that
I would have appreciated it then."

"All the kids were older than you, right?" Meg asked.

"They were. I didn't know them. Aaron went to jail, his
brother finished school and went to college, and I think his
sister dropped out of college and got married. None of them
ever came back here—until now."

"That's why we have that clipping," Gail volunteered,
pointing at the frame on the table. "The fire is still considered a high point in Granford history. Gruesome, isn't it? I

mean, three people died and one went to prison, and all we remember is how big the fire was."

Seth's cell phone rang. He checked the screen, then responded. "Art? What's going on?" He listened for a moment. "I'm at Meg's, and Gail is here with us." He listened, nodding, the ended the call. "He's coming over."

"Is Aaron . . . ?" Gail asked anxiously.

"He's holding his own. That's all Art told me."

7

Meg cleaned up the trash on the kitchen table while they waited for Art. Gail kept checking her watch, no doubt worried about getting back to her family, who would probably be wondering where she was by now. What would Art need to say in person that he couldn't have told Seth over the phone? Aaron Eastman was still alive; that was good news. Was there bad news?

It took Art twenty minutes to reach Meg's house, and she waited at the door to let him in. "I hope you don't have anything bad to tell us," Meg said anxiously.

"No. Actually, I wanted to talk to Gail. She still here?" he said.

"She is. Come on in. Coffee?"

"No, I'm good. Hi, Gail."

"Art," Gail said, looking nervous. "What's going on?"

Art sat heavily in the chair. "Your man is in fact Aaron Eastman, and he's got the documents to prove it. The downside is, he's not in any shape to talk to us. Before you have kittens, his condition is stable and there's nothing life-threatening. He'd lost a lot of blood, he was dehydrated, and the docs are worried about infection. That thing you used on him probably wasn't exactly clean. So I'd be stupid to interview him in his present condition. Maybe by tomorrow."

"Art, why's he out of prison?" Seth asked.

"He served his time—I checked. Nothing mysterious about that. You folks all know his story?" Art looked around the table.

"Seth just explained it to me, or at least the outline," Meg told him. "What was he convicted of?"

"Arson and involuntary manslaughter."

"How old was he in 1990, Art?" Meg asked.

"He was seventeen, but he was tried as an adult. Three people in his own family died because of him, plus the house was destroyed. The judge really threw the book at him with sentencing, because of the deaths, but Aaron was apparently a model prisoner and he just got out. Look, all this was before my time. I only know what my predecessor left in his records. Apparently the case for his being responsible for the fire is pretty clear, or at least enough to take to trial. But there's no evidence that he intended to kill anyone. Problem was, the kid was so stoned when it happened that he couldn't tell the police much of anything. Even when he sobered up, he drew a blank. No recollection of the event, period. His lawyer must have loved him."

"So what's he doing in Granford now, Art?" Seth asked.

Art shrugged. "I don't know yet. He's not talking. Revisiting the scene of the crime? Nostalgia? He didn't have any better ideas? He had a little money in his pocket, but I couldn't tell you how he got here from Norfolk, which is where he was held, or where he's been staying since he got out." He leaned forward, arms crossed on the table. "Look, Gail, the big question here is, do you want to press charges?"

Gail looked startled by the question. "For what?"

"Assault? Breaking and entering?"

Gail was shaking her head before he finished speaking. "Art, I left the front door unlocked, so he didn't break or enter anything. As for assault . . . I think I overreacted. I turned around, it was dark, and he startled me. I lashed out at him, and he fled. But at no time did he threaten me in any way. I never gave him a chance to say anything."

"So the short answer is no, you're not pressing charges?"

"Yes, the answer is no," Gail said firmly. "I feel terrible about what I did. And I want to apologize to him when he gets out of the hospital. How long do they want to keep him there?"

"Probably until tomorrow, unless they find something else they need to treat. I'd still like to talk to him before he vanishes into the woodwork, but he is free to go. You got any idea what he was doing at your place?"

Gail shook her head. "Not a one. You know the green, Art, and the buildings around it. There's the restaurant, the general store, and the Historical Society. Maybe the church. If he was looking for some human contact, those were his choices. He probably wouldn't go to the restaurant—too busy, too many people. He might have tried the church, if he was looking for a safe place to stay. I didn't see what direction he came from—he just showed up behind me. And I don't mean he was sneaking in like a thief—he was just quiet about it. That's all I know."

"I guess I can ask him when I talk to him." Art stood up. "Well, I'd better get back to business. I'll let you know if I learn anything else. But he's free to go wherever he likes."

Seth stood up, too. "I'll see you out, Art." The two men went out the kitchen door.

When Meg hadn't heard a car start up after a few minutes, she looked out the kitchen window to see the men
apparently engaged in conversation—with an alpaca. Not
Lulu—this one had darker fur. It looked surprisingly intelligent, as if it was closely following the men's conversation.
Meg turned to Gail, still seated at the table. "Have you met
our new neighbors?"

"No. Who are they?"

"More like, what are they? Come see."

Gail came over and joined Meg at the window, then burst
out laughing. "Is that an alpaca? That, I never expected to
see in Granford. What's it doing here?"

"We have new human neighbors a mile or two away.
Apparently their fences need some attention. This is the
second one we've seen. They seem friendly enough. How
do you know it's an alpaca? I didn't."

"The kids watch nature shows. Besides, they're cute."
Gail looked at her watch again. "Shoot, I've got to go. Maybe
Art can drop me back home. You think those two big, strong
men can persuade the alpaca to get out of the way so he can
move his car?"

"You can ask."

Gail turned and gave Meg a quick hug. "Thanks for helping me out. I feel so stupid about the way I handled poor
Aaron, and I'm going to tell him so. Talk later!"

Gail hurried out the back door, and as Meg looked on
she approached Art, apparently asking for a ride. The alpaca
responded to Gail's arrival with interest. Meg watched with
amusement as the three of them tried to persuade the animal
to move out of the driveway, but it took a while—it looked
like the alpaca was having too much fun playing with the
humans. Finally they succeeded, and Seth stood watch over
it as Art and Gail left in Art's car. Then Seth pulled out his

phone and made a call, presumably to the owner of the alpaca. She decided she might as well join him.

"You know, this is better than television," she said as she approached. "She looks so intelligent, almost like she was actually following your conversation. It is a she?"

"So says the owner. She'll be right over. This one is Phoebe."

Meg turned to greet the alpaca. "Pleased to meet you, Phoebe. So you found a new hole in the fence?"

"That's what Patty thinks. Maybe I can help her out with fixing it. These quick patches don't seem to be doing the job."

"May I remind you that you have about seventy-three other things on your plate? Fixing the neighbors' fence shouldn't leap to the top of the list."

"I'm just trying to be a good neighbor. You remember what Robert Frost said, don't you?"

"You mean, 'good fences make good neighbors'?" She sighed. "I probably can't stop you anyway. And I'd feel terrible if something happened to any of the alpacas. You want company while you wait?"

"No. There's no sense in two of us getting cold. I'll be in as soon as I've handed Phoebe over."

"Thanks." Meg retreated to the warmth of the kitchen. Now what? It was midafternoon. Bree didn't seem to need her. The ex-convict situation had been resolved, at least for the moment. Poor man: based on what little she had seen of him, admittedly under the worst circumstances, he hadn't looked evil. What kind of a person would set his own home on fire, knowing that his family was inside? It was unimaginable to her. Even if he'd taken God knew what kind of drugs . . . could those drugs override the innate person? Wipe out his sense of right and wrong? She didn't want to believe that, but she had extremely little direct experience with drugs, strong or weak.

And what had he been doing at the Historical Society the day before? Or in Granford at all? He couldn't have happy memories of the place. It was unlikely he knew anyone here anymore, or if he did, that they would speak to him. Gail had mentioned his brother and sister. Had they never returned to town after the deaths of their parents? Where were they now? Would they even speak to their brother, convicted in the deaths? Where could he go from here? Poor man.

Meg saw Patty Gardner's truck and trailer pull in, and Patty climbed down. When she spied Meg standing in the window, she waved. Meg waved back but made no move to join the party in the driveway. Patty and Seth conferred and apparently reached some kind of agreement. Then together they loaded Phoebe into the trailer, and Patty pulled away. Seth headed for the back door.

"What's the story this time?" she asked, once he had shut the door behind him.

"I'll go over in the morning to check out her fencing, and make some recommendations. This is their first venture in rearing animals, and they don't really know what they're doing. The former owners kept cattle in that field, and I'm guessing alpacas and cattle react differently to fencing. They need to get the right gauge for their needs."

"And you know this how?"

"I don't have the answer, but I know people who do. Don't worry—I'm not going to take over, just point them in the right direction."

"I'll hold you to that. What're you up to now?"

"I . . . don't know. You have some ideas?"

"I need to go grocery shopping, but I think I can handle that on my own. And Bree's going to be out tonight, if you recall."

"Ah. Yes. And it's Saturday night. Maybe a bottle of wine is in order?"

"An excellent idea, sir. You can open the bottle while I cook."

"An equitable distribution of labor, I believe."

Meg laughed. "What has gotten into us? We sound like a bad imitation of some old English novel. I have to say, I don't know what to do with myself when I don't have sixteen things to do. It's been months since I had anything like leisure time, and I'm afraid to start something frivolous because I don't trust it to last."

"'All work and no play . . .'" Seth began.

"Yeah, yeah—what is it with you and quotations today?"

"I'm as giddy as you are, I guess. Not that I don't have things to do—my client list is just about the right size, which probably won't last. But nobody is clamoring for a renovation right this minute. Want to go wander through big-box stores and look at bathroom fixtures?"

"Wow, you do know how to charm a girl. And we can do the rest of the errands on the way back."

"Deal," Seth said happily. "I'll go walk Max. Too bad we can't take him with us."

"I think the stores might have an issue with him. We can play with him later."

While Seth took Max out to burn off some energy, and accomplish a few other things, Meg studied the sparse contents of her refrigerator. She needed just about everything, which was sad. How long would it take her to get used to the annual cycle of managing an orchard? Long stretches of frantic activity punctuated by erratic intervals of waiting for the next apples to ripen, all the while hoping for some rain but not too much rain, and please, gods, no hurricanes or tornadoes. And then the three dark winter months, when all she could do was worry about her trees and wonder how many she would have to replace. Could she afford that new well pump this year? When should that be installed?

Luckily Seth operated on much the same schedule: crazy busy in the spring, summer, and fall, when everybody took one look at their homes during the longer days and wanted to fix things right away. It was possible for him to handle some projects in winter, but people didn't really want their houses torn up when they all were huddled inside trying to stay warm. So she and Seth should enjoy the downtime when they could, and do fun things. What was fun? She was having trouble remembering.

Planning a wedding was not on that list. Even a no-frills wedding. Maybe she was too old for all the fuss and feathers, but she didn't think she would have felt much different ten years earlier. A marriage ceremony was a milestone in contemporary culture, albeit possibly a waning tradition, but did it have to be so complicated? But maybe that was the point: it took a lot of work to make it happen, ergo it must mean something to people.

Meg and Seth spent a pleasant couple of hours scouting out plumbing supplies in the area. At least the company was pleasant, but Meg was overwhelmed by the variety of choices. She had to admit that she hadn't given much thought to the aesthetic qualities of bathrooms, certainly not her own, as long as everything worked. Seth did not press: this was an exploratory trip only, to give her something to think about.

"Have you seen anything you liked?" he asked, after the fifth store—or was it the sixth?

"Uh, maybe?" Meg said. "Can I sleep on it? Maybe the right one will float to the top of the heap. Or not—porcelain doesn't exactly float. Can we think about dinner now? I'm pretty sure I can decide between proteins at a supermarket at the moment."

They returned to Granford and stashed their groceries—and put the bottle of white wine in the refrigerator to chill. After that task was completed, Seth said, "I'm going to run out to the office and bring back some catalogs for you to look at. Just to remind you what you've seen, while it's still fresh in your mind."

"Fine," Meg said weakly. She admired his enthusiasm, but she wasn't sure she wanted to jump into the bathroom project right this minute. But still, she didn't want to disappoint him, because he was so excited about giving her something that she needed and would like, that he could do himself. It was sweet, if a bit exhausting.

He'd been gone no more than three minutes when someone knocked at the front door. She'd learned in the past that anyone who came to that door didn't know her, and often brought trouble. With some trepidation she went to the front of the house and unlocked the door, and opened it to find herself staring at someone she was pretty sure was Aaron Eastman, although he looked significantly better than he had the last time she'd seen him. She felt a flurry of panic: she was facing an ex-convict and possible murderer. Why was he here? What did he want?

He seemed to grasp her dilemma. "I'm sorry—I don't mean to bother you. I only wanted to thank you. The police chief said you were the one who found me in that shed, and if you hadn't, I might not have made it. Although that might have been a good thing. You know who I am?"

She studied the man's face: he looked drawn, and older than his years. And, if she was honest, pretty harmless. "You're Aaron Eastman. Would you like to come in?"

She hoped she wasn't making a mistake.

8

Aaron Eastman wavered on the doorstep, as if he couldn't believe Meg's invitation. She summoned up a smile. "I'm not just being polite. You look like you're freezing, and you're just out of the hospital. Don't worry—I don't bite." She stepped back and opened the door wider.

The man stepped in reluctantly, and looked around. "You know who I am?" he repeated.

"Yes, I really do. Come on back to the kitchen, and I'll make some coffee." She turned and walked toward the back of the house, and after a moment's hesitation, the man followed slowly.

Seth had already returned to the kitchen when they reached it, and Meg almost laughed at the shifting expressions on his face: surprise, then dismay, then a glance at Meg with one eyebrow raised. In the end his sense of politeness won out. "Hello, Eastman. I'm Seth Chapin, Meg's fiancé."

Aaron stood in the kitchen, looking back and forth between the two of them. "I didn't mean to barge in. I only wanted to thank Meg here for finding me and getting me help. I can go now."

"How'd you get here?" Seth asked.

"Some guy dropped me off in the middle of town—I think he figured I would catch a bus or something. Hitchhiking's still illegal, isn't it? Not that anybody would pick me up anyway, looking the way I do." He looked down at his clothes. They weren't the ones he'd arrived in, but most likely whatever discards the hospital had been able to scrounge up. At least they looked clean, if shabby.

"Come on, guys—sit down, will you? Aaron, is coffee okay for you?"

"Don't go to any trouble."

"It's not any trouble; I want some myself. So sit."

He sat. Meg got busy with coffee-making—again. Sometimes it seemed to her like an automatic reflex: when it was cold out, walk into kitchen, boil water, make coffee. In summer all she had to do was pull ice water or iced tea from the fridge. Basic Hospitality 101.

It occurred to her that Aaron Eastman had just spent twenty-five years in jail, in the company of only men, with an inflexible schedule. He must be at a loss now, when he had to make decisions about everything, like saying yes or no to a cup of coffee. Should she be direct? Or would that seem rude?

"Aaron, I've only lived in Granford for going on two years now, so I have no history with this place—unlike Seth, whose family goes back centuries. Gail and Seth between them explained to me what happened to you and your family."

"Gail . . . She that woman at the Historical Society?" he asked.

"Yes. She didn't hear you come in and she was frightened. She acted without thinking, and she's very sorry about it."

"I should of known better. I'm kind of out of practice with social things."

"How'd you get to Granford?"

"Caught a ride. Walked some. I wasn't in any hurry, and it was kind of nice to be able to do what I wanted for a change."

"Why'd you come back to Granford?" Seth asked, his tone neutral.

Aaron turned to look at him. "It was home. It was the only place I ever knew. I don't know what I was expecting to find. I mean, I know the house is long gone. My sister and brother live somewhere else. I thought maybe I should visit the cemetery, pay my respects to my parents and my grandmother. That's as far as I planned, I guess."

Truly a lost soul, Meg thought. *Nowhere to go, no one who cares.* "Would you like to have dinner with us?"

Aaron looked startled by the offer. "I don't want to make any trouble . . ." he began.

"Why would it be trouble?" Meg asked. "I'm making dinner anyway. I'll just make a bit more. You look like you could use a good meal."

He looked at her steadily, his expression unreadable. "Thank you. I'd appreciate that."

He turned to Seth. "Wasn't your dad a plumber near here?"

"Good memory," Seth said. "His shop was just over the hill, on the highway. He's been gone for over ten years now. I took over the business, but I'm trying to shift to more general building renovation and historic preservation."

"You would have loved our house, I bet. You must have been, what, ten, when it burned?"

"I was. I wish I could have seen it, up close—I work on a lot of old-house renovations around here. Until it burned, though, I didn't have any reason to go over to that side of town. Of course I had to go look after the fire—sorry. I've seen pictures of it before the fire, of course. It must have been at least twice the size of Meg's house here."

"Probably. It was one of those places that started out kind of like this—you know, simple—and then every generation decided they had to do something to it to make it bigger or finer. You'd have seen the front face, but behind it was kind of a jumble of additions."

"That's pretty typical of New England. Did it have . . ."

Meg turned away to hide a smile: the guys were talking guy stuff, about building construction. She'd better pull something together for dinner. She was pretty sure it didn't have to be fancy, if Aaron had been eating prison food for decades. Chicken, bacon, potatoes, herbs—she had plenty to work with. The coffee was ready, so she filled two mugs and set them in front of the men, then filled one for herself. This was not the evening she had expected, but it was probably going to be interesting, to say the least.

"You got any plans now, Aaron?" Seth asked.

Aaron shrugged. "I'm free to go wherever I want. I need to find a job, so I can eat, and sleep somewhere. From what I've been hearing, prices are kind of high around here, what with all the fancy colleges nearby. Maybe I'll head west."

"What kind of skills do you have?" Seth asked.

"Maybe you remember I was still a kid when I . . . was arrested. What I picked up in prison was mostly computer training. It was kind of fun, and challenging—and, of course, it kept changing. And it was clean, you know? But I don't know who's going to hire me, with a twenty-five-year hole in my résumé."

Meg flipped over the chicken in her pan, then turned to face the men. "Did you hope to stay around here?"

Aaron looked at her, his expression bleak. "What for? I don't know anybody here, not anymore. All people know about me is what their parents told them, that I was some kind of monster who burned my house down with my family inside. Why would anybody want me around here? And don't give me any BS line about how I've paid my dues and I'm rehabilitated and I deserve a second chance." Now there was a spark of anger in his eyes. "I've seen what happens to guys like me when they get out, and it's nothing good, most of the time."

It was hard to argue with him, Meg admitted to herself. He was right: a generation of Granford kids had grown up with the story of the fire and the deaths. And right now, Aaron was kind of an unknown quantity.

"Would you like a glass of wine, Aaron?"

"No thanks. I got clean in jail, and sober, thanks to AA. Haven't touched drugs or alcohol in years, and I don't plan to take it up again."

"Do you mind if Seth and I have one?"

"It's your home. Don't worry—I won't go nuts if I see you drinking. I was a stupid kid when I was doing all the hard stuff."

Meg was torn. She would enjoy a glass of wine, but it seemed wrong to flaunt it in front of Aaron. On the other hand, drinking was a fact of life in current society, and he'd have to get used to that sometime, unless he went to live in a cave in Alaska. She looked at Seth, and he gave her an infinitesimal shrug: it was up to her. She went to the cupboard and pulled out a pair of wineglasses, then handed the chilled bottle and a corkscrew to Seth. Then she turned back to the stove.

Half an hour later she was just ready to dish up when the

phone rang: Gail. She went into the front parlor to answer it. "Hi, Gail . . . What's up?"

"Sorry to interrupt you when you're probably sitting down to dinner. I heard from Art that Aaron Eastman had been released from the hospital, but Art didn't know where he was headed. I feel bad about it because I wanted to apologize to him for what I did. You wouldn't know anything, would you?"

Now, why would Gail assume Meg would know about the whereabouts of an ex-con she'd only just met? The awful thing was, she did. Karma? Lucky guess? "Gail, he's here. He came by to thank me for, well, I guess, saving his life, and I asked him to dinner."

That statement met with a long moment of silence from Gail. "Are you sure that's a good idea?" she finally said carefully.

"You mean, do I think he's going to murder me and make off with all my nonexistent valuables? No. Right now he seems like a sad man who could use a friend and a good meal. Besides, Seth's here to keep an eye on things."

"Oh," Gail said. "Did he say he was leaving town?"

"We've barely scratched the surface about his plans. If he has any. If you want to talk with him, maybe you should come over now."

"I . . . but . . . how . . ." Gail fumbled for words, then stopped herself. "Then that's what I'll do. My husband can keep an eye on the kids after dinner. I'll be there, say, eight?"

"Sounds good. We should be finished eating by then. Bye, Gail."

The two men looked up when Meg returned to the kitchen. "Gail said she's going to come over after supper," she announced. "Don't panic, Aaron—she just wants to say she's sorry to your face. She's a very nice woman."

Aaron did not look convinced. "Her family from around here? What's her last name?"

"Selden," Meg told him. "She's married, but she once told me that if she was going to be working at the Historical Society, she should hang on to her historical name."

"Eastman was an old name in Granford, too," Aaron said, to no one in particular. "And Chapin. How about Corey, Meg?"

"That's my father's name. But my mother was a Warren, and an ancestor of hers built this house. She inherited it, but she's never lived around here."

"So all of our great-greats would've hung out together, like, two hundred years ago."

"Probably," Meg said. "The 1790 census is only one page long, so they had to have known one another." She stood up quickly. "You guys must be starving—I know I am. Let me dish up."

Aaron seemed to relax over the course of the meal. It could have been the effect of a full stomach, or it could be that he had begun to trust them, Meg thought. She still wasn't sure that she trusted him completely, but she had no basis for judgment: she'd never met someone who had spent substantial time in prison. She didn't doubt that prison, particularly over the course of an extended term, could change a person . . . but for better or worse? Aaron had been a rebellious child when he was convicted; what was he now?

As the meal came to a close, Meg was faced with another problem: where was Aaron going to spend the night? Worse, she wasn't sure how to ask him, and if he said something like "I'll find something," would she feel right sending him out into the November night, when she was pretty sure he'd been sleeping rough? But what were her alternatives? Offer him a bed? He'd probably turn it down. Her couch? Better, maybe. A pile of hay in her barn? She'd slept there once, not

willingly, and it hardly fit the definition of basic hospitality—
at least, not in the current century. She looked at Seth in
mute appeal.

Somehow he got the message. "Aaron, I'm going to guess
that you don't have anywhere to go when you leave here
tonight."

Aaron neither confirmed nor denied what Seth had said,
but looked at him warily.

"We can offer you a couch here," Seth went on. Meg
cheered silently: he'd chosen her middle ground.

"I don't want to make any trouble," Aaron said.

"Aaron, it's no trouble," Meg protested. "I'd be more
upset thinking about you wandering around out there somewhere in the cold. You just got out of the hospital this morning, and you're in no shape to look after yourself. I don't
mean that as an insult; it's simply a fact."

Aaron regarded her, his expression blank, and Meg felt
as though she were being weighed. For what? Sincerity?
Good intentions? Stupidity or gullibility? Finally he said
simply, "Thank you. It's been a long time since anybody
worried about me."

Meg was spared from making a corny response when
there was a knocking at the kitchen door, and Meg got up
to let Gail in. Gail walked purposefully into the kitchen and
stopped in front of Aaron. "I am so sorry!" she said. "I didn't
mean to hurt you. Please say you forgive me?"

Aaron regarded her solemnly. "I forgive you. I should
have been more careful about how I approached you."

The tension seeped out of Gail, and she dropped into the
remaining seat at the table. "Thank you. You sure look better
than you did the last time I saw you."

Aaron gave a faint smile. "I'm tough. It looked a lot worse
than it was."

Gail leaned forward. "Can I ask you a question?"

Aaron nodded. "Ask away."

"Why were you at the Historical Society? I mean, why there? Why not the church or the store?"

Aaron sat back in his chair, weighing his response, Meg guessed. Finally he said, "You all know my history, right?" His eyes swept the small group; everyone nodded. "I don't think I did it. And there may be something at the Historical Society that can prove it."

9

Aaron's quiet statement brought a stunned silence to the table.

Finally Meg spoke. "Aaron, you were tried and convicted, and you've served your sentence. Was there something wrong about the trial?"

Aaron sighed. "Look, I know that a heck of a lot of people in jail claim they're innocent, and what's worse, most of them believe it. I've heard plenty of stories . . . well, never mind. You don't have to believe me, and I know nothing is going to change what's happened. I'd just like to have the chance to tell my side. And maybe have someone listen to me."

"Then I'll ask again," Meg persisted, "what didn't come out at the trial that could have made a difference?"

Aaron looked at the others around the table, and Meg knew that he was aware that he'd seized their attention. But was this a con? Or was he sincere?

Before Aaron could speak, Seth said, "The official story says that you were heavily into drugs when this happened. And that you were found passed out, outside the house, with no evidence that you'd been anywhere near the fire—no burns, no singed clothes, no smoke in your lungs. Have I got that right?"

"Yes," Aaron said. "I was what you might call a recreational drug user. I was not an addict. But I kind of liked to push the envelope, and I experimented with a lot of crap."

"So you were out cold on the lawn. Why did you get arrested? On what evidence?" Seth demanded. He paused for a moment before adding, "Was the fire due to arson?"

Aaron nodded, "That's what I was told. The fire started in the basement and spread through the house."

Seth countered, "There are plenty of ways a fire could start: bad wiring, a bunch of greasy rags burst into flames, a gas leak and a spark. Why did they look at you at all, other than the fact you were the only one to get out?"

"They found drug gear in the basement. I was playing around with making meth, which was pretty new back then, and the investigators thought that was the cause. The fire burned up, mainly, so it wasn't destroyed. That and the fact that I survived more or less nailed me, in their eyes." Aaron met Seth's gaze. "I could say, 'because they had nobody else to pin it on.' I mean, Mom and Dad and Gramma died in the fire, and I don't think any of them planned to commit suicide. My sister and brother were away at school. I don't think the police looked too hard. I was convenient. I was the bad kid, and everybody knew I didn't get along with my family. The police wanted to arrest someone and close the case, and I was handy."

"Come on," Seth said, sounding disgusted. "I never heard anyone say that Chief Burchard cut corners just to clear his desk. And since there were deaths involved, the state police must have been involved, and the state fire marshal. You're saying all of them conspired to pin this on you?"

Aaron shrugged. "I'm not saying anything, because I don't know how it happened. That's the only reason I'm here."

That answer didn't make Seth look any happier. "All right, then, let's look at this from another direction," Seth went on. "You said at the trial that you had no memory of the fire or of any of the events leading up to it?"

"Yes, that's what I said."

"Were you lying then? Or have you uncovered any buried memories, or whatever you want to call them? Have you received psychiatric counseling in prison? Did you try hypnosis?" Seth continued relentlessly. Meg wasn't sure whether she should step in: she had never seen him this confrontational. And Aaron was a guest in their home, even if he had kind of invited himself.

But Aaron did not back down. "You're right to be skeptical, Seth. No, I haven't tried to go digging up any memories of that night, but I have thought about what happened. I've had plenty of time to think. And, no, there hasn't been some big 'aha!' moment, where it all came back to me. I don't remember much about the trial, either. I'm not saying my attorney was incompetent, or that the prosecutor did anything wrong, but I think there was more to the story than came out then. Can I tell this from the beginning? It might make more sense that way."

Meg glanced quickly at Gail, who gave her a small nod; she was going to stay. When nobody objected, Aaron began, "I'm sure you all know the basics. Nice old New England family, living in nice old New England house for a couple of centuries. Dad does something in finance—I never did figure out what, exactly—and Mom does good works. She was a real throwback. Two-point-four white-bread kids—I was the point-four. Kids all went to Dad's alma mater, not far from here. Sister Lori graduated and went to Mount Holyoke. Older brother Kevin was in his last year. Younger brother—that would be me—got kicked out of school for various crimes and misdemeanors. I ended up at the high school in Granford, where I did exactly what my father expected: hung out with the wrong crowd and got into drugs. My grades went to hell. Mom and Dad stopped speaking to me, and Dad cut off my allowance, thinking I couldn't buy drugs if he did. Dumb move: I just started stealing small stuff from the house and dealing drugs to my high school buddies. It's a wonder I didn't get caught, because I was high most of the time, and not real careful. But it was just small stuff. What was the name of that police chief then? Seth, you remember?"

"Eben Burchard. He retired maybe nine years ago, and that's when Art Preston took over."

"What did you think of this Burchard guy?" Aaron asked, his tone carefully neutral.

Seth took his time answering. "I can't say I knew him well. I'd describe him as old-school, and he knew he had an easy niche in Granford. Heck, we didn't have any crime— maybe a fender bender now and then, a few Saturday-night DUIs, some cows getting out of a field. Easy to handle. But when the whole drug thing blossomed, he wasn't prepared to deal with it. He ignored it for as long as he could, but after a couple of underage kids OD'd, he knew he couldn't do that anymore. That's when he started talking retirement."

Aaron looked down at his place. "Can you tell me how tuned in he would have been when I was in school here?"

Again Seth considered carefully. "Are you asking if he

would have recognized what state you were in when you were picked up the night of the fire?"

"Yes." The two men held each other's gaze for several seconds.

Finally Seth said, "I don't know. I'm guessing it was late, and dark, and the fire was out of control, and he probably just wanted to get you out of there. Did he arrest you on the spot?"

"I don't think so. You're asking if he decided I did it then and there? Because he didn't go all soft and mushy and say how awful it must be that my parents were getting fried? Or maybe he assumed they'd gotten out of the building, or they were off skiing or partying somewhere."

Meg flinched at the harsh way Aaron referred to his family. Was he deliberately trying to antagonize Seth and her? But why would he do that? He didn't even know them.

"Were they supposed to be away from home?" Seth asked.

"Hell, I don't remember. I just kept my head down and talked to them as little as possible. And I'm pretty sure their date book burned in the fire, so I can't prove anything."

"So what did the police chief do with you, then, that night?"

"He had the paramedics check me out—or at least, that's what I'm told, because I really don't remember—and then he had me sit in the back of a police car, with a cop keeping an eye on me. And when it was pretty clear the house was past saving and nobody else was coming out, he had me taken down to the station to talk to me. I understand that I just kept saying, 'lawyer,' which I think pissed him off."

"Did you get a lawyer?"

"Hell, I didn't know any lawyers—I was seventeen. I didn't know if I could even pay a lawyer, so I guess they handed me over to a public defender, who was kind of a jerk."

"When were you charged?"

"Not until after the lawyer showed up, the next morning. I was about halfway back to sober by then. You ever come down from cocaine?" He looked at Seth and Meg, then shook his head. "Stupid question. Anyway, the high is great, but the low after really sucks. That's what I woke up to. They told me my parents were both dead, and Gramma, in case I'd forgotten, and I had no place to live, and, oh, by the way, did I set that fire? And all I could say was, 'I don't remember.' Which was true."

"And you're telling us you got railroaded?" Seth demanded. Meg thought he sounded angry. Why?

Aaron glared at him. "What the hell are you, an attorney?"

"No, I'm a plumber, and a builder, and a town selectman. You came here, remember? I didn't go looking for you."

"I came to thank Meg, not butt heads with you. You want me to leave, just say the word." Aaron was actually showing some emotion, which was a first since his arrival.

"Enough!" Meg said loudly. "Both of you, shut up." Luckily for her they did, because she had no idea where she was going with this. "Aaron, I appreciate that you came here to thank me. I'm glad I found you alive, because I don't want to think about the alternative. But I'm not sure how we ended up arguing about this, or what you think we're supposed to do now."

"Nothing," Aaron said. "Not one damn thing. You go back to your lives, and I'll try to figure out what I'm supposed to be doing with mine now."

"Aaron, do you believe you were responsible for the fire?" Meg said softly.

He gave her a long look. "I'll admit I did some stupid things when I was a kid, but I never wanted to hurt anybody. I never wanted to kill anyone or anything. Hell, I'd take spiders outside and let them go. I never kicked a dog in my life. I want to believe that under all the tough-guy stuff I was a pretty decent kid, and I probably would have straightened myself out, if I'd had enough time. Am I wrong to want to believe that?"

"I don't think so. I don't know you well enough to judge whether it's true. When you got out, why did you come to Granford? What were you hoping for?"

"I don't know. I thought maybe being in the place might jog my memory. Or maybe I should say a final good-bye and put the town behind me—I never had a chance to do that, after the fire. The town looks pretty much the same, but there's nothing left of the house, just a field with a bunch of shiny new houses on it. And like I said, I went to the cemetery. I wasn't in any shape to go to the funerals after the fire, so I needed closure, I guess. To make sure it was real. That they're gone."

"You aren't on some sort of crusade to prove that you're innocent?" Seth asked, but at least his voice was calmer.

"If I am, it's only for myself. Nobody else cares. I'm not looking to sue anybody, or get lots of publicity. I'd just like to know what really happened that night. If I did what they say I did, I'm prepared to live with that, and I've already paid the price. If I didn't, then somebody's guilty and they got away with it. But it's not your problem."

Meg and Seth exchanged rueful glances. If—a very large "if"—they decided to help Aaron Eastman, it wouldn't be the first time they'd been sucked into someone else's problems, Meg thought. And Granford had seemed such a peaceful town—until she had scratched the surface. She was not as naïve as she had been when she arrived, but what did they owe Aaron? They didn't know him. But wasn't there some kind of weird popular myth that if you saved someone's life, you were responsible for them forever after? Who'd made that one up? She did not feel responsible for Aaron's well-being, mental state, future employment, or anything else. She had fed him, and she might offer him a place to sleep for one night, or maybe two. And that would be the end of it.

Gail, quiet until now, spoke suddenly, startling Meg, who had all but forgotten she was there. "Aaron, you never explained what you were doing at the Historical Society. Why were you there? What were you looking for?"

Aaron leaned back in his chair and rubbed his face with both hands. He looked tired, which wasn't surprising. "A loose end that's been bugging me from the start." He leaned forward again, forearms on the table. "You know that my grandmother—my mother's mother—died in the fire, right? She was the person I was closest to. She wasn't a pushover, and she gave me grief when I went off the rails, but she always made it clear that she loved me, and I know that I loved her. Well, she'd moved in with Mom and Dad, maybe a year before the fire. Her mind was sharp, but she couldn't handle stairs, and she needed help doing other things. The house was big enough that Dad could set off a kind of in-law apartment for her—connected to the house, but private, you know? She had an aide who came in half days, but Gramma ate her meals with us, and I'd spend time hanging out with her."

"Aaron, what's this got to do with anything?" Meg asked.

"I'm getting there. When Gramma moved out of her house, I helped her clean it out. You can probably guess what the place was like: she'd lived there ever since she married, and she wasn't great about throwing stuff away. Not like a hoarder or anything, but there was a lot. I'd go over there, and we'd work together. I'd haul the boxes down from the attic, and we'd go through them, and she'd decide what to keep and what to toss. Gail, some of it was old family papers, and she wanted those to go to the Historical Society; Dad wasn't interested in keeping them. I was the one who delivered them, to whoever was running the place back then. I was going to ask if you'd kept them and where they were."

"You want to see those?" Gail asked, clearly surprised. "Because I'd have to do some digging to figure out where they might be."

"Thanks, but it's not just that. One thing I do remember. A couple of weeks before the fire, Gramma called me in and said she had a couple more boxes that should go to the Historical Society. She'd labeled them 'Family Papers.' I didn't think much about it at the time. I just took them and handed them over. It was only afterward I realized that we'd done a pretty good job of sorting out all the family papers from her old house, so what the heck was in the new boxes?"

"And you think that could have anything to do with . . . what happened?" Gail asked, incredulous.

"I know it's a long shot. But I remember thinking then that it was kind of odd. It could be nothing at all, or she could have slipped a few gears and put in all her old magazines, for all I know. But I'd like to see those boxes. If that's possible."

Gail said, "You've arrived at an odd time. We just built a new storage area under the old building, which will give us room to assemble all the collections that people have been giving to the Historical Society since we first opened. The problem is, they've been scattered all over town, wherever someone had room to keep them. And our early record-keeping left a lot to be desired. Bottom line is, I'm not sure where a lot of the stuff ended up—I'm still trying to track down some of it. Worst case, someone could have forgotten what it was and thrown it out. I'll look for your grandmother's stuff—it sounds like there's more than those last few boxes, although there's no guarantee that any of it was kept together—but I won't promise I can find it."

Aaron gave her a slight smile. "I'd really appreciate that, especially after I half scared you to death."

"And I nearly killed you with a vegetable chopper—which, by the way, is part of one of those wandering collections. So there's a kind of logic to it all."

Aaron stood up, albeit a bit unsteadily, his fatigue showing. "I should get out of your hair. You've been very kind."

Meg shot a glance at Seth. "Where are you going, Aaron?"

Aaron gave another shrug. "Not your problem."

Meg refused to believe that. "Aaron, you're welcome to stay here and sleep on our couch, like Seth offered." Seth gave her an odd look.

Aaron hesitated before answering. "That's more than kind, and I'm happy to accept. But what I really want is to take a shower."

It was Seth who replied. "No problem." So he'd cooled off. Meg rewarded him with a smile.

"Look at the time!" Gail exclaimed. "I've got to get home. Aaron, I'll start looking for your stuff as soon as I can. But tomorrow's Sunday, and I really need to spend some quality time with my family, after this week."

"No rush, Gail," Aaron told her. "It's already been twenty-five years. A couple more days won't matter."

"Great. Meg, Seth, thanks for including me. Aaron, I'll be seeing you again, I hope. Night, all!" She rushed out the back door, and Meg heard her car start up.

"Let me go find some blankets and stuff," Meg said. "We don't use the front parlor much, so it's chilly."

"I've slept in worse."

Meg and Seth spent a few minutes sorting out bedclothes

and pillows and such, and then Seth walked Max, and Meg made sure Lolly had food. Meg directed Aaron to the shower, and she could swear that his eyes lit up at the sight of it . . . with a door that closed.

"What do you think you're doing, Meg?" Seth asked, once he heard the water running.

"The man needs help. We can help. It's that simple. Do you believe his story?"

Seth didn't answer right away. Finally he said, "God help me, I think I do. But you're the one complaining about how many things you have to do. How did you manage to add looking into an old case of arson?"

"Don't ask me; these things just keep happening. If we're lucky, Gail will find the files and there won't be anything important in them, and Aaron will go . . . wherever." *And if we're not lucky?* Meg refused to consider that. "Can we go to bed now?"

10

Meg woke up with the sun and lay in bed worrying. Seth was right: why did she feel compelled to help some guy she didn't know, who hadn't been part of Granford for a quarter century, and who wasn't exactly popular with the few townspeople who remembered him? Even usually affable Seth had been wary of him.

But Meg believed Aaron. *Stupid, Meg—now you're going on gut instinct?* She couldn't see what he hoped to gain, other than peace of mind. Legally he was in the clear, since he'd served out his sentence. It seemed credible—barely— that the drugs had so addled his brain that he really didn't know what had happened that night. He was prepared to acknowledge his guilt, but he wanted to fill in the blanks. That she could understand.

Which left her with a couple of questions. One, why should she take this on? She had no obligation to him. Two, how on earth was she supposed to look into a crime that had taken place so long ago? The former police chief had retired long since, and Meg wasn't even sure he was still alive. Would Art be willing to share whatever records he had? There would have been an arson investigation, but would that be included in that report? The Eastman house had been far enough outside of town that there were no near neighbors, and apparently no witnesses had come forward. Were trial transcripts available to random citizens like her? Could Art request them? Was that public defender still practicing? And why did she care?

Because it was the right thing to do. It was an act of charity, of paying it forward. Sure, she was busy, but this could affect the rest of Aaron's life, and her problems with menus and invitations seemed kind of trivial in comparison. So she'd ask Art what information was available and what he could share. And maybe Gail would find those wandering boxes, which might or might not provide information about some aspect of this. Odd, what the human mind retained—or didn't: Aaron couldn't remember the death of his parents, but he clearly remembered helping his grandmother pack up storage boxes.

Seth stirred beside her. "Think Aaron's still here?" he mumbled into the pillow.

"I haven't checked. What're the odds?"

"On the one hand, he must be exhausted, so he could still be asleep. On the other hand, maybe he realized what a wild-goose chase this is and lit out. On the third hand, maybe he's telling the truth and he believes we can help him, which would mean he'll be waiting for us downstairs."

"Unless you've got a fourth hand coming, I'm going to get up and worry about breakfast. I should get downstairs before Bree walks into the kitchen and discovers a stranger there."

"Good point. I'll go start coffee and walk Max." Seth swung his legs over the edge of the bed.

"Did we have any other plans for today, before all this came up?" Meg asked.

"Not really. We should go see Rachel. Maybe Mom will want to come along."

How sweet of Seth to want to check in on his sister, Rachel, Meg thought. Rachel had already had two kids, but the one she was expecting now was, well, kind of unexpected.

Seth went on, "Rachel's getting pretty close to her due date, and we might not get another chance. Once the baby comes, it'll be a while before she can focus on a coherent conversation longer than two or three sentences."

Meg smiled. "And you know this why, Seth Chapin?"

"I've seen her with the first two, remember? Having a baby does something weird to your hormones. See you downstairs!"

Meg stretched like a cat, but when she heard two male voices downstairs, she decided she should get moving and join them. She dressed quickly and went down the front stairs. In the parlor, the blankets Aaron had used were neatly folded, the pillow laid on top. When she reached the kitchen, she was confronted by a sight of unexpected domesticity: Aaron sat at the table, a coffee mug in front of him, Lolly the cat settled on his lap, and Max sprawled on the floor at his feet, his gaze alternating between the stranger at the table and the pan of bacon Seth was frying.

"Good morning!" Meg said, helping herself to coffee. "Looks like you've made some friends here."

"I like animals. Mom would never let us have any; she said she had allergies. My theory is she didn't want any animals messing with the antique furniture."

"Well, as you've probably noticed, what furniture we have has seen better days, so those two can't do much harm. Did we tell you that my orchard manager lives upstairs, too?

So if you see a young woman at the door, that's probably her. She was at her boyfriend's last night."

"Got it. So she doesn't know about me yet. Your police chief didn't make a big deal about what happened in town?"

"At the Historical Society, you mean? No, and he doesn't jump to conclusions. But some people may have seen the ambulance."

"Food," Seth said, setting plates of bacon and eggs on the table, then another plate with a stack of toast.

"This looks great," Aaron said, and dug in eagerly. Meg avoided staring, but in reviewing what he'd said, how he'd acted, since he arrived, she thought that whoever had taught him manners as a child had done a good job, and apparently prison hadn't erased it all. He was well-spoken, too. How had he survived prison? Where had he been? Not that knowing the name would tell Meg much—she had zero familiarity with the Massachusetts prison system. Had Aaron been considered violent? She had no idea. He had no visible tattoos or scars, she noted, and then laughed inwardly at herself. Apparently she'd been watching too many sensationalized television shows. Were all prisons rife with gangs and drugs and violence and corruption? She couldn't exactly ask Aaron over the breakfast table.

After the food had disappeared, Aaron leaned back and stretched, dislodging Lolly. "That was great. Thank you. I should be going."

"At the risk of sounding rude," Meg said, "where are you going?"

Aaron shrugged. "I'll figure something out."

"You need to stay in Granford for as long as it takes to find those records, right?"

"Maybe. There may be nothing there, and I don't want to get my hopes up. I just think it's weird that that detail sticks out in my memory. Of course, if you're doing drugs, your brain isn't always rational."

"Why do you think that sticks out?" Seth asked, refilling his coffee cup.

Aaron thought for a moment. "Well, like I said, I thought we'd finished with all Gramma's papers, before she moved in with us. And then, I guess I thought she was acting kind of funny when she asked me to take the new stuff to the Historical Society."

"Funny how?" Meg asked.

"I don't know . . . kind of guilty, maybe? I mean, Gramma was usually pretty direct; she didn't let anybody get away with BS, and she was good at seeing right through me if I tried to lie to her. So even though my brain was kind of foggy, I got the impression that there was something peculiar going on with those particular boxes. But I couldn't tell you why."

"Well, let's hope Gail can track them down," Meg said firmly. "But what she told you was pretty much the truth. You've seen that building . . . well, maybe you don't remember it from that night. Anyway, it's tiny, and until a couple of months ago it had no on-site storage at all. So they decided to build under the building, rather than adding a new story or extension, to preserve its historic appearance. Seth played a part in that. Now there's plenty of space, so Gail has been trying to track down the collections that were stashed all over town so she can get them all together in one place and sort through them before shelving them. But she's only part-time; she's got school-age kids."

"Aaron, you mind if we cut to the chase here?" Seth asked. "You have any money? Anything else? I mean, you can't just wander around Granford sleeping in barns while you wait for Gail to track down what it is you're looking for."

"I can't complain if you ask, Seth. When you walk out

of prison, you get what you had when you went in. Period. This state doesn't believe in giving you any money to get started. Stupid, isn't it? I guess they offered to help me find a job and a place to live, but I just wanted some time to hang out, you know? And I didn't know if I wanted to stay around here or start new somewhere else. So I said no thanks. Hey, I know what I'm up against. I've got a criminal record, and it ain't exactly for a nice white-collar crime. I've got no diplomas, although I got my GED inside. I've got a few bills in the pocket. I don't expect anybody's gonna want to hire me. Heck, *I* wouldn't hire me. But my computer skills are pretty current, and I'm healthy."

Seth glanced at Meg again, but Meg had no wisdom to offer. The harvest season was pretty much over, and by the time he got up to speed on how to pick anything, it would definitely be past. Even if he helped Gail with her cataloging, the Historical Society had no money to offer him. Who did she know that was hiring, and wouldn't be concerned about Aaron's background?

"You have any construction skills?" Seth asked.

"Not exactly. I was a punk rich kid, remember? And they didn't offer too many shop classes inside; I think they got nervous about the idea of putting criminals and tools together."

"Can you cook?" Meg asked.

"Enough to survive. I can wash dishes, though."

Maybe Nicky and Brian need someone to help out, Meg thought. "Can you drive?"

Aaron grinned. "I used to know how, but my driver's license is a couple of decades out-of-date." Then his smile faded. "Look, guys, I've got a couple of hundred bucks in my pocket, and one change of clothes—or, no, I don't, since what I was wearing got pretty ripped up. Talk about a fresh start!"

"Clothes aren't a problem," Seth said. "Money is. I wish we could offer you something, even short-term, but we're not exactly rich and we barely get by. Both our jobs are kind of unpredictable. We could work out someplace for you to stay, at least until we get the documents sorted out."

Meg watched as an interesting variety of expressions crossed Aaron's face. He took his time before answering. "I appreciate that you're trying to help. Look, I hate having to ask for charity from anyone. I know I screwed up my life, my chances, but that doesn't make it any easier to beg. I have no clue where I'm going from here, so I'm focusing on the one thing that I can accomplish. One simple thing: find my grandmother's boxes and see if they have anything to do with how my family died. If there's nothing there, I'll move on. I'm not kidding myself that there'll be some piece of paper that proves that I didn't deserve to go to prison—that's fairy-tale stuff."

It's a no-win situation, Meg thought. She wanted to help Aaron. She was appalled that the state corrections system simply shoved released prisoners out the door and expected them to fend for themselves. Aaron had been incarcerated when he was little more than a child; how was he supposed to cope with a very different world now? No money, no home, no relatives to take him in, and no job prospects. No wonder so many ex-convicts turned back to crime—what other choices did they have? She wished she and Seth could take a time-out and talk about what to do, but it seemed kind of rude to leave Aaron sitting at the table while they conferred about him, as though he were an object that had to be managed.

In the end she turned to Seth and said, "What can we do?"

"I don't know," he said to her. Then he turned to Aaron. "Let me ask around, see if there's somebody who needs short-term help right now. I can fill them in on the situation, or at least part of it. And maybe the pickers know about someplace with spare rooms; some of them have already moved on, so there should be some vacancies. Does that work for you?"

Aaron looked like he was struggling between different responses, but in the end he said, "I would appreciate your help. I'll try to clear out as soon as I can."

Bree came clattering in the back door and stopped dead at the sight of a stranger at the kitchen table. "Uh, hello?"

Meg made introductions. "Bree, this is Aaron Eastman. He used to live in Granford, years ago. Aaron, this is my orchard manager, Briona Stewart. She lives upstairs."

Aaron had stood up, and he said politely, "Good to meet you, Briona."

"Bree," she said absently, studying Aaron's face and clothes. Then she turned to Meg. "He the convict from the Historical Society?"

"Bree!" Meg protested, even though she was right.

"What?" Bree shot back. "I live here. I've got a right to know who's here in this house."

"Yes, you do," Meg replied, trying to control her anger, "but don't be too quick to judge, until you've heard the whole story."

Aaron spoke again. "She's right, Meg. Yes, Bree, I was just released from prison, for a crime that happened twenty-five years ago. And my reentry into Granford has been a little rocky, since I managed to terrify Gail Selden into attacking me. But this is your home, and I don't have any right to make you uncomfortable. I won't be staying long."

"Huh," Bree said, still studying him. "All right. Meg, you'd better fill me in. And Mister Aaron Eastman, if I made assumptions about you that are wrong, I apologize. I should know better—I get that all the time, just because I'm young and black and a woman running an orchard."

"Thank you, Bree."

Before anyone else could say anything controversial, Meg said, "Bree, do you need me in the orchard today? Seth and I were thinking of visiting Rachel."

"She hasn't had that baby yet? Sure, we're clear. Have you fed the goats yet?"

Meg wondered what she was talking about—the goats had plenty of food at the moment—but then she realized that Bree wanted to talk to her alone. "Not today. Why don't you give me a hand?"

Outside, Meg and Bree crossed the driveway and went into the barn, where they couldn't be seen. "What the hell you playing at?" Bree demanded.

"I'm trying to help someone who could use a little help," Meg said tartly. "What, you think he's going to murder us in our beds and rob the place? Good luck with that; there's nothing to steal. He was in prison for something that happened when he was younger than you are. And he might not have done it."

"Oh, right, now you're playing the bleeding-heart card?"

"No. I'm not that naïve, Bree. But there are some odd angles to this, and I said I'd help."

"Like you don't have enough else to do?"

"I know. You're right. But I feel sorry for him. And what if he really wasn't guilty?"

"You believe that?"

"I don't know. Maybe. And I don't know how much we can find out, or how to prove anything. It was a long time ago. Look, Bree, this doesn't affect what you're doing. I'll give it a couple of days. If we don't find anything relevant, he'll be gone, I promise."

"I'll remind you of that. You know, you keep taking in strays, and things are getting crowded. Cats, goats, a criminal.

I hope you aren't planning to add an alpaca?" Bree nodded toward an approaching animal that Meg hadn't noticed.

"Oh, sugar. This is the third time one's gotten loose. Seth's going to have to check out the fences sooner rather than later."

"Well, at least it's not my new roommate."

11

Back at the house, Seth called Rachel and his mother, both of whom were delighted by the idea of getting together. Lydia Chapin happily accepted the offer of a ride to Amherst, where Rachel and her husband ran a bed-and-breakfast. At least during normal times: Rachel's unexpected pregnancy, ten years after the birth of her son Matthew, had kind of put that on hold. Luckily her husband Noah's schedule gave him some flexibility to deal with the children.

Lydia lived just over the hill from Meg, in a house similar in age and style to hers. Meg had always hoped that the same hands had built them both: the Chapin and Warren families had lived side by side since the later 1700s. She was waiting outside, well wrapped against the chilly wind, when Seth and Meg drove up. She hopped quickly into the car.

"I'm so glad you suggested this, Seth," she said.

"I can't take credit for it; it was Meg's idea."

"Well, it's a good one. I hate to say, I haven't spent nearly enough time with Rachel as I should. Oddly enough, my job seems to have picked up recently."

"I'm not getting over to Amherst much, either," Meg admitted, "but the orchard eats up all of my spare time, and more. Although things are finally tapering off now."

"That's good. I'd ask how the wedding plans are coming, but I assume you'd tell me if there was anything I need to know. So, what's the story about the convict at the Historical Society?"

"Lydia!" Meg protested. "How do you hear these things?"

"I talk to people. And now I'm talking to you. If I've got any part of this wrong, you can correct me. What happened?"

Meg recounted the events of the past few days, starting when she came upon Gail covered with blood. Lydia made the appropriate horrified noises. Meg stopped short of Aaron's arrival the prior evening, although she wasn't sure why. Lydia was a very fair-minded person, and would give anyone a second chance.

"I remember the fire at the Eastman house," Lydia said pensively. "It was big news then. Of course, this town doesn't often have much to talk about."

"Did you know the Eastmans?" Meg asked.

"Ken and Sharon? You really have to ask? We weren't exactly in the same social circles. Seth's father, Stephen, was a plumber, and Ken Eastman was a financial wizard of some sort. We had no money to speak of, so we weren't on his radar. But the fire, now, everybody knew about that. I gather that Seth sneaked over there to check things out, although he'd never admit it to me."

"My lips are sealed, Mom," Seth said, his eyes on the road.

"It was a terrible thing that three people died. Of course, this was before everybody had smoke alarms in every room.

I could understand why the mother couldn't make it out; she had some mobility issues. But her son and his wife? Of course, maybe they were overcome by the fumes before they could move. And Aaron doesn't remember anything?"

"That's what he says," Seth told her. "That's what he's said from the beginning."

"Do you believe him?" his mother asked.

"More or less. Look, you and Dad did know Chief Burchard, right?" Seth said.

"Sure. He was a nice guy."

"What did you think of him?"

"Seth, are you fishing for information on that poor man? He was honest, if that's what you're asking—I mean, didn't take bribes to look the other way. Not that there was much to look at anyway. If anything, I'd say that he was a bit too laid-back. He liked to play the good ole boy, shaking hands with all the guys, paying silly compliments to the women."

"Are you saying he was lazy?" Meg interrupted.

Lydia thought for a moment. "Not lazy, exactly. Just prone to taking the easiest path. You know, if it looks like an elephant and smells like an elephant, it probably is an elephant, and he wasn't going to look any more closely."

Meg laughed. "I love the image of an elephant in Granford!"

"You know what I mean," Lydia said, laughing with her. "It never would have occurred to him that someone might have dressed up a horse in a gray tarp and stuck a hose on the front, and sprayed it with the, uh, residue from his manure pile."

"And it worked just fine for him, for years. He retired happily. Is he still alive?"

"I think so, over at the retirement center in Holyoke. But I don't know if he's still got all his faculties, if you know what I mean."

It took Meg a second to work out what she meant: interviewing him about something that had happened in the distant past probably wouldn't be fruitful. Or maybe it might be, Meg thought, since in many cases older memories were clearer to people with dementia or Alzheimer's than something that had happened the day before.

"Here we are," Seth said cheerfully, having stayed out of the more recent parts of the conversation. "Mom, you brought lunch?"

"Of course . . . that box in the trunk. You'll carry it in, won't you?"

"Yes, Mom, like I always do."

Which freed up Lydia and Meg to march up the front steps of Rachel's handsome Victorian home and ring the doorbell—or rather, twist it, since it was an authentic one installed in the door. Noah opened the door quickly. "Come in, come in, please." He stepped back to let them enter.

Rachel was enthroned on the plush-covered settee in what had once been the front parlor, her feet raised on a tufted ottoman with fringe. She was draped in paisley shawls. "Rachel, are you trying to look Victorian?" Meg demanded, with a smile.

"How'm I doing?" Rachel shot back.

"Well, you definitely look like a lady of leisure, with a dash of Jabba the Hutt thrown in."

Rachel smiled. "That bad? At least it won't be for much longer. Sometime in the next two weeks."

"Everything on track, dear?" Lydia asked, settling herself on an overstuffed armchair.

"So my doctor tells me. Hi, Seth!" Rachel called out. "Oh, goody—you brought food, Mom. Just put the box in the kitchen, Seth, and see if you can find some clean plates. So, ladies, what's the dirt?"

Now Meg, Seth, and Lydia exchanged glances. Rachel

most likely had not heard of the excitement on Friday, Meg
reasoned, because if she had, she would have asked directly.
It was good that the news hadn't spread beyond Granford,
but did they want to talk about it now? And if so, what spin
should they put on it? Rachel, the baby of the family,
wouldn't have heard much about the Eastman fire when she
was growing up.

Seth disappeared into the kitchen, and reemerged two minutes later with sandwiches on paper plates. Rachel beamed at
him. "Thank you, big brother. Now, what about drinks?"

"Coming up." He headed back toward the kitchen.

Rachel leaned toward Meg and Lydia and said, "I'm really
going to miss being waited on like this. One of the perks of
late pregnancy." Then she sat back and said in a louder tone,
"So either nothing at all has happened since the last time I
talked to any of you, or something big has happened and you
don't know how to tell me. I assume it's door number two?"

Seth reappeared with glasses and bottles of soda, which
he set on the table. Then he sat down next to Meg and helped
himself to a sandwich.

"Yes." Meg said. "Listen, Rachel—"

Rachel interrupted her. "Let me guess. It's more fun, and
I need to exercise my brain. Unless someone we all know
has died?"

"No, nothing like that, dear," Lydia said. "It's—"

Rachel held up one hand. "Nope, let me do it. So nobody
near and dear has died. Is somebody dead?"

Seth volunteered, "Yes, but—"

Rachel covered her ears with her hands. "What part of
'me do it' do you not get? I'm bored out of my mind and I
feel like a whale, so let me have my fun, okay? Now, if there
had been a murder, or a significant local citizen had passed
away unexpectedly, I probably would have heard that on the

local news. Likewise, if somebody died and no one knows who he or she is, there might be an appeal for help. Ooh, I have it! It's a cold case!"

"Uh, sort of?" Meg said.

"And somebody died in the past."

Meg silently held up three fingers. Rachel stared at her. "Three people died in the past? All at once or serial?"

Meg held up one finger this time.

"Three deaths, same time. In Granford?"

Meg, Seth, and Lydia nodded in unison, and Meg wondered if they looked like a row of bobblehead dolls. "Wow," Rachel said. "That's pretty rare. How did they die?"

"That's going to be a little difficult to mime, Rachel," Meg said. She looked around the room and her eyes lit on the fireplace; she pointed at it.

"Three people died in a fire," Rachel said to herself. "In Granford. Arson?"

More nods. "Was anyone arrested?" Rachel asked.

Nods again. "Got it!" Rachel crowed. "The Eastman fire."

"Rachel, how do you know about that?" Lydia said.

"Uh, well, I never quite told you, Mom, but when I was a kid we used to ride out there on our bikes. If you were there at the right time of day, you could almost believe you could hear the screams of the people trapped inside. Let me tell you, we moved a lot faster on the way back."

"Rachel," Seth said, "they razed what was left of the building right after it burned; there was nothing there."

"Except some rubble and holes," Rachel said. "Don't be so literal, Seth. We were kids, and we were looking for some spooky thrills. We grew out of it. So what the heck does the Eastman fire have to do with now?"

"Aaron Eastman is out of jail," Seth said. "He showed up at the Historical Society on Friday, and Gail Selden panicked and sliced open his arm, and Meg walked in right after he disappeared, but Meg found him yesterday and he went to the hospital, and then he showed up on our doorstep to thank Meg for saving his life, and he ended up telling us his whole story, and then he spent the night."

"Breathe, dear brother. So the bottom line is, last night you hosted an ex-convict who is part of Granford's history. What's he like?"

"Fortyish, but looks older. Quiet, sad. Nothing scary about him."

"Why'd you give him a bed for the night?"

"Actually it was a couch."

Rachel waved a dismissive hand. "Whatever. I'm going to guess that he thinks he was framed."

"Sort of," Meg said. "The fact is, he doesn't remember anything about the night of the fire. He more or less sleep-walked through the trial, with a public defender. He spent twenty-five years in jail, wondering if he was capable of killing his family at seventeen. He's still not convinced. So when he got out, he came back to Granford, I guess to see if anything jogged his memory. So far all he's gotten is some stitches, thanks to Gail."

"What does he think he can find, this much later?" Rachel asked.

"Maybe nothing," Seth admitted. "He knows it's long odds, but he wants to try. And he sure doesn't have much else to look forward to in his life. He finished high school in prison, and he's taken some additional courses, but basically he has no money, no home, no education, and a criminal record."

"So of course you and Meg volunteered to help him," Rachel said, smiling.

"Gail's helping, too," Meg added, "since she feels guilty for almost killing him."

Rachel turned to her mother. "Mom, what do you think about this?"

"I only heard the story on the way over today, and I haven't met the man yet. But I trust both my son and Meg: if they think Aaron Eastman's story may have some truth in it, then I'm on their side. Give the man a chance to find out what he can."

"Then I'm in. Where do we start?" Rachel said, rubbing her hands together.

"Wait a minute, Rachel," Meg protested. "You're not in any shape to take on an investigation of a long-ago crime."

"Meg Corey, my brain works just fine, even if I do move like a hippopotamus. The kids are at school all day, and Noah is working, and have you looked at daytime television lately? Trash. And I've seen every DVD of every movie I've missed over the past few years. So having something to do that involves nothing more strenuous than thinking would be a godsend. Maybe a few phone calls. Or online research, if I can reach my laptop around Pumpkin here." Rachel laid a fond hand on her very round belly. "Do we have a deadline?"

Meg could see her point, and she felt briefly ashamed that she had assumed that Rachel wouldn't be capable of participating in their probably futile exercise. "Well, Aaron is going to have to find a job of some sort, and we have no idea how he's going to do that. If we could prove he's not a killer, it might help."

"Good point," Rachel said. "Can I meet him?"

"Rachel," Seth began, "I know you're looking for an antidote to your boredom, but do you really think chatting with an ex-convict is the best way? I mean, no matter what kind of a guy he is underneath, he's been in jail for all of his adult life. He's got a lot of catching up to do."

Rachel's expression came close to being a pout. "If I'm

part of this, I'd really like to look him in the eye and decide for myself if he did the deed."

"He's not a trained seal, Rachel," Meg said. "He's not ours to parade around. I'll ask him, and if he agrees, we'll bring him to see you."

"Fair enough. So, what've you got so far?"

12

"What've we got?" Meg and Seth swapped glances before turning back to Rachel. "Only what Aaron has told us himself," Seth said.

"What about the police report?" Rachel demanded.

"Rachel, let me remind you we only heard about this yesterday—last night, in fact. We haven't had a lot of time to dig up anything," Seth said, sounding exasperated. "But to answer your question, whatever investigation went on took place under Art Preston's predecessor, Chief Burchard. I have no idea where his files might be stored. I can ask Art. In theory it shouldn't be a problem, since I think police reports are public documents. Best case, Art has them on file somewhere, or has already pulled them."

"Want me to start a list?" Rachel asked.

"Whatever makes you happy," Seth told her.

"Great. Give me a pad—over there, on the table. Making lists seems to be part of my nesting behavior," Rachel said.

Seth handed her a lined pad and a pencil. "Thank you. Okay, next. Trial transcript: who keeps those, and where can you get them?"

"Uh, I don't know?" Seth replied. "It's never come up for the town, as far as I can remember."

"Well, then find out. So, between those documents you should have the official description of the event, the evidence presented, and the witnesses called."

Meg smiled. "Rachel, have you been watching *Law & Order* again?"

"You bet. What evidence was there?"

"Aaron said drug materials were found in the basement near where the fire started, which pointed to him," Meg said. "He admitted they were his. Aaron was found outside the building, passed out, but there was no sign he'd been anywhere near the fire."

"Who was inside the house?"

"Aaron's parents and his grandmother—his mother's mother," Meg replied.

"Where were they found?"

"Rachel, I have no idea!" Meg protested. "And no, I don't know if there was an autopsy on any or all of them. From what Aaron has told us, I'd guess that somebody like the medical examiner looked at them and said they died in the fire. It seemed logical. I suppose you're going to suggest they could have been strangled or poisoned or drugged into unconsciousness before the fire started?"

"Well, it is possible, isn't it?" Rachel demanded. "I mean, if there was no autopsy, you can't say they weren't, can you? So if everybody was found neatly laid out in their own bed, that tells you one thing. If they were found on the floor clawing at a locked door, that's a different story."

Meg sent Seth a *what have we gotten ourselves into?*

glance. Rachel was absolutely right: they hadn't even begun to think this through.

"Was there anybody else who wanted the family members dead?"

Meg sighed. "I'm getting tired of saying this, but we don't know."

"Other relatives? Who stood to inherit?"

"Ditto," Meg said.

"What was the insurance situation?"

"Ditto. May I remind you that this happened a quarter of a century ago?" Meg said wearily. "Maybe you and your brother have some vague memories of what happened, but I wasn't even here."

Rachel answered quickly. "Look, Meg, if I remember the event, and I was a babe in arms when it happened, then other people might. Nobody noticed any skulking ninjas or Druids bearing torches running around in the woods?"

Meg giggled.

"The nearest neighbor lived about half a mile away, and they didn't notice anything until the fire was fully engaged," Seth informed Rachel.

"Didn't I read a story somewhere about someone who lit a mouse on fire and threw it into a building, to start a fire?"

They all looked at each other and burst out laughing. "So we need to find someone who raised mice in Granford at that time?" Seth asked. "Or someone in trouble with the SPCA? Or just somebody with a really twisted imagination?"

"Well, if you can find a fire report, maybe we can eliminate the mouse scenario. You need to know for sure where and how the fire started." Rachel stretched and shifted her weight on the couch. "Thanks, guys—at least you've given me something to think about other than Pumpkin. Look, I've got to pee, which is a major production, and it's time for my nap. Why don't you let me think about what you've told me, and then when you find all those documents, we can confer. And I really would like to meet Aaron, if he doesn't get scared by hugely pregnant women."

"I think we can safely say he hasn't seen many lately. If ever," Meg said.

"I'll talk to Art about getting hold of the documents," Seth volunteered. "And I've got to find something around here for Aaron to do. It sounds like it may take more than twenty-four hours to pull all this together, what with legal documents and whatever Gail can track down, and he can't just hang out at our house."

"Are you set for child care when Pumpkin arrives?" Meg asked, changing the subject.

"You mean, after school and stuff like that? Mostly. I may need to call on you and Mom now and then, but not full-time. I'll let you know when the time comes. Soon, I hope!" Rachel skewered Meg with a wicked gleam in her eye. "How're the wedding plans coming, huh?"

"Moving along nicely, thank you," Meg shot back. "I've still got a few weeks left." And a lot of details to deal with—and now an old crime to unravel. Why was life never simple?

They said their good-byes, and Seth, Meg, and Lydia headed back to Granford. Lydia said tentatively, "Rachel's right, you know. There's probably official information to be had, but it's going to take some time to dig it all out, unless Art has already started the ball rolling. Has he made any comments to you?"

Seth shook his head. "I haven't really talked to him since he took Aaron to the hospital. Gail told him she wasn't going to press charges, so he has no further involvement. He wasn't in charge when the fire happened. Bottom line is, he's within his rights to wash his hands of the whole mess right now."

"Will he, Seth?" Meg asked. "You've known him longer than I have."

"I really can't say. I don't know how much Aaron told him, or wants to tell him. Not that Aaron has a choice, if he wants to get to the bottom of this. Art's our best avenue to getting the legal documents. If we're lucky, he's got most of them at the station, or at least in storage somewhere nearby. Hey, maybe they've even been digitized."

"In your dreams," Meg muttered to herself. "You'll call Art when we get back?"

"Oh yeah. He'd love to have his day off interrupted by me so he can dig into a closed case he wasn't even part of. But then, technically this isn't current police business, so maybe it's better that he do it on his time, not town time."

"Thank you." Meg turned to face Lydia in the backseat. "Rachel seems upbeat. Are the kids old enough to help when the baby comes?"

"I hope so," Lydia replied. "At least they're past the stage where they'll be jealous of a new baby. And Noah's great with kids, but he's got to work to pay the bills. Somehow I doubt that Rachel will be getting the bed-and-breakfast up and running again any time soon. My guess is that next summer is the earliest it could happen. At least Pumpkin should be sleeping through the night by then."

"Are you going to take any time off when Pumpkin arrives?"

"To help out?" Lydia said. "Maybe. We haven't hammered out the details. And there are parts of my job I can take home and work on anywhere, so I could be at Rachel's to pick up the kids or take them to sports things. It'll work out, I'm sure. People have been doing this for a long time. Do you know when your parents will be arriving, Meg?"

"We haven't fixed a date. I assume they'll be driving, anyway."

"I was wondering if they might like to stay with me," Lydia said cautiously. "Unless they'd prefer the privacy of a hotel?"

"That's very kind of you, Lydia. I'll ask them." The truth was, Meg had no idea how her parents would feel about that, but it was nice of Lydia to offer.

"But I warn you—I might be tied up with Pumpkin, so they might get only a bed and a wave from me."

"Don't worry about it," Meg said. "I can feed and entertain them." *Assuming I have a working bathroom*, she added to herself. "And I don't think they'd stay long."

"Why not?" Lydia asked. "They don't get to see much of you."

Whose choice was that? Meg wondered. She loved her parents, and she thought they got along reasonably well, but there had always been a certain formality between them, almost as though they were guests in each other's lives. "Well, I'll leave it open-ended, and they can decide. It's not like we're planning an exotic honeymoon, so we'll be around." Hopefully without an ex-con in residence. "Did Seth tell you he's giving me a new bathroom?"

"Seth always was a romantic," Lydia said wryly. "When's that going to happen?"

"As soon as Meg here picks out the fixtures. The rest is easy," Seth said.

"Oh, so I'm the one holding up the project?" Meg said, swatting him on the arm.

"In part. I hadn't factored in a criminal investigation."

"So that's mine, too? Which do you think will take longer?" Meg shot back.

"It depends."

"On what?"

"On what Art has on hand, which he could lay hands on today. There may be other stuff he can't access until tomorrow. Or there may be stuff he can't access, ever."

"So call Art as soon as you get home."

"Yes, ma'am."

"Lydia, you want us to drop you off first?" Meg turned to ask.

"I guess. Although your life seems a lot more interesting at the moment than mine does. Will Aaron Eastman still be around?"

"I don't know. I have no idea where else he'd go, but I doubt he wants to be cooped up in the house."

They arrived at Lydia's house, and Seth turned off the engine. "So, you getting out?"

"I guess." Lydia sighed. "Look, if your Mr. Eastman is around for dinner, can I come over? I can tell him a bit more about the Granford he remembers, and what's changed. If he's interested, I mean. If he'd rather be alone, I'll understand."

"I'll give you a call, Mom," Seth said, and watched as his mother unlocked her door and went inside with a parting wave.

"So, home?" he asked Meg.

"And you're going to call Art, unless our guest has ridden off into the sunset, leaving a brief note behind."

"It's a plan," Seth said, pulling out of his mother's driveway. He pulled into Meg's ninety seconds later. They parked and entered the kitchen together.

Bree was sitting at the kitchen table leafing through what looked to Meg like an agricultural catalog. "How's the mom-to-be?"

"Large," Meg replied. "Where's our guest?"

"Well, another alpaca showed up, and I called the Gardners,

who came over to pick it—her—up, and they started talking to Aaron. He said he had the time to fix their fence, and he asked me if he could borrow some tools, because, duh, he doesn't have any. So I let him go through some of yours, Seth—the ones you keep in the barn, not your office. So they all went off merrily to fix the fence. Aaron said he'd be back for supper, unless, of course, Patty Gardner insisted on feeding him. But he'll be back sometime, anyway."

"Interesting," Seth said. "Did he tell them he'd just gotten out of prison?"

"Hey, I couldn't hear their conversation, and I'm no snoop. Would it matter? He's just fixing a fence."

"I guess not," Seth replied. He glanced briefly at Meg. "I have to make a phone call." He hung up his jacket by the door, then walked into the front room to call.

"What's that about?" Bree nodded at Seth's departing back.

"We told Rachel a bit about Aaron, and she took the bit in her teeth and ran with it—well, figuratively, anyway. She made a list of information we needed, starting with the original police report. Then the trial transcript. Then we regroup and decide what more we need. I think Rachel is bored."

"You gonna do it?" Bree asked.

"That's why Seth is talking to Art right now. As far as we know, Aaron has no current legal issues, so this isn't an official investigation from Art's viewpoint, now that Gail has said she won't press charges. He'd be doing us a favor, that's all."

"You expect to find anything new, based on some old paperwork?" Bree asked.

"I honestly don't know. If we get hold of the documents, it may be a dead end. Or it may take a while to get them, if they're available. Seth and I have no legal standing here, and I'm not sure what rights Aaron has. Damn, it's complicated." Meg thought for a moment. "What's your take on Aaron? You have no history with him, past or present."

Bree gave Meg's question the attention it deserved. "I think he's very controlled. Reserved. Doesn't trust people—yet. Maybe that's not him, but that's the way he's acting. Maybe even kind of shell-shocked—I can't imagine being kept out of society for twenty-five years and walking into the way things are now. So he's being cautious. And I don't think he's made any plans, which might be a good thing because if he had, they'd probably be irrelevant now. Enough?"

"I agree with everything you say, Bree. And he must feel very isolated. The last thing he knew, his parents were dead and he was told he'd killed them. I don't know if he's had any contact with this sister or brother—that's something else to add to Rachel's list. But basically, Aaron has no one and nothing; he's starting over."

"So of course you have to fix things for him," Bree said sarcastically.

"I'm just trying to help!" Meg protested. "And before you say it, yes, there's this wedding coming up. But it's nothing fancy! Just friends and a few relatives getting together for a party that happens to have a legal ceremony included."

"If you say so," Bree said. She stood up. "What's happening with dinner?"

Seth reemerged from the front of the house. "I just invited Art over, which didn't make his wife too happy. We have food?"

"We'll figure something out," Meg said, and started digging through the refrigerator.

13

 "Hi, Meg," Art Preston said as he walked in the back door. "My wife says you owe her big-time, and she's already thinking about what she wants from you. Hey, Seth."

Seth raised his hand in greeting, but Meg rushed to explain. "Hi, Art. I apologize, but all this has come up kind of quickly. I mean, two days ago I had no idea who Aaron Eastman was, and now he's coming to dinner. You don't have a problem with that, do you?" Meg ended anxiously.

"Hey, I've only seen the guy when he was semiconscious. He had ID on him, and once I figured out who he was, I checked for a record and found that he was a free man. Didn't know about his Granford history—wow. And then Gail said she and the Historical Society didn't want to press charges. I didn't even get a chance to tell Eastman myself, because by the time I got back to the hospital yesterday he'd checked himself out. Since he has no insurance, the hospital didn't fight too hard to keep him. And of course he didn't leave any forwarding address. So he popped up here?"

"Yes, late yesterday. He said he wanted to thank me for saving his life. Maybe that's an exaggeration."

"Maybe not, Meg. If he'd spent another night in that barn, he might not have made it. The hospital had to pump some blood and fluids into him before they stitched him up. But at least they declared him more or less healthy. And then he walked out. Wonder how he found you?"

"He must have asked somebody. I didn't even live here when he did, and I don't have the same name as the people who did. And I'm pretty sure he didn't even know my name."

Seth handed Art a beer. "Just call her 'Angel of Mercy,'" he said. "So he shows up on the doorstep, and what does she do but invite him in, feed him dinner, and let him bunk on the couch."

Meg was beginning to get angry. "Seth, what did you want me to do? He was just out of the hospital, and he had nowhere else to go!"

Seth backed off quickly at her reaction. "I'm sorry. It was a decent thing to do."

"And I had you here to protect me, if he tried anything funny. Which I really don't think he was in any shape to do."

Art regarded them both with amusement. "Can you two stop bickering long enough to tell me why I'm here?"

"Since I seem to have assumed responsibility for the man, I'll explain," Meg said. "Aaron Eastman still doesn't remember what happened the night of the fire that he's supposed to have caused. But there's one item that he does remember from before the fire that's been bothering him for twenty-five years. He wants to find out if it meant anything, or if it's just a loose end. He asked us to help. Now we're asking you to see what files you have or can get, Art."

"Meg Corey, you are a piece of work. You're asking me to look into a cold case that was prosecuted when I was about fifteen? And a guy was convicted and went to prison for?"

"Exactly. Look, we're not asking you to investigate, only to find out what records and documents are available and how to get them. The Granford police records, court records, a report on the fire, that kind of thing. Can you do that? Please?"

"You aren't going to tell me what he told you about?" Art finally said.

"No, because it won't even be in the records, and even he admits it may not be relevant. But Seth and I are coming at this with fresh eyes. The thing is, there might have been questions that weren't asked, if you know what I mean."

Before Art could answer Meg, Seth said, "Art, how well did you know Chief Burchard?"

"Eben? I'd known him maybe ten years before I took over his job. I worked with him, remember? I can't say that we socialized—he was a lot older than me."

"What kind of a man was he?" Seth pressed.

Art stared at him, and it wasn't friendly. "What are you asking? Did someone pay him off? Was he asleep at the wheel? What?"

"I'm not implying he took bribes—besides, the only people with the money in this story were the Eastmans, and they were dead, so who was going to bribe him? I guess I'm wondering more whether he took the easy way out sometimes. From all I've heard, the Eastman fire was pretty cut-and-dried: the fire started, three people died. We don't have all the details, but the obvious assumption is that the fire caused the deaths. Aaron told us that his drug kit was found in the basement, near where the fire started. Again, the assumption would be that that was where and how the fire started, he panicked and got out fast while the others didn't, and that's why he was convicted. But isn't it possible, just barely, that there was something else going on?"

"To draw an obvious conclusion is not a sign of bad police work, Seth," Art said stiffly. "Why should Chief Burchard have looked for complicated explanations when the simplest one fit just fine?"

"Art, I'm not saying he was wrong. I just want to put Aaron Eastman's mind to rest. We're not asking you to involve yourself or any of the town resources, only to get us what documents you can. Any digging to be done, we'll do it."

"And if you find something, it'll end up in my lap," Art grumbled.

Seth grinned at him. "And if we don't, ours is the only time we've wasted. Can you just check the police department's files? Please?"

"All right. If you'll get me another beer and then feed me. At least I can tell my wife with a straight face that this was police business."

"Deal."

The back door opened, and Aaron Eastman walked in and stopped dead at the sight of Art. "Sorry—am I interrupting something? Wait, do I know you?" he asked Art.

"I'm the one who hauled you off to the hospital on Friday night, after Meg here found you." Art stuck out his hand. "Art Preston, Granford chief of police. And apparent sucker for a sob story."

After a momentary hesitation, Aaron shook Art's hand. "You know who I am."

"I do."

"Did these guys explain why I'm still here?"

"They tried. Maybe I should hear it from you?"

"I'm not doing anything illegal, if you're worried about that," Aaron said defensively.

"Nope, I'm just curious," Art told him. "I count these two"—he nodded at Meg and Seth—"as friends, and you seem to have convinced them of something. So if they trust you, I guess I'll have to. I'd like to hear your side of it. You stayin' for dinner?"

Aaron looked at Meg. "Am I welcome?"

"Of course you are," Meg said promptly. "Now all I have to do is figure out what we're eating."

"I vote for pizza," Seth said. "Saves time and effort."

"That okay?" Meg asked the group. She got nods all around. "Then pizza it is. What do you all want on yours?"

They spent a couple of minutes working out toppings, and then Seth phoned in an order and agreed to pick it up. When he was finished, he gestured to the others to sit, and then he sat down as well. "Bree told us you were alpaca-wrangling today. How'd that go?"

"Silly-looking animals," Aaron said, "but they're nice enough. The fencing over at the Gardners' place is a joke, for anything bigger than a bunny rabbit. They asked if I'd be willing to repair the whole thing, and said they'd pay a fair rate. I had to tell them about my past, but they didn't seem worried about it. And they've got a spare room out in their barn—I guess the place used to have a resident farm-hand before they bought it. Add a space heater, and it'll be fine. I hope you don't think I'm not grateful to you, but I'm kind of looking forward to working outside for a while. Anybody see any problems with that?"

"I think it's great, Aaron," Meg said before anyone else could speak. "The alpacas are cute, but I'm getting a little tired of finding them in my backyard. How long do you think it will take?"

"No idea. But they quoted me a flat rate for the job, plus the room, so it's not like I'd be shafting them by stringing out my time." He looked at the faces around the table. "If we solve anything here, or find out it's a dead end, I'll make sure the job is finished before I leave."

"Aaron, no one was thinking that you'd abuse their trust," Meg said. "But it might be a good thing if you were sticking around for a couple of weeks. Look, we've just told Art here that you asked us to look into something that was bothering you from before the fire, but we didn't give him the details. Are you willing to lay it out for him?"

Aaron shrugged. "Why not? There's nothing that can be used against me. Art, sorry if I don't have a very high opinion of local cops, but nobody ever really asked me about my side of the story. I'm not saying it would have made any difference in the end, but it was my life that they were screwing with, and it would have been nice to be heard."

"Aaron, I don't know the history of the case," Art told him. "You can tell me whatever you want; I'll listen."

Aaron started in on his saga once again, after accepting a beer from Meg. Seth had heard it before, so he went off after about fifteen minutes to pick up the pizzas. Listening to the story, Meg didn't hear any changes from the first version, but it was a pretty simple story, and Aaron had finished before Seth returned with dinner.

Aaron's tone remained flat throughout his narrative, almost as though he was describing someone else's story. Of course, he'd no doubt gone over it hundreds of times in his head, so he would know it by heart. He ended without fanfare, and looked at Art, waiting for a reaction. Meg knew that Art was a fair man, so she was equally curious to see what he would say.

Finally Art spoke. "Let me get this straight, Aaron. You

don't remember what happened, but you do admit the drug stuff was yours and you used in the basement, where the fire started. You don't remember anything about earlier in the day, and you have a fuzzy memory of waking up outside on the lawn while the fire was at its peak. Have I got that right?"

"Yeah, but . . ." Aaron began, but Art stopped him with a raised hand.

"In the interest of fairness, I'll admit that I've heard that a traumatic event can interfere with short-term memory, and add drugs to that and maybe I'll buy your *I don't remember* story. But it seems to me that your idea that there's some secret hiding in these documents is pretty thin."

"You think I don't know that?" Aaron shot back. "But it's the only thing out of the ordinary that I can remember from right before the fire. Look, I spent more time with Gramma than with anybody else in the family. She was acting odd about those boxes."

Art nodded noncommittally. "So you're thinking that there was something fishy going on in the family, and that your grandmother knew something about it, and that these mystery boxes she told you to deliver might have some of the details? That's kind of a big leap of logic, you know."

"That's the only explanation I've come up with," Aaron said. "Unless Gramma had gone senile all of a sudden, but I didn't see anything like that. She wanted to be sure whatever was in those boxes was safe and out of the house."

Art was now in full cop mode, and Meg was glad to see that he was slipping from a guest role into that of an interrogator. "What would she have wanted to hide? Something valuable? Stolen? What did the boxes feel like?"

"Sort of heavy, I guess. Like stacks of paper or books. Not like wrapped-up objects, unless they were made of metal, which would've made noise. We'd already cleared out her house, and my folks weren't much into collecting things. If I had to bet, I'd say paper."

"And she never explained?"

Aaron shook his head. "She didn't. But then, she didn't say, *Don't tell your parents about this.* It was more the way she gave them to me. Anxious, I guess. Maybe somewhere she left a note explaining what was in them, but it would have been in the house, so it's long gone."

"Did she have a lawyer? A will?" Art asked.

"Toward the end she was pretty much stuck in the house; she didn't drive anymore. She did have a will, but it was one of those real simple ones that said something like, *I leave everything to my only daughter*, and so on. I found a blank form at the library and copied it for her, but she didn't ask for help filling it out. I can't tell you if she added anything to that, but she would have had no reason to tell me anyway. Was it ever found?"

Art shrugged. "I don't know. Probably destroyed in the fire, unless she had a safe deposit box somewhere, or maybe a lawyer. Did she still get mail?"

"Sure," Aaron replied. "She wasn't like a prisoner. It was her physical mobility that was a problem—she was past eighty—but her mind was okay. Look, Chief, the more I tell this story out loud, the sillier it sounds, even to me. I was stoned most of the time, so maybe I added something, or, more likely, forgot something. Or I was just paranoid, seeing things that weren't there. Maybe those boxes really were nothing more important than her diaries. I'd just like to know."

Seth arrived with the pizzas. Meg doled out paper plates and more drinks, and called upstairs to Bree, who'd been in her room to avoid the whole discussion with Art, to alert her that food was on the table. Bree came down, grabbed a couple of slices, then retreated to her room again. Once everyone had food in front of them, Art cleared his throat, and the other three turned in unison to hear what he was going to say.

Art laughed at their response. "Hey, guys, I'm not about to make some big pronouncement here. This is all new to me, remember? But I'll tell you what I've got so far. The most important thing is to find those boxes, and you've already got Gail working on that. She's probably the only person who has a hope of tracking them down. Okay." Art held up one hand and started ticking off points on his fingers. "So either she can't find them, and the story's over." One finger. "Or she can find them, and there's nothing important in them." A second finger. "Or she finds them and we get a real surprise and this whole thing blows wide open." And he opened his hand wide as if mimicking an explosion. "If that happens, we can all reconsider. Tomorrow I'll track down our in-house files on the fire—you're lucky there, Aaron, because when we moved into the new building a year or more ago, we did go through the files and sort them, and since we had room, at least for now, we kept them within the department. So it won't take me long to find what you need. Then we wait on Gail. Now can we eat?"

"Thank you, Art. I appreciate it," Aaron said quietly.

Art waved a slice of pizza toward Meg and Seth. "Thank these two."

Aaron smiled at them and went back to eating.

14

Not long after Art had left, Meg was startled to see Lydia's face at the back door. When Meg let her in, Lydia said cheerfully, "I thought I'd bring you that recipe you asked for earlier."

Meg stifled a laugh. "Yes, Lydia, you may come in and meet Aaron."

"Am I that bad a liar?" Lydia walked into the kitchen. "Hello, Aaron, I'm Lydia Chapin, Seth's mother. I just didn't want you to feel like some zoo specimen that everyone had to inspect. But Meg's told me about what's going on with you, and I'd like to help. I knew your parents slightly, but we weren't exactly friends."

Aaron had stood up when Lydia entered—those good manners again—and he extended his hand. "It's nice to meet you, Mrs. Chapin. I don't mind; I guess I'm pretty much a curiosity around here."

"Lydia, please. Well, it's rude, but I thought I should at

least see you face-to-face, if I'm digging into the details of your personal life."

"Have you eaten, Mom?" Seth asked. "I'm sorry we ate all the pizza."

"Yes, I waited until I thought you'd be done. And I'll be on my way—it's getting late. But I'm glad to have finally met you, Aaron."

"Thank you for your help, Lydia. I appreciate it."

"Will you be staying around long?"

Aaron looked at Meg and Seth before replying. "I . . . don't know. A couple of weeks, anyway."

"Then I'll probably be seeing you again. Night, all." With that Lydia breezed out the way she had come in.

"Sorry," Seth said. "I was going to call her, but we got busy. I hope you don't mind, Aaron. We weren't planning to drag all of Granford into this."

"I know. No problem," Aaron said, and lapsed into silence.

The rest of the evening passed cordially, and Meg was pleased. Aaron left first, pleading a need for sleep; Seth told him he'd try to find him some additional clothes, and offered to direct him to local supply stores so he could get the materials he would need for the fence repair project.

"You have a way to get around?" Seth asked.

"Yeah, the Gardners have an old pickup they said I could use to haul supplies. I didn't drive over tonight because I like walking back and forth to this place—clears my head."

Art had left, but he had agreed to help, within limits, and Meg couldn't ask for more. Now the next step rested on Gail's shoulders. No, that was a confused metaphor, Meg realized; she must be more tired than she thought. So, she would call Gail in the morning, after she'd sent her kids off to school. And she'd keep her fingers crossed that the boxes would turn up somewhere. And maybe she'd bake something and take it over to the Gardners, to thank them for offering Aaron work, and to welcome them to the neighborhood—and to check out the alpaca herd. She was having trouble imagining a whole bunch of the silly fuzzy creatures together.

The next morning Meg could hear Seth in the kitchen before she could drag herself out of bed. After a quick shower, she joined him. "You're up early. Busy schedule?" she asked, helping herself to coffee. She sat in one of the kitchen chairs, and Lolly immediately jumped on her lap— she must be getting cold.

"That's what I'm trying to figure out. You?"

"I'll call my parents today. Was Lydia serious about having them stay at her house? We didn't have much chance to talk to her last night, since you forgot to call her."

Seth looked guilty. "No, but I'll call her today and ask about her inviting your folks, if you want."

"Good," Meg said. "Anyway, I know the last time my mother was here, she said the hotel in Northampton was kind of expensive, which is no surprise, since it's the nicest one around. Well, maybe the one in Amherst is good, too, but I'm pretty sure that costs just as much. Not that they're hurting financially, as far as I know. It's more a question of privacy. Although I'm sure they'd get along fine with Lydia." *Maybe.* "I can't remember that we ever visited much of anyone that way."

Seth was still studying a pad on the table. "Meg, you're dithering. Just call your mother and ask what she wants to do. Mom won't be insulted if your parents would prefer a hotel."

Yes, Meg thought, *that would be the sensible, adult thing to do.* So why was she waffling? "I've got to check the responses to the wedding invitations. I told people they could reply by e-mail, but I don't seem to get much time to read it."

"Don't worry so much. Most of the people we want to be there live in Granford, and we'll probably see them before the day."

"Nicky needs a head count to buy food," Meg reminded him.

"Oh. Well, tell me how the responses are coming, and I'll nudge the ones who haven't replied, if I see them. Did you invite a lot of out-of-towners? Old college roommates or high school friends? Any relatives I don't know about?"

"No," Meg admitted reluctantly, obscurely embarrassed that she seemed to have so few friends. "I've lost touch with most of my college friends, and it's not like I'm recruiting a herd of bridesmaids. Have you talked to Art about being best man?"

"Nope. How about you and Gail?"

"Nope. Are you sure we're getting married?"

Seth looked up at her then. "Of course we are. I just want some friends there."

"My mother will be horrified by the whole process. But then, I'm not inviting any of her friends, so they'll never know to criticize." She stood up, dislodging Lolly, and went to the refrigerator to find breakfast. "What are you so busy working on?" she asked, over her shoulder.

"Trying to figure out when to install the new bath. I think I can break some time free next week, depending on when I can wrap up a couple of small projects."

"Please don't tell me you're going to rip out the plumbing the week of the wedding!"

"Don't worry; this'll only take a couple of days. Well, except for finishes. So, have you made any decisions about tiles yet?"

"Seth! We've been a little busy. I really hope Gail finds those boxes for Aaron and we can put that whole problem to rest. It was nice of the Gardners to give him some short-term work. Did you have a hand in it?"

"Nope. Although I do feel sorry for the guy somehow—it can't be easy for him."

"I'm glad Art's on board. And it sounds like he should be able to find the police records quickly, which is another plus. I wonder when Rachel will have the baby. She really did look ready yesterday, didn't she?"

"She did. Has Mom said anything about Thanksgiving?"

"Not to me. I'll talk to Lydia about it. Any other problems I need to solve? World peace? Global warming?"

"That's for next week." Seth smiled at her, and Meg's heart turned over. He looked so happy, and somehow she could claim at least part of the credit for that. All the rest was just . . . details.

Bree interrupted them during a long clinch. "Hey, I thought I was making plenty of noise. You want me to leave and come back again?" she said.

"No, we're about done here," Seth said. "Meg, you go pick out tiles and fixtures. See you later." He strode out the back door toward his office, a man with a plan.

"Wow, he's in a good mood," Bree commented, as she poured a mug of coffee.

"Yes, he is, all things considered," Meg replied.

"What things?" Bree demanded. "Invading alpacas? That Big Event you keep avoiding talking about? This cold case that just fell into your lap?"

"That's just the short list. Add to that, I have to call my mother. Are we picking today?"

"Yup, but just for a few hours. You should help. I think the fresh air will do you good, clear the fog out of your brain."

"You could be right. So I can postpone all the unpleasant stuff I'm apparently avoiding until this afternoon?"

"You got it."

Bree had proved right: Meg felt better after a few hours of simple physical exercise. The autumn air was brisk and cool, and most of the trees around her property had lost their leaves. The last rows of late-ripening apples provided a bright spot of color, and Meg would be sorry to see the red highlights go. It had been a good harvest. Maybe not financially, but she was much more comfortable now with the process of picking and the details of marketing, and even with working with the pickers. Bree hadn't said so yet, but she was pretty sure they'd all be coming back next season. And if she was very lucky, by then she'd have a new pump for her spring, and new irrigation lines laid down. One spell of watering by hand during a long heat wave, with a tanker, was more than enough for her.

She had just about finished up her row when her cell phone rang, and she recognized Gail's number. She answered quickly. "Hi, Gail. What's up?"

"I think I've found them. The boxes, I mean. Aaron's boxes."

"Gail that's terrific? You have them now?"

"No, but I know where they're stashed. Where's Aaron?"

"He's got a part-time job, mending fences for the Gardners. Can you retrieve the boxes by the end of the day?"

"I think so. But I've got the kids to worry about, and supper . . . I know how much Aaron's going to want to see these, but I'm kind of jammed up."

"Aaron's not the only one! We talked to Art last night, and he's going to try to find the police records of the fire—he thought they'd still be in the new police department offices. And I have to admit, since Seth and I seem to be in the middle of this, we'd really like to see them, too. Any chance we could all meet after supper?"

"I think so," Gail said, after a moment's thought. "Can you reach Aaron?"

"Shoot, obviously he doesn't have a cell phone. But I know where he's staying. I was going to go over there and see the alpacas at home. Or maybe Seth can track him down. One way or another we'll get in touch with him, and I'll call Art. But I'll wait to see if you can actually take possession of the boxes first, okay?"

"I'll let you know. If this is going to happen, I've only got an hour or two before the kids get home. Gotta run!"

Meg felt ridiculously pleased that this whole tangled mess might actually be moving one step forward. She waved to catch Bree's attention, then called out, "Bree, are we about done here?"

"Yeah, we're good," Bree yelled back.

"Then I'm going down to the house." She made her way down the hill. Once inside, she wavered: eat lunch, or call her mother? Lunch could wait: she knew she'd feel much happier once she had discharged one responsibility, and she was still riding high on Gail's news. She decided to use the landline, in case Gail called back on her cell.

Her mother was on speed dial, so Meg hit that. Her mother answered on the third ring. "Well, my goodness, I thought I remembered a daughter. How are you, darling?"

"The usual. Busy, overworked."

"I'm glad to hear that. So I can assume that this theoretical wedding hasn't been called off?"

"Mother, I gave you the date as soon as I knew it. I'm just calling to firm up plans."

"Well, I believe it'll be too cold in December to hold this in a New England meadow, or in your orchard. I assume you have a venue?"

"I do—Gran's. The restaurant."

"Oh, right. Lovely place. So those nice young chefs are doing the catering?"

"They are." At least one thing was settled—knock on wood, barring disasters.

"And your delightful professor friend Christopher will be officiating?"

"He will." Assuming he had requested the license, and that hadn't gotten hung up somewhere in the labyrinth of state offices. Another thing she should check. "Actually I was calling so we could decide when you'll be arriving, and where you'll be staying."

"Well, dear, I thought you might be a bit preoccupied, so rather than stay at your house I assumed we'd find one or another hotel. Early December's not a particularly busy time of year among the colleges, is it?"

"Not that I've noticed, Mother. But I did want to suggest one other alternative. Seth's mother has invited you to stay with her, if you like."

"Oh, how nice of her! May I discuss it with your father?"

Her mother's typical stalling tactic. "Sure," Meg said. "Don't worry—Lydia won't be offended if you say no."

"Let me think about it. Are you planning anything like a honeymoon?"

"Not yet," Meg said cheerfully. "So you can stay around after, if you want."

"I will let you know, as soon as I've talked to Phillip. Is everything else all right? How's Seth?"

"Seth is happy as a hog in . . . well, you know. He's got as much work as he can handle, but it's what he loves to do. You want to know what his wedding gift will be?"

"Of course, dear. What is it?"

"A new bathroom," Meg said triumphantly.

Meg's mother was silent for several beats. "How very thoughtful of him. And both personal and practical."

"Yes, it is. I think it's sweet. How's Daddy?"

"He's fine. His knees have been bothering him, with this cold weather, so he hasn't been playing as much golf as he'd like." She hesitated before saying softly, "Are you happy, Meg?"

Meg replied honestly, "Yes, Mother, I am." *And thank you for asking.* "Let me know what you decide about where to stay."

"I will do that. We'll talk soon! Bye, love."

There, one duty done. As if planned, Meg's cell phone rang as soon as she'd hung up the landline. "Hi, Gail."

"Got 'em!" Gail crowed. "Can you and Seth bring Aaron by, say, seven thirty? To the Historical Society building? I want to show off our new heating system—the place should actually be warm."

"I'll call Seth now. See you later!"

As soon as she had ended the call to Gail, she hit Seth's speed dial number. He, too, picked up quickly. "What's up?"

"Gail's found the files! She wants us to bring Aaron to the Historical Society after dinner, for the great unveiling. Can you stop by the Gardners' and tell him, or would you rather I went over?"

"I think I can manage that, maybe around four thirty. I was going to swing by my house and see what clothes I've got that might fit Aaron. Or maybe I should ask Mom—she's probably got loads stashed in the attic. Either way, I'll collect Aaron and bring him over for supper, if that's okay with you."

"No problem; the afternoon is clear. See you later!"

Meg hung up again, feeling very pleased with herself.

15

Since she was freed from orchard activities for the rest of the day, and it seemed kind of early to start cooking dinner, Meg decided to do a quick Internet search on the Eastman fire in Granford. It never ceased to amaze her how much older material kept cropping up online, and she wasn't disappointed. Archived newspaper reports from the time informed her that early in October 1990 the Eastman blaze had gone to three alarms. When the first fire truck had arrived, the house was already fully engaged, and there was no chance to enter the house and search for anyone. Putting out the fire was further complicated because there were no hydrants in the neighborhood—the house was set well back from the street in a rural part of town. Tanker trucks would have been useless against a blaze of that size. The best the firefighters could do was try to keep the fire contained and away from the surrounding woods. Apparently a few other people had shown up, but all they could do was huddle together at a safe distance, watching the house disintegrate, before describing the fire to the newspaper writers.

The only mention of Aaron at first was that the Eastmans' youngest son had been at home but was found outside the house in what appeared to be a state of shock. His two older siblings were both attending school outside of Granford and were not affected. Although it could not be confirmed until after the fire was fully extinguished, it was presumed that Aaron's parents and his grandmother had perished in the blaze.

Having read three versions of that account in three different newspapers, Meg sat back and reviewed. Basically she hadn't learned anything new, except for the absence of hydrants, something she hadn't thought about. Everything matched what Aaron had told her. She debated briefly about reading the follow-up stories from the first few days after the fire, which would segue into Aaron's trial and conviction, and decided against it. She didn't want to hear the story from third parties: she wanted to hear what Aaron had to say, in the present. She didn't want to prejudice herself, either pro or con. Aaron was being fair. He admitted his memories of the event, then and now, were missing. He just wanted to know the truth, to know what he was really capable of, so that he could get on with his life.

If there was no new evidence, or if anything they unearthed pointed even more strongly toward Aaron's guilt, would Aaron be able to live with himself? Knowing what he had done? He had so little to look forward to from life. Maybe he would see suicide as a viable option.

Not if she could help it. But she'd already saved him once. Was she supposed to save him again?

Shutting down the computer, Meg set about making an elaborate casserole, mainly to distract herself from her troubling thoughts. Bree came in, took one look at her activities, and said, "Looks good—I'll leave you to it," before disappearing up to her room. Meg was just pulling the casserole out of the oven to cool when Seth and Aaron arrived, and Meg was surprised to see that it was nearly six o'clock. "Hi, guys," she said. "Let this cool off a bit and we can sit down and eat. Bree?" she called up the stairs.

"What?" Bree shouted in return.

"Dinner in five," Meg replied.

"On my way," was Bree's answer.

After ten minutes, they were seated around the kitchen table with heaped plates in front of them, and Max and Lolly had been fed. Aaron was wearing clean clothes, and looked like he was trying to bottle up his anticipation. This small piece of the family puzzle meant a lot to him, and Meg hoped he wouldn't be disappointed. "How'd it go with the alpacas?" Meg asked him.

Aaron smiled, which made him look younger. "They are so funny. Really curious, you know? Every time I wanted to do something along the fence, a bunch of them would follow me, watching. I swear they were talking about me."

"How much work is involved?"

"Some parts are going to have to be completely replaced. Others I can repair, at least for now. I don't know what those people were thinking when they bought that particular site— most of it's on a steep slope. I gather they're from a city. And why they chose alpacas doesn't make sense to me, either."

"Hey," Bree responded, "alpacas are hot these days. I took a class in animal husbandry at school, and if you can find an outlet for the fur, they make economic sense."

"I didn't know that," Aaron said. "Thank you."

"Anything more from Gail?" Seth asked. Aaron's eyes flickered toward Meg's face.

"What's going on with Gail?" Bree demanded.

"She found the family papers that the Eastmans donated to the Historical Society, back before the fire, and we're going over there after supper to take a look at them."

Bree cast a dubious glance at Aaron but didn't say anything.

"Hey, I talked to my mother today," Meg announced in a cheery tone. "Seth, I told her about Lydia's invitation."

"What did she say?"

"She said she'd talk to Daddy."

"And how do you read that?" Seth asked.

"It'll probably be no. I told her Lydia wouldn't be offended. Are you insulted on her behalf?"

"No. I'm not surprised, is all."

"So you two are getting married?" Aaron said. "How long have you known each other?"

"I moved to Granford two years ago January." Meg debated briefly with herself before adding, "And was accused of murder almost immediately. I'm not sure Seth believed I didn't do it, at first, so I had to figure out who did. As you can see, it all worked out."

Aaron smiled at his plate. "That's sure one heck of a romantic story."

"It is, isn't it?" Meg said complacently. "And did he tell you he's giving me a new bathroom as a wedding present? We don't seem to do anything the traditional way."

They wrapped up dinner quickly, conscious of the coming meeting. Bree asked, "You want me to clean up so you can head into town?"

"That would be great, thanks," Meg said. "You guys ready to go?"

"I guess," Seth said. Aaron just nodded. "I'll drive," Seth added.

It took them all of five minutes to reach the Historical Society on the green. The lights were on inside, their golden glow spilling out into the night, and Meg could understand why Aaron would have been drawn to the building, even if he hadn't had an agenda. After Seth parked and they climbed out of the car, Meg sneaked a glance at Aaron's face. He looked somber—and frightened? He had spent years pinning his hopes on this one meeting, and Meg hoped he wouldn't be too upset if it didn't produce the results he hoped for.

Gail opened the door before they reached the granite stoop. "Please, come in." Aaron hung back, as if unsure of his welcome, and Gail added, "You, too, Aaron. We're even now, right?"

"Thank you, Gail." Aaron followed the others into the building.

After she'd shut the door, Gail turned to face them. "I set things up in the basement. Ooh, that's an ugly name for a great space. Seth, help me out here—what should I call it?"

"The archive? The library?"

"'Library' will do, I guess. Or maybe we should have a naming contest among our members. Anyway, there's a nice large table there, and the light is good. And it's warm, as promised. Follow me."

Dutifully they trooped through a door at the rear and down some new stairs to the lower level. Meg inhaled: the place still smelled of fresh paint, now combined with the musty smell of old paper. As Gail had told them, there was a table about eight feet long, which currently had two chairs on each side. A dozen or so bankers' boxes occupied one end of the table. "You found all of them?" Aaron asked.

"All that I know about. You think something is missing?"

"No, no," he hurried to reassure her. "Look, you can tell

those three on one end are different—not the same kind of boxes. Those have got to be the last ones Gramma sent over. Have you looked in them, Gail?"

"No, Aaron, I thought you should have the first look. You want to start with those three?"

"Okay. Uh, they're still taped shut."

"Let me get some scissors," Gail said. While she ran upstairs, nobody spoke. Meg noticed that the three nonmatching boxes were the only ones that were taped shut. Why?

Gail was back in thirty seconds, and handed the scissors to Aaron. "You can do the honors."

Aaron stood up and pulled one of the boxes closer to him, then ran one blade of the scissors around the lid, cutting the tape. Meg found she was holding her breath. What would emerge? Dust? A large rat? A million dollars in bearer bonds? Aaron wiggled the lid off, then stood staring at the contents. "I don't understand," he said to no one in particular.

"What's in there, Aaron?" Meg asked.

He glanced at Gail, who nodded her encouragement, and then he reached in and pulled out what looked like a bundle of financial ledgers. Not antique, not even close. Aaron extracted three ledgers, followed by a stack of manila folders. "I don't know what these are."

He reached for the second box and opened that. This time he pulled out a bundle of green-and-white-striped paper, which Meg recognized as outdated computer paper. The third box contained more folders, and Meg spied what she thought read "Insurance" on at least one of them.

When Aaron had opened all of them, and sorted through the piles—with surprising patience—he sat down and shook his head.

"Not what you expected, Aaron?" Gail asked.

"I don't know what I expected, but it wasn't this. These look like business records."

"For what business?" Meg asked.

Aaron pulled one of the ledgers toward him. "Eastman Investments."

"Your father's company?"

"No, or at least I don't think so. He worked for a big Wall Street firm, in their Boston office. He traveled a lot on business. Why would my grandmother even have these? And why did she think they were important?"

"What're the dates on them?" Seth asked.

Aaron leafed through a couple of volumes. "Late 1980s, up to the first part of 1990. So they were pretty much current when Gramma handed them to me."

"Do you think your grandmother was, well, of sound mind when she gave these to you?" Meg asked.

"I always thought so."

"Well, if she was, then she must have had a good reason to think these were worth saving," Meg said. "And worth getting out of the house, out of harm's way."

"May I suggest something?" Gail asked suddenly. When everyone nodded silently, she said, "Why don't we set those aside for now and see what's in the other boxes? If it's more of the same, that will tell us something. If it's not, then something else. Agreed?"

"That makes sense," Seth said. "Let's put the stuff back in the first boxes first, so we don't get things mixed up."

The transfers were accomplished quickly, and they did a cursory check of the other boxes. All turned out to contain historic papers relating to the Eastman family, collateral families, and Granford history. When they had finished the first pass, Gail said, "Under normal circumstances, I would be thrilled to see this collection, and I promise we'll take good care of it. But it doesn't begin to explain the contents of those other boxes. What the heck is going on? Or should I say, was going on twenty-five years ago?"

"I wish I knew," Aaron said. "That was my father's stuff. There's no reason for Gramma to have it, much less hide it. You all agree that she didn't want it found, at least right then?"

"Seems likely," Seth said. "Tell me, what was your grandmother like? Educated? Did she have a job at any point?"

"Sure, until she couldn't work anymore. She was smart and observant. It made her really mad that she couldn't do what she had been able to; she kept cursing her body for giving out on her." A brief smile passed over Aaron's face. "And she got really bored when she had to stop working. She told me she'd read every book she wanted to, and even reread her favorites. She hated television. I guess that's why she was happy to let me spend time with her—at least I was entertainment."

Meg was listening with only half an ear, trying to figure out what the odd cache of documents could mean. She didn't like the results she was coming up with. "Aaron, forgive me if I sound tactless, but did either of your parents inherit money?"

"Gramma had enough to get by on. Dad didn't come from a rich family. Maybe the house was worth a lot. Why?"

Meg ignored his question. "You said he worked for a big Wall Street firm—as I remember it from business school, things started to get kind of rocky in the financial world right around then, in the eighties. Did that affect your family's lifestyle, as far as you can remember?"

"Meg, I was so out of it then, they could have brought home a pet elephant and I wouldn't have noticed. As far as I remember, there were no big changes. They bought new cars every year or two, and they were nice cars, if you know what I mean. They took vacations to fancy places. My brother and sister were still in expensive boarding schools. But I'll admit I could have missed a lot."

"Let me ask you one more thing, Aaron: did your grandmother like your father?"

Aaron stared at her for a moment, then laughed. "To quote Gramma, my father was a pompous ass. He was condescending to her, and she hated having to depend on him for anything—although she had money of her own and contributed to the family budget. As far as I know, she paid him for her room and food, like she was a boarder. And Mom didn't complain; she took his side. So no, Gramma didn't much like dear old Dad. Why are you asking?"

Meg chose her words carefully. "The only reason I can see for your grandmother to collect these documents and hide them off the property is because there was something fishy about them. You said your father did something in finance, right?" Aaron nodded. "But these look to me like documents from a private investment scheme. Which could have been perfectly legal, and he might have suffered some reverses in his primary job and needed some additional income. Or it could have been, well, something less than legal. Your father might have been running some sort of scam or Ponzi scheme. You probably missed the whole Bernie Madoff scandal, which was a very large and successful fraud, so it's been known to happen. Let's say that your grandmother knew or guessed that something was not right, so she hid the documents from him—kind of her ace in the hole, if he got too difficult. Maybe she wanted to protect your mother. Does that make sense to you? Anybody?"

"How does that connect with the fire?" Seth asked.

"I don't know . . . yet. If he'd been found out, would your

father have committed suicide, Aaron? And taken his wife and his mother-in-law and possibly you with him?"

Aaron shook his head. "Nah. Dad thought he was invincible—and smarter than everybody else. He probably would've found a way to get out as much money as possible and then settled on a Caribbean island somewhere."

"Then we need to take a close look at these documents. I can do some of it—I used to be a financial analyst—but I didn't specialize in corporate accounting."

"Mom can help," Seth said. "She knows bookkeeping. Although she probably doesn't see this many zeroes very often."

"Then we can work together for a first pass. Aaron, this may be nothing, so don't get too excited."

"That's okay, Meg—I know you're trying. But I think you're right. As far as I know, Gramma had all her marbles right up to the end, so if she took these and had me help her hide them, then she had a reason."

Meg wasn't sure whether she wanted to find something or not.

16

They left the boxes at the Historical Society and headed for home. Meg and Seth dropped Aaron off at the Gardner property, then proceeded to Meg's house. Aaron hadn't said a word along the way, beyond "Thanks."

At Meg's house there were lights on in the kitchen and in Bree's room. Seth turned off the engine and they sat in the relative darkness. "Well," Meg said, and stopped, unsure of what she wanted to say.

"I agree," Seth said. "That was . . . interesting. Not what any of us expected. But what the heck do we do with the information?"

Meg shrugged. "I'm not sure. Maybe the grandmother was falling into dementia, no matter how much Aaron protests, and she collected random stacks of paper and believed they were important and squirreled them away. Aaron wasn't in any shape to judge. Or maybe she was bang on and she was somehow trying to protect her daughter from her sleazy husband. If he *was* sleazy. We don't know that yet, and won't until we see what those ledgers mean. What I still don't see is how any of this connects with the fire."

"Well, suicide is still on the table, if dear old Dad was a swindler and couldn't stand the shame of being revealed. Or it could be murder, planned or accidental. Maybe the fire was meant as a warning, but it got out of hand."

"Seth, do we have to go there? Why can't it simply be a single tragic event, unrelated to anything else?" Meg asked.

"It may yet be. I'm afraid we aren't giving Aaron much closure. Although you'll notice he was right, that there was something odd going on, and his grandmother seemed to know it. Too bad she didn't leave a file explaining what she thought she knew."

"Nothing from Art yet?" Meg asked.

"Not that I know about. Of course, he may have a few other things to do in his job, apart from tracking down dead files for us."

"I know that; you don't have to be sarcastic. Seth, what do you think of Aaron, now that you've spent some time with him?"

Seth considered. "I think he was a smart kid who got into trouble, but lots of kids do that and survive. I think he got sandbagged by the fire and the deaths, so he never had the chance to come out the other side and become an adult. He seems to be intelligent; maybe he could have made something of himself, given the chance."

"But if he didn't start the fire, someone took that chance away from him. That's almost criminal itself, that he should have been deprived of a rewarding, meaningful life, however he would have chosen to define that."

"I can't argue with that."

"So what do we do now?" Meg demanded.

"For the moment, we get some sleep. Tomorrow or whenever, you and Mom go through the financial records. I'll check in with Art about the rest of the documents. And we hope that something jumps out at us."

"I hate to bring this up, but do you think there's any risk involved, to anyone? I mean, if—still an 'if'—Aaron didn't do it, the person who did is still out there and has believed he got away with it for twenty-five years. What would he do now? Go after Aaron? Or us, who seem to be snooping around?"

"Why do you assume it's a 'he'?"

"Okay, he or she. It wouldn't take much strength to start a fire. It would take some planning, which of course women excel at."

"Of course," Seth said with a smile. "As for what you really asked, I don't know. It's possible. On the other hand, if this person has felt safe for this long, he—or she—probably doesn't think there's any threat now. And there may not be: most of the players are long gone, and who knows where Kenneth Eastman's original records are, if they survived at all? Or maybe there's a statute of limitations on fraud and it's all moot. Who's going to remember enough to change the script now?"

"Will you tell me when you think we've invested enough energy in this, so we can stop?" Meg unbuckled her seat belt and turned to face Seth. "Do you think I'm doing this just as a pretense, so I don't have to think about the wedding?"

It was hard to read his expression in the dark. "I don't know. Are you?"

"I don't think so. But I seem to be obsessing about the wrong things. Or maybe after such a crazy busy season, with not enough pickers, I don't know how to slow down, so I'm creating my own tempests in teapots."

"I don't think so, Meg. Aaron deserves a fair chance, and I'm not sure he got one. But we don't have to make it a crusade. We need to strike a balance."

"Agreed. Can we go in now? I'm getting cold."

The next morning Art called while they were still eating breakfast. Seth answered, but what Meg could hear of his conversation was not very helpful. "Uh-huh. Yeah. When? All right. What do we need to do?" When he finally hung up, he sat down at the table again and resumed eating.

Meg swatted his arm. "What did he say?"

"He's got the police report in hand, but it's pitifully thin. He can get hold of the court proceedings, which weren't included, but not before this afternoon. The state fire marshal's report is included in both."

"Did he read the report?" Meg asked.

"If he did, he didn't comment on it. I'd tread lightly here, Meg. I won't say he was close to Chief Burchard, but he is loyal to him—they're both cops. So don't go charging in and telling the world that Burchard handled it wrong."

"But what if he was covering something up? Even if it was only that he was incompetent or sloppy, but he realized he might have messed up?"

"You're going to have to prove it to Art. And also keep in mind that forensics have changed in the past twenty-five years. There are a lot more tests they would run today that they simply didn't have back then. Burchard had to make a judgment call, based on what he had to work with at the time."

"I get it, Seth. I'm not clueless. So when can we look at the files?"

"You are an impatient woman—except when it comes to weddings, I guess. He said he'd drop off what he found after work today. Maybe he'll have the court documents by then, or at least a computer link we can use."

"Great. Are you going to talk to your mother about reviewing Kenneth Eastman's documents, or should I?"

"Why don't you? I don't know what her schedule is like these days, so you two can work something out between you. You have any idea what you're looking for?"

"Something that smells wrong. No, don't laugh, Seth. Of course, what I'd really like is an official prospectus for whatever dear old Dad was flogging. If it's a publicly held fund, it should be available, or at least archived somewhere. If it's not, our only hope would be to find someone who invested with him, assuming they received all the paperwork and kept it. And if we find a copy, then we compare it with the documents from the boxes. It would be nice to have his own bank records, but I think that's too much to hope for. Anyway, if there's more money coming in than is going out to the shareholders, there may be a problem. Ditto if there's no money and he's making payouts from the new investments."

"I see what you're trying to do, but what's the point? Even if Dad was cooking the books, he hadn't been found out, as far as we know."

"But he could have been teetering on the brink, which is what pushed him to act," Meg protested.

"Maybe. But he still ended up dead, so he didn't benefit in the long run. You could check out his will, to see how he handled his estate, but I don't know if there would be a final tabulation. And if he'd run through all the money he'd taken in, or he kept it in some secret account, his death would have ended things."

"Interesting point, though. I wonder what it would take to get a look at the state of his bank accounts when he died. Did he leave everything to his wife, who was also dead? Or to his children, simply divided among them? Could Aaron legally inherit, since he was convicted of killing them? Assuming, of course, there was any money at all."

"Meg, I don't have answers to any of these questions. You'll have to do your own digging. Have you thought about tiles?"

It took Meg a moment to follow his leap of logic. "For the bathroom, you mean? I was wondering if you meant Kenneth Eastman was playing some kind of game, like a shell game, or maybe dominoes—that uses tiles, right?"

"Bathroom, ma'am?" Seth said, nudging her back to the question.

"Right. Where do you want me to look?"

"We've seen the big-box stores. Check online and see if there are some smaller specialty shops. They might be more expensive, but they might have more interesting stuff, and it won't be that big a space if you fall in love with purple granite or something."

"I do not think I could face purple in the morning. What's the most flattering?"

"There's a reason why so many bathrooms are pink, Meg. Makes people look better when they see themselves in the mirror."

"Oh. How about peach? Or cream?"

"Just go look, will you? Bring back samples and you can see how they look in the space."

"Got it. You on a job today?"

"A couple, but they're wrapping up. Say hi to Mom when you call her."

Whistling, Seth deposited his dishes in the sink, grabbed a jacket, called to Max, who came eagerly, and headed out the door.

It was still early enough to call Lydia, in case she was working today. She was lucky to have some flexibility in her work hours, but like Seth's, the larger company she worked for had busy and less-busy seasons, and this was probably one of the busy ones. She hit Lydia's speed dial.

Lydia answered quickly. "Hi, Meg—I was just on my way out the door. What's up?"

"I'll be quick. Art's got Aaron's records, and he's going to drop them off after work today. But I wanted to ask if we could go over Kenneth Eastman's financial records at the Historical Society and see what we can figure out. Is there a good time for you?"

"Do we have to do it at the Historical Society or will Gail give you custody of the papers?"

"I don't know, but I can ask. Why?"

"It would be easier if everything was in one place, so we could cross-check things if we need to. I could come by for supper and we could at least get a sense of what's what. If Gail doesn't mind. Were you going to include Aaron?"

"I don't think so. For one thing, I don't think he knows much about finance or his father's activities. For another, I'd like us to be as objective as possible. And it would save time if we didn't have to explain ourselves along the way."

"Makes sense," Lydia agreed. "So I'll come by about six, all right?"

"Sounds good to me. See you later!" Meg ended the call.

Bree came down the stairs. "Wow, you two were up early. Anything I need to know about?"

"Seth's got some projects he wants to finish up so he can start the bathrooms here. I guess he wants to finish them before the wedding. I know that sounds crazy, but he thinks he can do it. Listen, Bree, there's something we really haven't talked about yet."

"Right, like where I'm going to live," Bree said bluntly, as she popped toast into the toaster.

"Exactly," Meg said, relieved that she didn't have to dance around the subject. "You know that the room and board are part of your salary, don't you?"

"Yeah, I do. And I know how much we're bringing in here, and what you can afford to pay me. And we'll need another picker next year—maybe Hector will come back."

"I was wondering if you and Michael had any plans for moving in together."

Bree laughed shortly. "We're fine the way we are. I mean, he's a good guy, but we aren't that tight. And he's got roommates, so his rent's really low, even for Amherst. And no, I don't want to move in with a bunch of guys, particularly those—they're real slobs."

"Would you be comfortable staying on here after Seth and I are married?"

"Heck, I might as well be: he's always here anyway. What, you want to throw me out?"

"No, nothing like that. In fact, this new bathroom will make things better for everyone, I hope. But there are other options to explore."

Bree buttered her toast and sat down at the table. "Like what?"

"Well, there's Seth's house," Meg began.

"That's vacant again?" Bree asked.

"Yup, it is. So it's available, if you want it."

Bree looked uncharacteristically uncertain. "Thanks for the offer, but it seems kind of big for just me. And I don't much like having roommates—I like my privacy. You got any better ideas?"

"Maybe Lydia would like company? Look, Bree, I'm just throwing out ideas here. In a perfect world, where would you choose to live?"

"You asking if I like my job? I do, although I can't

promise it'll be forever. But I've still got a lot to teach you."
Bree grinned at her.

"You didn't answer the question," Meg said, returning
her grin.

Bree got a faraway look in her eye. "Rebuild the chicken
coop."

"What?" Meg replied, startled.

"You heard about these new tiny houses?" When Meg
shook her head, Bree explained. "They're really tiny—
maybe five hundred square feet, but you've got everything
you need, mostly built in. Look, I don't want a place that
requires a lot of fuss. I don't have a lot of things, and I don't
want any more than I have. So I don't need a lot of space. Is
this making sense to you?"

"I think so. Think Seth knows about this?"

"He probably knows more about the chicken coop."

"Okay, then let me think about it. And please don't ask
Seth just yet. If he gets into it, it'll distract him from everything else that he's supposed to be doing."

"So what else is new? It probably couldn't happen before
spring anyway, but he could think about it over the winter.
So it's status quo for now? Plus one bathroom?"

"Two. One off the master bedroom—and why isn't it
mistress bedroom?—and a powder room down here."

"What a luxury!"

"Oh, and Lydia will be coming by for supper, and then
we're going to go over Aaron's mysterious documents."

"You need me for that?"

"Only if you're fascinated by accounting ledgers."

"I'll pass. But I can help with dinner."

"You need me in the orchard?"

"Nope. Everything's under control. Enjoy the moment—
how often can we say that?"

17

Meg checked the time: too early to call Gail, whose children would still be at home. She decided to leaf through the bathroom catalogs Seth had left for her, to try to visualize what she wanted. Quickly she realized that she had never given much thought to bathrooms. All right, there would be a shower for the new one upstairs, since a bathtub wouldn't fit in the reclaimed space. Did she want a prefab one? Fiberglass? Corian? Would she rather have a tiled one? What about overhead lights in the shower stall? She giggled at that: who couldn't find their own body parts in a space that measured three feet by three feet? Or tell whether they'd scrubbed a particular patch? On to sinks: Freestanding? With cabinet? How big a cabinet? Would this be the only storage? Where would the towels live? Plastic, tile, or stone? What would be easiest to keep clean? Least slippery?

This is ridiculous. Now Meg understood why she'd never

given it any thought. She searched her memory and couldn't come up with a single example of a bathroom she'd walked into and said "wow." Any bathroom should be warm and well lit; safe; easy to keep clean; and as roomy as possible given the available space. Period. She could recall a few, mainly when she had traveled, where it was impossible to sit on the loo without her knees hitting the wall, and she was by no means a large person. A test run might be useful, although the plumbing running through the walls kind of dictated the layout. But apart from that, she hoped that Seth had an opinion about the decor, because she certainly didn't.

Once she'd finished ranting to herself about bathroom planning, it was late enough to call Gail.

"Hey, Meg," Gail answered cheerily. "Just sent the kids off to school. Anything new? Where's Aaron now?"

"Fixing the alpaca fence, over the hill, at least for a few days. Art says he's retrieved all the police files, or will have by the end of the day. I don't suppose you want to join us to go through them?"

"I wish I could," Gail said, with true regret, "but I've got a ton of stuff to do at home, and I'm not sure my family recognizes me anymore. You'll have to give me a quick summary tomorrow."

"That I can do. Lydia and I want to go over those three mystery boxes of Eastman files. Are you comfortable releasing them to us so we could bring them here, or would you rather we worked at the Historical Society building in town?"

"Just the three boxes of financial documents? I think I can trust you with them. Not the earlier boxes, though, because there may be some good historical stuff in there. You want to come by and pick them up later?"

"You give me a time and I'll be there."

"Before three, when the kids get home. Or, wait—I've

got some errands to run. Why don't I just bring them by on my way home? Will you be around?"

"Sure. We're pretty much done with apple-picking. Give me a call when you're on your way."

"Will do. Bye for now!"

It was barely nine o'clock, and Meg didn't know what to do. Feed the goats? Or she could stroll over to where Aaron was supposed to be working on the fence and see how he was doing, but she didn't want to talk to him again until she had more information, afraid of either getting his hopes up or disappointing him. She could clean out the basement. Or the attic. Or both. But those ideas didn't appeal to her. What was it Bree had said about tiny houses? She could investigate those on the Web, and decide if it made sense to talk to Seth about the idea. It was creative, she had to admit, and it would solve a couple of problems. Bree didn't seem to mind the idea of living in a chicken house. But when would Seth find the time to convert it? Would he entertain the idea of letting someone else do the work, or (gasp) buying a ready-made kit?

She became so engrossed in her searches that the next time she checked, it was time for lunch. She found sandwich fixings in the refrigerator, and poked around looking for inspiration for supper. One plus about cooler weather: she could go back to cooking stews and thick soups, which, along with some hearty bread, made a perfectly good meal. Finally enthusiastic, she collected ingredients and started assembling them.

Gail called shortly after two, and appeared in her driveway a few minutes later. Meg went out to greet her and to help carry the boxes. "Let's put them in the dining room," Meg instructed her. "We rarely use that. Funny, isn't it, that we give so much space to a room that doesn't get used, while we crowd into the kitchen to eat?"

"Hey, it's cozier that way, and think of the heat you save," Gail said cheerfully. "Plus you get a nice big work surface. I'll get the last box and you'll be all set." Gail went back out to the car and returned bearing the third banker's box. "So that's it," she said, panting. "Hope you have fun with them. I'm afraid the contents wouldn't make any sense to me. I don't have a head for numbers—just history, apparently."

"You have time for a cup of tea?" Meg asked.

Gail looked at her watch. "I have approximately seventeen minutes. Boil fast."

Meg had a steaming cup in front of her in three minutes. Gail applauded her speed.

When Meg sat down with her own tea, she said, "Gail, there's something I've been meaning to ask you."

Gail dunked her tea bag one last time, then looked at Meg. "What's that?"

"Would you consider being my matron of honor?"

Gail looked blank for a moment, and then her expression turned to glee. "For the wedding? Of course I would! Wait— don't you have any old friends who claim first rights? Colleagues? Former roommates?"

"Gail, you *are* a friend. And you've been part of my life here in Granford since I arrived."

Gail's eyes filled. "Oh, Meg, I'd be happy to. Remind me when and where?"

"Friday, December fourth—the week after Thanksgiving, in the evening. At Gran's. And that is just about all I know. But of course your husband and kids are welcome." Meg made a mental note to tell Nicky to provide some kid-friendly food.

"And here I thought people planned for years. You're talking weeks?"

"I know. I'm behind the curve. But I can't get my head

around some big fancy—and expensive—event. We just want friends and family around us, and good food and drink, and everybody happy."

"Sounds perfect."

"Good. This is anything but formal. And it's not a sit-down meal—I envision people grazing on lots of interesting stuff."

"Well, if Nicky's cooking, it's going to be good. Thank you." She took a swig of her tea, then glanced at her watch again. "Who's the best man?"

"We hope Art Preston, but I don't think Seth's asked him yet."

"Good, good. Is there more to the wedding party? Your folks, Lydia, Christopher?"

"Gail, there isn't really a wedding party. We just need someone to stand up for each of us, and to sign the right documents."

"You mean I don't get to throw you a shower?"

"That's really sweet of you, Gail, but I don't think it's necessary. I'm trying to keep this low-key and simple."

Gail sighed dramatically. "Well, if that's what you want. Is there anything else that I can help with?"

"I've got a whole list of things we haven't done yet, but I'm not sure what you can do about them."

"License, rings, and someone to officiate—they're important. I'm sure half the guests will take pictures. Good food and drink, but not too much. It'll be great. Just let me know if you need help." She stood up. "Gotta run. Call me tomorrow and tell me if you've found anything interesting in the boxes."

"Of course." When Meg stood up to see her out, Gail grabbed her in a quick hug, then turned and hurried to her car. Meg waved as she pulled away.

Well, she thought, *it's turning out to be a pretty good day.*

She'd finally managed to broach the question to Bree about where she wanted to live, and discovered a solution she hadn't even considered. She'd asked Gail to be her attendant. They might have an answer to at least some part of Aaron Eastman's mystery by the evening. Maybe she should give Christopher a call and see if everything was on track for his special license? Or was she bound to encounter bad news somewhere along the way? Well, sooner was better than later: if she found out now that there was a glitch, there was still time to fix it. Who else could perform marriages in Massachusetts? *No, one step at a time. Call Christopher.*

Of course he wasn't in his office: he still taught at the university, and he also spent time in the new research building on campus that he had helped launch. She left a message at his academic office number, and made a mental note to try again later.

She still had time on her hands. Maybe this would be a good moment to take a hard look at the records for her harvest, since there would be few chances to come before it ended. Of course, she'd asked Bree to do it, since Bree was the official manager, which made it part of her job. She didn't want to undercut Bree, or make it look as though she didn't trust her. Still, Bree had never pretended that she enjoyed the financial side of the orchard business. She took much more pleasure in working with the trees—pruning, fertilizing, spraying (organically and responsibly!) against various pests, and even the nitty-gritty stuff like watering and picking. Bree did not shy away from hard work. So it was only fair that Meg pick up the parts that fit her own skills—like finances.

But she'd already asked Lydia to come over later so they could review the financial documents in the boxes, so she didn't think this was the right time to dig into her own. Might as well focus on making dinner.

Art stopped by just after five, and Meg let him in. "You look like a cat who hasn't eaten in days," Art said with a smile. "And here I am carrying a can of cat food."

"All right, I'll be polite. May I offer you some refreshment, sir?" Meg said with exaggerated courtesy.

"No thanks—my wife is ticked off already, so I can't stay long. Seth around?"

"I don't know where he is at the moment. Maybe the two of us should swap tracking devices as wedding gifts—then we'd always know where we were."

"They could probably build a chip into your rings. Ain't technology great? By the way, Seth finally got around to asking if I'd be his best man."

"Will you?" Meg asked, with a tinge of anxiety.

"No, I was planning a skiing vacation in the Alps that weekend." At the sight of Meg's expression, Art burst out laughing. "Of course I will, Meg. Seth and I are joined at the hip, aren't we? And this way I can keep the crime rate at your wedding down."

"Ha-ha," Meg said. "Well, I'm glad to hear it, anyway. Gail's going to be my matron of honor. Will your wife be there?"

"Probably. She enjoys a good party, not to mention the food at Gran's."

"Good. Now have I played nice long enough? Are you going to let me take a look at the files?" Meg wondered whether Aaron was going to show up suddenly; better to keep the files under wraps until she had a better idea what was in them.

"Yes, ma'am." Art pulled out a heavy envelope from under his arm, and even before he opened it Meg was disappointed: it was no more than two inches thick. Was that all it took to decide the course of a man's life?

"Is that all there is?"

"From Granford and the state fire marshal, yes. The court transcripts are another story, but I'm working on it."

"Have you read the file?" Meg demanded.

"Yeah," Art admitted. "Didn't take long."

"What did you think?" Meg tried to keep her tone neutral.

Art sighed. "There's not much there, Meg. The fire was determined to have been set, so it was not electrical, or a careless cigarette, or a forgotten candle. It started in the basement and spread quickly, because the building was old and drafty and the wood was dry. Your buddy Aaron had himself a little hidey-hole down there where he could carry on his less-than-legal activities out of sight of Mom and Dad. He managed to get himself out of the building, God knows how, but there's no evidence that he tried to help anybody else get out. That didn't go over well with the jury. That and he showed no remorse at the trial. Both probably contributed to his long sentence."

Meg didn't like what she was hearing. "Where were the parents found?"

"In their beds. Probably overcome by smoke. As was the grandmother."

"Sad," Meg said, almost to herself. "So nothing new?"

"Not really. To be honest, I don't think Chief Burchard dug very hard, but I can't see any reason why he should have. I don't know if I would have, in his place. It looks like the proverbial open-and-shut case. I know that's not what you want to hear, Meg."

"Oh, Art, I don't know what I want," Meg protested. "A few days ago I'd never heard of Aaron Eastman or the fire in Granford. A jury convicted Aaron, and even he isn't sure whether he did it. Look, I really appreciate your digging up the files, and there's no way I want to throw mud at the Granford police, past or present."

"Am I hearing a 'but'?" Art asked.

"The Aaron Eastman I see now seems so harmless. Even after twenty-five years in prison. Isn't that supposed to harden people? He just wants to know what really happened. If everything points to him, he says he'll accept that. But I still want to see what's in those financial files—that's sort of the wild card here. You don't have to do anything more. Seth and I, and the rest of Seth's family, I guess, will take it from here."

"Good luck with it, Meg. I mean that. Well, I'd better be going," Art said, as he turned toward the door.

"Wait." Meg stopped him. "Can you find out where the brother and sister are now?"

"Better than you can, with the Internet these days? Maybe. I don't recall if we interviewed them before the arrest; they were both at school at the time, not in Granford. If we did, it would be in the file."

Maybe they said they weren't in Granford, but both had attended schools that weren't all that far away. Did they have any reason to burn down their home? But then, did Aaron? "Could you take a quick look for them? Please? I'll let you know if I come up with any more questions, once I've looked at the files. Thanks again, Art. Now go home and enjoy dinner with your wife."

"On my way," Art said, and walked out the door.

18

Lydia arrived shortly before six. When she walked in, she said, "Mmm, something smells good!"

"I hope it *tastes* good," Meg said. "I've been so busy this year I may have forgotten how to cook. How was work?"

"Busy. Funny, what goes on at a big construction company is exactly like what Seth is facing: everybody suddenly gets busy when fall comes. It's like they can see snow looming on the horizon."

"How long have you been working there?" Meg asked, tasting her soup. *More salt*, she thought, *and maybe another herb. Or two.*

"Since not long after Seth's father died. I think I told you'd I'd been keeping the books for the family business, and those skills transferred pretty directly to the position I've got now. Of course, the company was a lot smaller when I started, and it wasn't really a full-time job then, but it worked for all of us. I enjoy it; the people are nice, and the size of the business now is about right. I can't imagine working for some huge corporation, or even the university. Listen, Meg . . . I'm not sure how much I can contribute when we look at the files tonight. I mean, I may know numbers and accounting, but high finance? Not so much."

"Don't worry. I hope I've got that covered, if I haven't already forgotten everything I used to know from my banking days. But once you get past the size of the accounts, it's pretty much the same principles. And I appreciate having a second set of eyes looking at things."

"You really want to find something that would exonerate Aaron?" Lydia said carefully.

"'Exonerate' might be too strong a word. I don't want to go into this with any preconceived ideas, and everything attached to the trial may have been done by the book, with the right result. I want to give Aaron peace of mind. Wouldn't you hate not knowing if you'd done something awful? So if there's something in these papers that suggests that his father might have been doing something shady that might have led to his death, I want to know."

"Maybe it's a blessing, Meg," Lydia responded. "Could you live with yourself, with that knowledge?"

"I can't begin to guess, but I do know that Aaron asked me to help him find out. That's all. I know I shouldn't be giving big chunks of time to this, much less dragging other people into it, but I feel sorry for him. And he didn't have to come back."

"Did he have a choice, Meg?" Lydia asked. "It's the only place he knows; he was only a kid when he went to jail. He has no resources. Where would you have him go? And what do you see as the best outcome now?"

Meg shook her head. "Lydia, I really don't know. If he

did start that fire, he isn't any worse off than he was. If he didn't do it—if he was framed, or nobody found the right evidence or asked the right questions—that creates a whole new set of problems. But let's take this one step at a time. Tonight you and I will sift through his father's papers and see if anything seems 'off.' If we find something odd, we can look further. If not, we give the whole batch back to Gail and tell Aaron we tried. Good enough?"

"Works for me," Lydia replied. "Hi, Seth," she said to her son as he walked into the kitchen. "How're things?"

"Busy!" he said, giving his mother a quick hug. Then he turned and gave Meg a longer one, which ended only when Lydia said, "Hello? There's someone else in the room, you know."

Bree came in from outside, bringing a blast of cool air with her before she shut the door. "Do I smell dinner? Hi, Lydia."

"Yes to dinner," Meg said. "Get washed up and I'll serve. You, too, Seth. Lydia and I have a busy night tonight."

"First dibs on the bathroom!" Bree said, as she dashed up the stairs. Seth's mouth twitched as he looked at Meg. "I hope we won't have to worry about that for much longer."

Once they were all settled at the table, with steaming soup, hot rolls, and wine or their beverage of choice, Meg reviewed what she'd done all day. She glanced at Bree before she mentioned the tiny house concept, but Seth seemed intrigued, and that launched a spirited conversation about housing needs around the table. Meg waited until the end to say, "Art dropped off the police files."

"And?" Seth asked.

"I didn't look at them yet, but in Art's opinion they don't hold anything that we didn't already know. But he went as far as admitting the notes were kind of sparse. I did ask if he could help track down Aaron's brother and sister."

"Why? They weren't around at the time of the fire," Seth countered.

"It's just another loose end. I guess I'm curious to see how they turned out, and how much they were affected by losing their parents in such an awful way. I wonder if they know that Aaron is free now? Or if they've kept in touch with him?"

"Have you asked Aaron?" Seth said.

"No. I didn't want to talk to him until I had something to report. Either we find something or we don't, and then he deserves to know, but right now I don't want my sympathy for the man to color my opinion." Meg took another spoonful of soup. "I looked at bathroom fittings today, in those catalogs of yours."

"And?" Seth asked.

"I have no idea what I want. You want to pick?"

"I had another idea today," he said. "What about authentic pieces? I know a couple of salvage places that carry the old stuff in good condition, at fair prices. Unless you're committed to shiny new things?"

"That sounds great to me, considering this place started out with an outhouse and maybe a few chamber pots. Do things like you're talking about meet current code? I've always heard Massachusetts is pretty sticky about details like that."

"Don't worry. I can retrofit them and you won't even notice. What about tile floors to match? Tile walls, at least half high? Easy to clean."

"Great."

Seth raised a glass. "Here's to one more item checked off the list!"

After supper, Seth volunteered to clean up, Bree disappeared upstairs, and Lydia and Meg moved to the dining room. "Where do we start?" Lydia asked.

"Since we don't really know what's in here, I'd say

chronologically. Maybe after that we can sort them by type, like bank statements, client reports, and so on."

"Works for me," Lydia said. "So we line them up on the table, earliest at the back, newest at the front?"

"Fine. Let's get started."

The sorting was both harder and easier than Meg expected. The entire date range, covering less than ten years from the early eighties to the date of the senior Eastman's death, was represented. But the longer Meg sifted through the documents, the more she had the feeling that these were discards—not the final copy. Some had items scribbled on them, but she planned to wait until the organization was done before taking a closer look at those. But the general condition of many of the pages led Meg to wonder if maybe the grandmother hadn't been scrabbling through the trash to retrieve them. At least Kenneth Eastman hadn't shredded them, so they'd survived. But Meg realized she had been wondering how the grandmother had gotten her hands on the pages, and so many, over time. Had there been a copy machine in the Eastman house? And why were these documents at the house at all? Didn't Eastman have an office to go to? She wondered if this was a cross-section of all the documents in his home space, or whether there had been far more that had been destroyed in the fire.

After a couple of hours, Meg and Lydia had everything lined up in piles by year and sorted by type within each year. They stood side by side along the table and looked at them. "Well, what have we learned?" Meg asked.

"There's a lot more from the later years than from the earlier ones," Lydia offered.

"True. The business was growing? And I'm wondering where Aaron's grandmother got all this—was she riffling through the wastebaskets?"

"I had the same thought. They look kind of shabby, don't they?"

"They do. The other question, of course, is why did she collect these?"

"I did find what looks like a client list," Lydia volunteered. "It goes back a ways." Lydia riffled through a stack and came up with a two-page document, which she handed to Meg. "Notice anything?"

Meg scanned it quickly. "Mostly Granford names. I'd bet you most of those families appear on the first census."

"So if he was working in Boston, he was recruiting his friends and neighbors for his own business?"

"Lydia, did you see any Boston letterhead?"

Lydia shook her head. "Now that you mention it, none at all. He had his own—nice-quality stock. Maybe Aaron got it wrong; he was pretty vague about what his father did for a living, mostly because he wasn't paying attention. Maybe his dad was no more than a small-town financial advisor with pretensions. Although he handled some pretty big sums."

"Not exactly a titan of Wall Street?" Meg said, smiling. "I'd say I could ask a friend in Boston to check it out, but it was so long ago, they wouldn't know about him personally."

"Google the man," Lydia said.

"You Google, Lydia?" Meg asked, surprised.

"Of course I do. I'm not ancient. Although I'd bet either of Rachel's kids could run rings around me, electronically."

"I'll look up the obituary. There must have been a nice one." Meg booted up her laptop and then searched for Kenneth Eastman, and quickly found a multicolumn obituary with a professional photo. "Here we go. It says he was employed by a company of Boston and New York. I vaguely remember the name: I think it was one of the ones that merged with another or two or three when the investment-banking bubble burst. But the implication in the obituary is that he was still working for them at the time of his death."

"Stop and think about who may have written that obit," Lydia said. "One of the kids? How much did they know about Dad's activities? Maybe they grabbed an old CV from somewhere. Or maybe it had been written in advance by the paper and nobody updated it. Any way you look at it, he may not have been working for that firm when he died, but we have no way of knowing how much earlier they had parted ways. What's the earliest date for his own company?"

"Looks like 1983," Meg said. "So now we've got one more puzzle. Well, leaving that aside, what do the reports tell us?"

"That his clients were doing really, really well," Lydia said. "In a very unstable market. I remember thinking back then that I was glad we didn't have any money invested, with three kids and a small business supporting us all, because we probably would have lost it."

"Interesting point, Lydia," Meg answered. "Are you saying that the numbers look too good to be believable?"

Lydia looked Meg in the eye. "I'm saying that's a strong possibility."

Is that the smoking gun? Meg wondered. "Lydia, how much longer do you want to spend on this tonight?"

"Hey, we're just getting to the fun stuff." Lydia grinned. "How about this: we pick one client and follow him or her from start to finish? See how their account performed? How many trades? Ups and downs?"

"Lydia, you do know something about finance," Meg said.

"I know enough to know that when something looks too good to be true, it usually is. Especially when money is involved."

Meg pulled a client statement at random from the 1983

pile, and she and Lydia went searching through the other stacks of paper. At the end, they had a tidy handful of copies. "Looks like a nice, steady rise in the balance, but not many payouts. Which is not unusual—Eastman may have persuaded his clients to reinvest the income. If they didn't have an immediate need for the money, it makes some sense, especially if the funds were doing so well."

"Hold on," Lydia interrupted her. "We've got a couple of duplicates in the stack . . . and those doubles don't show the same figures." She handed several pieces of paper to Meg.

Meg scanned them quickly. "Funny, the changed pages all seem to show an increase over the original calculations. Of course, this is only a couple of statements out of who knows how many. But he made sure the returns looked really good."

"Did this guy have a secretary?" Lydia asked. "Or an accountant working for him? Most bigwig banker types don't bother themselves with basic math and sending out reports."

"I haven't seen any evidence of that," Meg said, "but this isn't everything. Or maybe his lovely socialite wife was doing the books, the way you used to for your husband."

"Goodness, Meg, do I detect a hint of sarcasm? I can't imagine Mrs. Eastman doing anything so mundane. Not that we ran in the same circles or anything; she didn't mingle with the Granford masses."

"But maybe her husband didn't want to let anyone else in on what he was doing," Meg said, "so he kept it all in the family."

"Maybe," Lydia said, unconvinced. "I wish we had some bank statements. At least then we'd know where the money actually was."

"Trying to get those would be a royal pain, Lydia," Meg told her. "Even if we could locate the bank, or even banks, there's no guarantee that we could get hold of the records. We don't necessarily know what name he used for the account. And I'm pretty sure it would take legal action for us to get copies. I doubt we can convince anybody to help us on that."

"But there could be an inventory when the estate was settled, right?" Lydia said with a gleam in her eye. "And wills and probate are a matter of public record."

Meg stared at her, impressed. "Lydia, you are brilliant."

"Where do you think Seth got his brains?"

19

Lydia left not long after that, pleading eye fatigue and the need to get up early for work. Meg tidied the piles of papers, fed Lolly, and walked Max one last time, then trudged up the stairs to her bedroom, where Seth was propped up in bed reading. "Mom gone already? I would've come down to say good-bye, but I didn't want to disturb you two—you looked pretty wrapped up in what you were doing."

"She just left. Are you disappointed she didn't kiss you nighty-night before she left?"

"I think she's passed that torch to you. Did you find anything useful?"

"I think so," Meg said cautiously. "Do you want to hear about it now, or wait until tomorrow?"

"Give me the condensed version now; I can wait for the details." Seth put down his papers and rolled over to look at her.

She settled next to him. "Okay. From what we saw tonight,

Lydia and I both think that Kenneth Eastman was running his own investment business and cooking the books. He was altering clients' reports to make them look better, but he wasn't paying out much. Which suggests to me that his mother-in-law was onto him and was stashing documents that could prove it, possibly to protect her daughter. That's what was in the boxes."

"Interesting. Why do you think that?"

"Because the numbers look outstanding, even after the stock market went to pieces in the eighties."

"I'll take your word for that. But how does that help Aaron?"

"It doesn't, directly, but it could provide a motive for a lot of different things. Maybe the side business was tanking and Dad took the easy way out. Maybe he didn't plan to die, but only to collect life insurance on his wife or her mother—whom he'd already labeled as physically impaired—or the insurance on the house."

"Setting a fire to achieve any of those ends sounds pretty risky."

"Well, of course it is: look at what happened."

"Do you have anything like proof?" Seth asked.

Meg's shoulders fell. "No. It would help if we could see his bank statements, or the terms of the insurance payout, assuming there was one. Arson wouldn't disqualify Kenneth Eastman for that, would it?"

"Only if he set the fire."

"Which doesn't seem likely, because he wouldn't have been found dead in his bed if he had. What've you got on for tomorrow?"

"More of the same. I thought we might grab an hour or two in the afternoon to go visit Eric in Hadley. You remember him, don't you?"

"The guy with the barn full of bits and pieces of buildings? Sure," Meg said.

"He's got bathtubs and sinks, too."

"Aha! Then I will be delighted to accompany you. What did you think of Bree's idea?"

"Kind of intriguing. I've been reading about those small houses. I'm not sure the chicken house is structurally up to it, but it would be fun to design one."

"Maybe you could get an article in the paper out of it: from chicken house to people house."

"Something to think about. You ready for bed?"

"I am. Funny how exhausting reading financial statements can be."

The next morning Seth was up before Meg once again, and when she arrived in the kitchen he had already finished breakfast. "I walked Max. Maybe we can take him with us later. He's been cooped up a lot lately. One o'clock sound all right for the great bathtub hunt?"

"Sure. I'm going to make some phone calls this morning, and then maybe dig into the orchard summaries for the year. I'll give Rachel a call; I've got something she could look into without moving off the couch, if somebody hands her a laptop."

"Sounds good. See you later!" Seth went out the back door whistling.

Meg sat savoring her coffee and waited for some wisdom to surface about what she and Lydia had seen last night. Had Dad Eastman really torched his own home? Had he intended to kill his mother-in-law? Had she left any money? She made a quick note to add that to the list of things she wanted to ask Rachel to look for. Dad had the so-called in-law apartment constructed for Gramma, so he would have had a key, and could have locked her in. And then gone back to bed? That sounded absurd.

Maybe Mom Eastwood had been working on the dark side of the business, which would have given her the opportunity to slip her mother the possibly incriminating documents, when she could. But she wouldn't have planned to die as part of a cover-up, nor to kill her mother. Maybe she just wanted to know there was a backup copy of the documents in her mother's hands, sort of an insurance policy. Meg was sorry that she couldn't ask any of the offspring about the state of the Eastwood marriage, but the senior Eastmans had shipped the children off to boarding school, and Aaron, while still living at home, would have been too stoned and self-absorbed to notice much of anything, by his own account. Or maybe Mom had drugged her husband and set the fire and lain down to die, unable to face the shame of public exposure. Which still wouldn't explain why her mother had died. Had anybody done autopsies? Had they done a tox screen for any of the dead, which might have shown drugs in their systems, administered so that they would go quietly?

This is ridiculous, Meg told herself. She was creating increasingly dire scenarios based on next to nothing. Could she eliminate or enhance one or more of them? First she should read the police and fire reports, and maybe give particular attention to the discussion of the fire. Second, she could hunt down information on the parents' estate, which might include the payment from the insurance company or companies. Or would those have gone directly to the kids? Or rather, two out of the three of them? Could Aaron benefit from life insurance policies, if he'd been convicted of causing the fire that killed his parents, even unintentionally? That was something she could ask Rachel to check. She was reaching for the phone when it rang, and she jumped before gathering her wits and answering it.

"Ah, Meg, it's Christopher. I hope it's not too early to call?"

"Of course not; I keep farmers' hours. How are you? We haven't talked much lately."

"Fine, fine. I received your message and apologize for the delay in returning it."

"No bad news, I hope."

"No, none at all. Everything appears to be on track for that rather unique license you requested I obtain, and I'm looking forward to the event. Any additional details?"

"I'm working on it. Seth and I want to keep the wedding simple and informal, so nobody has to fuss too much. We're just gathering together our family and friends to celebrate."

"A very sensible approach, my dear. Is Briona still working her magic?"

"She is indeed. No doubt you heard about our trouble with one of our pickers a couple of months ago?"

"I did. A tragic thing, although it may herald a change from the old guard to the new. The times keep changing."

"That they do. Anyway, Bree was great throughout, and it can't have been easy for her, with kind of mixed loyalties. She does much more than keep the orchard going."

"I always had faith in her abilities; she's an outstanding young woman. Well, I won't keep you. We can touch base shortly before the event, in case there are any changes."

"I look forward to it, Christopher. Thank you for getting back to me. Bye!" As they ended their call, Meg mentally made another check mark on her to-do list. Next she needed to set Rachel to hunting for whatever online information was available. As long as she was still willing. Meg had little concept of what it must be like to be hugely pregnant; from what she'd read, it consisted mainly of having to pee a lot and watching your ankles swell up. And, of course, getting up and down would be a challenge, with your center of gravity completely whacked out. While she wasn't ruling it out, she wasn't hurrying to have a child right away. But then, she wasn't getting any younger, and she had a suspicion that Seth would love to have a child, even if he hadn't said so directly. *Enough, Meg!* That wasn't a decision she had to make this minute, or even this year.

She cleaned up the kitchen and sorted through her cooking supplies—definitely in need of restocking yet again, after feeding so many extra people recently. Mainly she was killing time until it was a reasonable hour to call Rachel. She couldn't make up her mind whether Rachel would be trying to sleep as much as possible, knowing that would quickly become a luxury when the new baby arrived, or whether she'd be so uncomfortable that she couldn't sleep at all. Plus the kids had to be out of the house for school. Maybe she'd risk calling now, and if Noah answered, she just ask him to tell Rachel to call.

Rachel answered on the first ring. "Hi, Meg. You have an assignment for me?"

"How did you guess?" Meg said, laughing. "Did you talk to your mother?"

"Yeah, I called her early this morning, before she left for work. Sounds like you had a fun evening. I'm jealous!"

"I can't think of many people who would think sifting through old financial records would be fun."

"Shows you how bored I am. What can I do to help?"

"Find out anything you can about Kenneth Eastman—anything about the company, his finances, his will, the estate, insurance policies, you name it. And if either his wife or his wife's mother pops up along the way, make a note of that, too."

"You have the mother's maiden name?"

"Shoot, no. You can probably find it online somewhere, like in an engagement or wedding announcement."

"I'll find it. What're you looking for?"

"Fiscal malfeasance."

Rachel giggled. "Ooh, I like that term. You think he was cooking the books?"

"Something like that. Bilking the neighbors, scamming God knows who. There's something fishy in there. Of course, it may have had nothing to do with his death or the fire. But it sure looks suspicious."

"You've got the police report?"

"Yes, and the fire report, but I haven't had time to go over them in detail yet. I can scan the relevant parts and e-mail them to you. Doesn't look like there's much there anyway. Hey, anything new with you and Pumpkin?"

"My doctor just keeps saying 'soon.' No help at all. I mean, I could have told her that much. So I appreciate the distraction from you."

"Happy to oblige. I just hope we find something that points somewhere. Wow, that sounds really stupid," Meg said.

"I know what you mean, though. I'll let you know what I come up with by the end of the day. How's that brother of mine?"

"Busy. We're going to go looking at antique bathtubs this afternoon."

"Ooh, lucky you. Are you going to sit in them to see which one fits best?"

"I hadn't thought of that, but it's probably a good idea. Minus water, though. Take care, Rachel. I'll talk to you later today."

"Happy bathtub hunting!" Rachel said cheerfully and signed off.

Meg scanned the Eastman materials and sent them off to Rachel, spent a couple of hours assembling the documents from her orchard sales and expenses, then made some sandwiches, assuming Seth wouldn't have eaten lunch when he arrived. He rolled in just before one and, as Meg had predicted, wolfed down a sandwich quickly.

"Ready to go?"

"I am. Rachel said I should try the bathtubs on for size."

"You talked to her? Anything new?"

"I gave her a working assignment: to find all the Eastman documents online pertaining to his business, insurance, estates, etc. She was thrilled to have something to occupy her mind. She said she'd report back by the end of the day. Nothing new on the baby. The official medical estimate is 'soon.'"

"Typical. Okay, let's head out." Once they were in Seth's van—he seemed optimistic that they would find what they wanted, and he hoped to be able to transport the items—he said, "Did you read the official documents?"

"I did. They were disappointing."

"In what way?" Seth said, turning onto the road toward Hadley.

"Chief Burchard stuck to the simplest possible explanation: Aaron started the fire, then fled, but didn't get very far, so he was found on the lawn, without a mark on him."

"Did he assign a motive?"

"Not really. Aaron was a 'troubled youth' involved with drugs, period. The parents were model citizens. The whole thing was tragic. End of story."

"The prosecution went for manslaughter?"

"Yes. They wouldn't commit to saying that Aaron deliberately killed his family, but they danced around it. He wasn't injured, he didn't try to help them out of the house, he didn't go for help from anyone else, he didn't seem remorseful when he was found or at any time after. It could have been a judgment call, and they took his youth into account. Despite his drug use, he hadn't been in any official trouble with the law, before the fire. If they suspected he was dealing at the high school, there was no mention of it."

"What did the fire report say?" Seth asked.

"I think you should look at it—you'd probably understand it better than I would. There was some line in it about the balloon framing allowing the rapid spread of the fire, which is why the building was fully engaged when the fire department got there."

Seth was silent for several beats. "That can't be right," he finally said.

"Why?"

"Because the Eastman house was built in the later eighteenth century, like yours and mine. Balloon framing didn't come into use until the nineteenth century."

"I don't understand," Meg said.

"Balloon framing means the studs run from the bottom sill to the top of the structure, which, as you might guess, leaves nice open channels for air flow—and fire. If there was any insulation back then, it would have been something flammable, too, like straw. Colonial timber-frame construction, on the other hand, has more interruptions within the studs, so the fire can't spread as quickly. It may be splitting hairs, though—it was an old wooden building, so it would burn fast. Where did the fire start?"

"In the basement, where Aaron apparently kept his drug stuff, away from prying eyes."

"And where was the parents' bedroom, where they were found?"

"Directly above, on the second floor. Why?"

"There would have been ample time for them to realize what was happening and get out of the building. What about the grandmother's space?"

"That was added toward the back, at the same end of the house."

"And that was relatively new, so modern fireproofing standards should have been in place. Again, she should have had time to get out. Something's not right."

They'd reached Hadley while they talked. "Well, let's see what Eric's got for us. We can resume this discussion later."

"Lead on!" Meg said.

20

They spent an entertaining couple of hours wandering through Eric's large, rambling old barn, loaded with architectural salvage, both large and small. Seth wanted a bathtub to replace the existing modern one in the main bath, plus a sink to replace the existing one there; another sink for the new bath, part of the laughingly entitled master suite; and a third sink for the new powder room. The shower for the master suite would be tiled, they had decided, but there were plenty of modern tiles available. They found a small mirrored cabinet that would fit over the sink, suitable for toiletries and prescriptions but not much more. By the end, they'd found everything they wanted, and Seth spent some time haggling over the price, in a friendly way, with his buddy Eric. While they dickered, Meg prowled around poking at other odds and ends, wondering if she'd ever take home decorating seriously. As long as there was something for people to sit on and eat off of and light to see by, she was more or less content, although she did draw the line at plastic furniture. Other than that, she enjoyed picking up odds and ends that appealed to her, with no particular plan in mind.

Finally Seth retrieved her from the maze. "All set. There's too much stuff for me to carry, so Eric's going to deliver them by truck. The bathtub's going to take two of us to get upstairs, and I need to get the plumbing into place and make sure the floor is up to the task before that can go in."

"Whatever you say, dear," Meg said primly, but with a mocking tone in her voice. Seth raised one eyebrow at her. "So I guess we need to look at tiles before that happens?"

"Yup. Let me check my calendar when we get back. Anyway, I think we're ready to roll."

"When did you plan to start?"

"This weekend, if nothing else crops up."

"Oh. Wow." Somehow Meg had been envisioning this in a misty distant future. Like . . . after the wedding. "How long will it take?"

"Two, three days? I promise that I'll make sure you have workable plumbing throughout, anyway, although you may be surrounded by bare lath for a few days."

Meg smiled at him. "I am descended from hearty pioneer stock. I'm sure I can cope."

"Attagirl!"

The phone was ringing as they walked into the house, and Meg grabbed it up to see Rachel's number.

"Hi, Rachel. Everything okay?" she asked anxiously.

Rachel laughed. "I keep forgetting everybody is hovering over their phones waiting for baby news. No, Pumpkin is still taking her own sweet time. I'm just reporting on the information you requested."

Seth was still standing by, but once Rachel had assured

her that she was all right, Meg waved Seth away. He pointed toward his office, at the back of the property, and Meg nodded vigorously to show that she understood, then turned her attention back to Rachel. "You've already found stuff?" Meg asked.

"Sure—you just have to know where to look, and how to ask nicely. So, you want to hear?"

"Of course I do!" Meg said quickly.

"All right. I started with the Hampshire County probate court, because that's in Northampton. If you don't already know it, wills and deeds are a matter of public record, so anyone can ask to see a will. A lot of the current documents are online, but we're looking for something from twenty-five years ago, right? Now, in theory you're supposed to show up in person to ask for a copy, or fax or mail a written request, and pay for the copying fee for a hard copy. But I know the clerk there—we were in high school together—and I explained I was very pregnant and she'd be doing me a really big favor if she could fax me the information ASAP, and she said yes. It helps that she just had a baby last year, so she knows what it's like."

"And?" Meg said, getting impatient.

"I've got the will! And not only that, but since the Eastmans both died in the fire, the courts had to identify all the beneficiaries and creditors, and include an itemized inventory of the assets and liabilities."

"Who was the executor?"

"Court-appointed, since the kids weren't in any shape to handle it. He did an okay job. I can give you his name if you want, but I don't know him."

"Hold on to that for later. What did the assets look like?" Meg asked.

"Well, the insurance on the house and contents was the

biggest chunk, followed by the land itself. Surprisingly little in any bank accounts."

"Did they list a business account?"

"Sure did, but there wasn't a whole lot in it."

"How much, roughly?"

"About five hundred thousand."

"Brokerage accounts?"

"Yes, but they're pretty skimpy, too. Didn't you say this guy had a lot of clients?"

"Your mother and I found a list that said so."

"Can you send me a copy? Anyway, if that's true, then either the auditors missed something, or there's something really funny going on."

"That's about what we concluded. Interesting. I wish we could get the records of bank transactions, but we don't have any legal standing. It would be nice to know what kind of deposits Eastman was making."

"Can't help you there," Rachel said cheerfully. "One other thing: I looked up who can benefit if he—and I quote—'feloniously and intentionally kills the decedent,' according to the statute. Here's what it says: 'The decedent forfeits all benefits under this article with respect to the decedent's estate.' That includes the property. So if Aaron was hoping to score some cash from Mom and Dad's deaths, he was out of luck, although he might not have known that. But you didn't really expect that, did you?"

"No. Although he might have been stoned enough to think it was a good idea at the time. So the other two children inherited everything?"

"Yup. In case you're wondering, the age of majority in Massachusetts is eighteen, so the boys—or, after Aaron's conviction, his brother—required a guardian."

"But the sister was over eighteen, wasn't she?"

"Yes, but reading between the lines, I think someone decided she wasn't a fit guardian. Or maybe she didn't want to do it. Have you met the sibs?"

"No, but I'm beginning to think I'd like to. So, bottom line, how much did the children inherit?"

"Not a whole lot, oddly enough. Dad Eastman had a whole lot of debts, and by the time they were paid off, there really wasn't anything left over."

"What happened to the investors?"

"That's a different search, but I'm going to guess that they settled for less than the full amount they claimed, if they got anything at all. Nobody could find any more money squirreled away, unless it's in some offshore account that nobody knows about, and all the records were destroyed in the fire. Unless you've found anything that points in that direction?"

"No, nothing like that. So the obvious conclusion is that Mom and Dad were living way beyond their means, and scamming their neighbors as well as some outsiders, and the whole house of cards was about to fall down."

"So does that point to a joint suicide? One that took the grandmother, too?"

"I'd really rather believe that they wanted to burn the house down to collect the insurance."

"And forgot to get out of the way?" Rachel laughed. "Anyway, the insurance proceeds wouldn't have covered the full amount they owed investors, would it?"

"I don't think so," Meg told her. "But it might have given them a little breathing room. I don't pretend to understand the mentality of a financial scammer. Maybe it's like with a gambler: they think the next hand or roll of the dice or whatever will fix everything."

"So, what now, Sherlock? Or do you prefer Nancy Drew?"

"Seth said there was something odd in the fire report."

"Really? What?"

"Something about the description of how the fire spread not matching the architectural structure of the period."

"Trust him to pick out a tiny detail like that. But he does know houses. So what's he think? The fire inspector got it wrong? It's a typo? Or somebody got paid off to falsify the report?"

"I, uh, don't know. For one thing, we didn't talk about it, because I don't know that much about what he was talking about. For another, the fire report came from the state, not from a local inspector."

"Ah, but did the state inspector rely on a report from someone around Granford? Did he ever come out and actually look at the place?"

"I don't know, Rachel. By the time the fire was over, there wasn't much to look at, as far as I can tell. Maybe a cellar hole and some parts of the foundation."

"Check on it. Look to see who reported what."

"Rachel, I'm beginning to think you've got a devious mind. You've just accused a state official of deliberately falsifying a report."

"You think that never happens?"

"Well, yes, I guess it does. But why? Who benefits?"

"Follow the money. And see if there's anyone still around Granford who remembers the details. Oops, gotta go—the kids are arriving. Talk soon!" Rachel hung up quickly, leaving Meg holding the phone, bemused.

She was startled out of her reverie by a knocking at her front door. As she headed toward it, she thought that she ought to make a sign saying FRIENDS: USE BACK DOOR. EVERYONE ELSE: GO AWAY. Front-door visitors usually arrived bringing bad news.

She pulled the door open to find a fortysomething woman in well-worn jeans and a bulky sweater standing on her stoop. "Are you Meg Corey?"

"Yes. What can I help you with?" Meg sent up a quick prayer that it wasn't someone looking for a contribution to something or other worthy.

"I'm Lori Eastman. I'm looking for my brother Aaron. At the police station they said you'd know where to find him?"

Meg was momentarily stunned into silence, and then her mind started whirring briskly. "Come in, please. How did you—"

"Find out he was out? He sent me a letter when he knew his release date." Lori stepped into Meg's hallway and looked around. "Nice house—kind of like ours used to be. Anyway, he didn't have my address because I moved a few months ago and it took a while for the letter to catch up. But he did say he wanted to visit Granford one last time, so I just headed here. I live in Vermont now, so it wasn't a long ride. Is he still in town?"

"Uh, yes, he is. Hey, where are my manners? Come on through to the kitchen. Can I get you coffee? Tea?"

"I didn't plan to stay long; just tell me where to find Aaron."

Was she hostile or just nervous? Meg wondered. "He doesn't have a phone, and I'd have to explain where to find him. Please, come in. I'm glad you're here, because I have some questions."

"About what?" the woman asked. Definitely hostile.

"About the fire that killed your parents."

Lori Eastman looked like she wanted to turn tail and run. "Why the hell would you want to know about that?"

"Because Aaron wants to know what really happened that night."

"And he asked you? Who are you?"

"A friend, I hope. I live here, at least for the past two years or so, and I run an orchard. I met Aaron . . . well, it's complicated. I don't have an axe to grind, and I want to help Aaron. It won't hurt to sit down and talk for a few minutes, will it?"

Lori wavered for a moment, then shook her head. "I guess not."

"Good," Meg said firmly. She gestured toward the kitchen, and let Lori precede her. Once there, she asked, "Can I get you something to drink?"

"Water's fine."

"Please, sit down. Oh, do you mind if I call my fiancé? He's interested in Aaron's story, too."

"Whatever," Lori said. Now that she'd agreed to stay, at least for a short while, she seemed kind of passive.

Meg stepped into the dining room and hit Seth's speed dial number—which seemed ridiculous because he was no more than a couple of hundred feet away. When he answered, she said, "We've got company—Aaron's sister is here."

"I'm on my way."

21

Seth arrived in thirty seconds. "Wow, that was fast," Lori said. "You're the fiancé?"

Seth extended his hand. "I'm Seth Chapin. My family lives just over the hill there, but I've got an office in one of Meg's outbuildings here—that's where she called me."

"I wish I could say I remembered your name, but I never really spent much time hanging out in Granford. Where's my brother?"

Meg stepped in. "Everybody, please sit down. Aaron's not far away, Lori, but I was hoping we'd have a chance to talk with you. You said he'd written to you?"

Lori gave her a dirty look, then sat reluctantly. "Yeah, but he didn't say much, just gave his release date. He didn't ask for anything, but he said he thought I should know he was out. I might've had like five letters from him all the time he's been in jail."

"Were you two close when you were growing up?" Meg asked. "There's only a few years between you."

"He was the bratty little kid for most of my life, and then he was the druggy little kid, and then he was in prison. Doesn't make for a warm and wonderful relationship, you know?"

"Are you married, Lori?" Seth asked. "You have any kids of your own now?"

"Married, yes, more than once, but not right now. One kid, who doesn't talk to me. Why does it matter to you? Hey, you never explained how you connected with Aaron. What are you, some kind of missionaries or do-gooders?" Lori's head swiveled back and forth between Seth and Meg.

The woman's behavior was verging on rude, Meg thought, although being sat down by two strangers and more or less interrogated could upset anyone. Why had Lori even bothered to come to Granford if she was so uninterested? "No, neither," she answered. "Here's what happened." Meg outlined the events at the Historical Society, and Gail's attack, and how she had found Aaron the next day. How he had come by to thank her, and ended up staying for dinner, and then overnight. And how somehow they had found him some work, which meant he had a way to stay around town, at least for a short while.

At the end of Meg's narrative, Lori demanded, "Why the hell would he want to stick around here? The place can't hold many happy memories."

"Where should he want to go?" Seth countered. He looked about as fed up with Lori's lack of sympathy as Meg felt. From what she'd seen so far, Meg decided she liked Aaron better than his sister.

"Got me," Lori told him. "Me, I'd go make a new life for myself, somewhere else. New place, new name, all that."

"You were at college when the fire happened, weren't

you, Lori?" Meg asked. She was having trouble picturing Lori as a preppy type.

"Yeah. Bunch of snobs. That was a bitch of a phone call to get in the middle of the night, when the fire happened. Oh, you poor dear, your parents were fried to a crisp." She mimicked a fluty old-lady tone.

Meg wondered briefly who had made that call. "Did they mention Aaron when they called?"

"Yeah, they said he was alive. Like that made up for two dead parents."

"And your other brother? Kevin?"

"Ditto. We both arrived the next day, or maybe I mean the same day. After the sun came up, anyway."

"Did someone come get you? A friend or neighbor?"

"We didn't have any friends in Granford. My folks had drinking buddies at the nearest country club, but I never saw any of them at our house. No relatives nearby, either. My brother and I each had a car, and we came separately."

That was news to Meg. "Could students at Deerfield have cars back then?"

"Only seniors, with permission. When I was at Mount Holyoke, they didn't care, except you had to find your own parking." Lori looked back and forth between them again. "What's it to you, anyway? I just thought I should check in with my brother. It's been twenty-five years, you know."

"You never visited him in prison?" Seth asked.

"Hell no. Creepy. And I was pissed at him." For someone who had said she was in a hurry, she certainly didn't seem to be rushing now.

"Why?" Meg asked.

"He killed our parents! And Gramma! And he burned the house to the ground. We came out of it all with squat, Kevin and me. I had to drop out of college. Kevin was lucky—his first semester at school was paid for, and the school oh-so-generously gave him a scholarship for his last semester. The insurance money just about covered the bills."

"Did Kevin go to college?" Meg asked.

"Yeah, but not right away. He took a year off, and then he started. He was smart and he did well in school, so he got financial aid. I think those places take pity on orphans. He must have written a hell of an admissions essay."

"What did you do after you dropped out, Lori?" Seth asked.

Lori stood up and started pacing around the kitchen. Then she stopped and leaned against a counter. "What is this, an interrogation? I did this and that. Traveled. Had some jobs. Got married, had a kid. Got unmarried. And that's my life in a nutshell. Like I said before, why should you care?"

"Lori, are you sure Aaron set that fire?" Meg said softly.

Lori stared blankly at her. "What? He was convicted! There was evidence, and a trial. Who else could it have been? And why are you asking this now? It's ancient history."

"Because Aaron still can't remember that night, and that troubles him. He's not claiming he didn't do it, but he'd like to know for sure, if it's possible."

"Good luck with that!" Lori said. "If there ever was any evidence pointing to anybody else, nobody ever mentioned it, and it sure as hell is long gone now. And I don't doubt that Aaron can't remember it; he was stoned every time I saw him, those last couple of years. That was his rebellion, although I'm not sure Mom and Dad ever noticed. Me, I went another way—slept around and mouthed off to my professors. I never was college material, but our folks just didn't want to hear that. We had to be the perfect little family. Nice house, nice cars, nice kids. Maybe I should be glad Aaron broke the ice, so I could act out, too. They were so busy trying to handle him, they didn't pay much attention to me."

"And Kevin?"

"I guess Kevin was the poster boy for the family—the goody-goody kid. Hey, they got one out of three right."

"Do you know where Kevin is now?"

Lori shrugged. "Last I heard, somewhere in the Midwest. I think. We do not exchange Christmas cards. He thinks I'm a lazy tramp. I think he's a pompous asshole. Takes after Dad, I guess."

Meg was amazed that Lori had kept talking as long as she had. The more she learned, the more she saw the Eastmans as a classic dysfunctional family, worried about outward appearances, short on emotional connections. On the outside everything had looked nice and shiny—handsome old house, professional dad, three kids in good schools. But the cracks had already been showing, before the fire happened. "How'd you get along with your grandmother?"

"Gramma?" Lori looked surprised at Meg's question. "Okay, I guess. She was old, but she was pretty sharp. She'd listen to me. Dad kept trying to make it out like she was senile and helpless, but that was a load of crap. She had arthritis pretty bad and couldn't get around easily, but her mind was all there."

"Did she like your dad?"

Lori gave Meg a searching look. "That's kind of a weird question to ask somebody you just met. What mother-in-law ever thinks her daughter's husband is good enough for her darling?"

"Is that a no?"

"Yeah, I guess. Dad treated Gramma very politely, if you know what I mean. Like, 'How're you feeling, Virginia?' 'Can I get you a cup of tea?' 'Is the television loud enough for you?' Like she was a helpless idiot." Lori's tone was simpering. "He had that addition built on so she could live with us."

"Was she financially independent?"

"You mean, did she have money of her own, so she didn't need Dad's charity? Sure, as far as I know. I mean, we didn't sit around the table talking about the family budget. We kids got our tuition paid and a nice allowance and a car, so we didn't ask questions."

"So let's go back to my earlier question: do you believe Aaron deliberately set that fire?" Meg asked.

Lori glared at her. "I don't know, and I don't much care. It's water under the bridge, isn't it? Even if he didn't, what's knowing anything different gonna change?"

Meg ignored her question. "What would Aaron's motive have been?"

"Like I know? He was a stoner. Maybe he took the wrong pill and started seeing pink dinosaurs and thought the only way to get rid of them was to set them on fire. If he'd thought it through, he'd've known that it wouldn't get him any money. I mean, not if he was convicted."

"So it wasn't that he hated your parents enough to want them dead?"

"I think 'hate' is kind of a strong term for what he felt. He didn't respect them. He didn't like them. He tried to ignore them and stay out of their sight as much as possible. And they were fine with that."

"He told us that he got along well with your grandmother," Meg said. In fact, she thought, Aaron's description of her matched Lori's pretty closely.

"Yeah. Actually, looking back at it, she was kind of a cool old lady. She didn't judge us, and she stood by us. Which is more than I can say for Mom and Dad."

"Were your parents getting along well?"

Lori gave a short bark of laughter. "Define 'well.' They weren't planning a divorce, as far as I know. They were polite—no throwing things or getting drunk and yelling. Kind of a chilly environment, overall. Family dinners were a trip—real silver and china and crappy food. Mama was a wannabe."

"Why do you say that?" Meg asked.

"She wanted to fit in with the ladies. You know, playing bridge, going out for lunch, getting her hair done. They used to do that in those days, or at least when she first got married. But now that I think about it—which I don't spend much time doing, believe me—all that was kind of over by the time she died. The old model just wasn't working anymore, but Mom didn't have any better ideas, and she was too old to rewrite the script."

"Did either of your parents ever get counseling?" Seth asked suddenly.

"Like, see a shrink? Or couples therapy? Hell no. That would mean they had to admit there was something wrong with them and their perfect family. Why does that matter?"

"I just wondered if there was ever an official evaluation—if one or both of them was depressed, say. Or suicidal. Or homicidal."

Lori stared at him, then burst out laughing. "Wow, you two sure are a pair! I come here with a simple question—where is my brother?—and now you're trying to psychoanalyze the entire family? Why the hell do you care?"

"Because I asked them to help." Aaron's voice came from the kitchen door: somehow he had managed to slip in while the rest of them were talking. "Hello, Lori. Here I am."

The siblings held each other's gaze from opposite sides of the room. Meg realized she was holding her breath. How would they play it?

Lori spoke first. "Oh God, Aaron, you look so much like . . ."

"Dear old Dad?" Aaron spat out, his tone sarcastic.

Lori shook her head. "No, Mom. I'm the one who took after Dad. Damn—you're pretty close to the same age she was when she . . . died."

"I look older." He paused before saying, "Thanks for coming. Why did you?"

"You wrote to me," Lori told him. "I figured either you were dying and it was my last chance, or you wanted to apologize for screwing up everybody's life."

"Thanks." Aaron's voice was flat. He probably heard what he expected to hear, Meg thought.

This was stupid. Meg hadn't asked Lori to be here, and then Aaron had walked in, and now they were acting out some ridiculous Greek drama in her kitchen. Seth wasn't helping much at all, although if a fight broke out, maybe he could break it up. "Listen up, people!" Meg said loudly. Everyone turned to look at her. "This is my house, and if you want to fight, take it somewhere else. If you want to talk, I'll feed you dinner and then you can do whatever you want. What's your choice?"

"You don't have to stay, Lori," Aaron said, once again in that curiously neutral voice.

"It's been so long, Aaron," she replied softly. Then she shook herself. "Sure, why not? There's nowhere else I have to be. Where are you hanging out, Aaron?"

"Over the hill. I'm fixing the fence at an alpaca farm. I'll be leaving whenever that's done. I just stopped by to ask Seth here if I could borrow some tools."

Lori startled Meg by bursting out laughing. "Alpacas? You and those silly fuzzy things? Wow!"

Aaron smiled reluctantly. "They're actually kind of nice, once you get to know them. Want to take a walk while dinner's cooking? If that's okay, Seth?"

"That's fine. It won't take long."

After Lori and Aaron had disappeared out the back, Meg and Seth exchanged bewildered glances. "This is really weird," Meg ventured.

"It is. How do we keep finding ourselves in the middle of things like this?"

"I wish I knew. Anyway, I've got to think about dinner. Think spaghetti will work?"

"I don't think those two will care."

22

It was a disjointed dinner. Meg wondered if Emily Post had ever addressed the issue of acceptable topics for discussion in the company of a recently released prisoner who had once been convicted of homicide. Or patricide plus matricide. Having cooked dinner, Meg allowed herself a glass of wine with her meal, and Lori seized on the opportunity to follow suit—and then some. Seth remained quiet and watchful.

Meg considered then rejected a number of subjects. *What was life in prison really like?* was at the top of the list. She had never been inside one, and what little she knew came from television programs or movies. Was it violent? Did the inmates live in constant fear that they would be harassed or even attacked by others? Or was that a gross exaggeration, and the worst problem was really boredom? Of course, boredom could lead to violence, just to create some excitement. No, she couldn't ask that.

She settled on "You said you took some computer classes, Aaron?"

"Sure. I had to do something, and I'd already read half the books in the prison library."

"Hey, some people write 'em in prison," Lori said, more loudly than necessary. "I bet you'd have publishers beating down your door for your story. If you had a door."

"I can't write about what I don't remember," he said, surprisingly mildly.

Lori waved a dismissive hand. "Ah, make it up. Who cares now?"

"I do, Lori," Aaron said. His simple statement produced silence all around.

Finally Lori got the message, and said in a more sober voice, "I'm sorry, Aaron. Look, you really don't remember what happened that night?"

"Yes."

That brief statement seemed to stump Lori. "How can you not? I mean, you've had years, decades, to think about it."

"I have, and I've had shrinks to help. It's a blank, just not there at all. I blame the drugs: I did a lot of mixing up, without a clue about how they might work together. Didn't you ever experiment?"

Lori shook her head. "Nah. I was scared to look for anybody who was dealing—maybe I was just paranoid, or afraid of getting ripped off. Now, alcohol—that's another story. A whole lot easier to get, and it's even legal, mostly. You aren't drinking?" Lori nodded toward Aaron's glass, which contained water.

"Not since I went to prison. If I could forget such an important event in my life as killing my parents and destroying my own home, I don't even want to guess what any drug—and alcohol is a drug, big sister—could do to me now."

"You're a drag," Lori said with a hint of contempt. "You used to be more fun. And you've already done the worst thing possible, right?"

"How could you tell I used to be fun?" Aaron asked, brushing off his sister's negative comment. "You never spent any time with me."

Meg wondered if she was supposed to jump in and change the course of the discussion, but she had to admit that she found the sibling dialogue interesting. Luckily Seth stepped up. "So, computers. What skills did they emphasize in your courses?"

Lori looked confused by the change of subject, but Aaron turned his attention to Seth. "Well, it depends on when you're asking about. Over twenty-five years, I saw a lot of changes in that industry, so I kept taking courses, and there wasn't much repetition of the same material, let me tell you. Most recently . . ."

Meg listened with half an ear. She chided herself for forgetting that while Seth had chosen to work with his hands, he had an undergraduate degree from Amherst, one of the most competitive colleges in the country. He still read widely—when he could stay awake after a long day of physical labor. He appeared to be surprisingly well-informed about current computer issues—certainly more than she was. She felt a surge of affection for him; he was being kind to Aaron without being condescending, which wasn't easy for anyone.

Lori looked bored and restless. She stood up suddenly. "Where's your bathroom?"

"Upstairs. On the left, at the top of the stairs. I can show you . . ." Meg started to say, but Lori was on her way.

"Don't worry, I'll find it," she called back over her shoulder.

The three remaining people at the table exchanged looks. "Aaron, why do you think she's here? You said you two were never close," Meg said.

"Curiosity? I don't think she has much of an attention span. Maybe nowadays someone would say she had ADD, but back when she was in school nobody talked about it much, not like today. Not many girls had the problem."

"I think I can see what you mean. But she got into a good college."

Aaron nodded. "And Dad made a nice contribution to get her there. Plus she didn't last long—made it through one year, and had barely started her second when . . . the fire happened. Hard to say which came first, the drinking or the flunking out."

Meg shot a glance at Seth. "Do you want us to ask her to stay? I mean, here with us?"

"Only if you want," Aaron said. "I mean, I'm glad I had a chance to see her, but I don't see us being best buddies for the rest of our lives. Do you?"

He had a point, Meg conceded. "What about your brother?"

"What about him?"

"Do you want to see him? Do you want to get the three of you together, even if it's only once?"

"For a happy family reunion? Or a final farewell? Meg, I know that you mean well, but I'm not sure what the point is. It's been a long time since I felt much of anything for either of them."

"Kevin might know something about that night, might have seen or overheard something," Meg countered stubbornly.

"How? He was at school."

"He had a car," Meg shot back. "So did Lori. Either or both of them could have been at the house in an hour or two. You were wasted, and you can't remember a thing. Prove that they *weren't* there," she challenged him.

Finally Aaron looked surprised. "The police never talked to them? There's nothing in their files?"

"They were never considered suspects, if that's what you're asking. They had you."

"Huh," Aaron said. He thought for a moment. "Maybe I should see him. But I don't know where he is. He didn't keep in touch."

Lori came back at that point. "You mean, like I did? I think Kevin was happy to put the whole mess behind him. And no, I don't know where he is at the moment. Last I heard he was in"—she shut her eyes for a moment to concentrate—"Chicago or something. He ended up as a do-gooder, running inner-city programs for starving people or sick children or something like that."

"He finished college?" Aaron asked.

Lori nodded. "In social work, that kind of thing."

Meg broke in. "Lori, why didn't the two of you stay in touch?"

"Because Kevin is boring and a prig. Lousy combination. We have zip to say to each other."

"But do you know where to find him? Or how?"

"Try the city first—it could be some public agency. Or Google him."

"Or try the college alumni association," Seth suggested. "And I'll remind Art—he has more means to do this than we do."

"Who's Art?" Lori asked.

"The Granford chief of police. And a friend," Meg told her.

"So he's mixed up in this, too?" Lori said. "Jesus, Aaron—couldn't you have just fallen off the grid like a normal ex-con? Now you're asking favors from hometown police chiefs?"

Aaron shrugged, and nodded across the table to Meg and Seth. "I didn't; they did. But I appreciate it. And if Kevin's as annoying as you say he is, he'd probably jump at the chance to patronize his bad-seed brother."

"Ooh, and having the two of us together to look down our noses at Kevin would be too good to miss. I'm in," Lori said gleefully. "But I'd better figure out where I'm staying while we track him down."

Meg sighed inwardly. She should ask Lori to stay with her, but . . . Luckily Seth preempted her. "My house is empty at the moment—you're welcome to stay there. Aaron, you could join Lori there if you want."

"And abandon my alpaca pals? I think I'd better stay where I am, but Lori and I can spend some private time together at the house. Thanks for the offer, Seth. Lori, that work for you?"

"Whatever. We should get out of these people's hair."

"I'll take you over and show you what's where at the house, Lori," Seth volunteered. "Aaron, you want to come with us?"

"Sure. I can walk back to the farm from there."

Seth turned to Meg. "I should be back in half an hour, no more."

Meg smiled at him. "I'll try to stay awake that long."

It was slightly longer than half an hour before Seth returned, but Meg had expected that. She had cleaned up the kitchen, taken a shower, and was happily settled in bed reading when he clomped up the stairs. "How'd it go?" she asked.

"I really have to figure out what I'm doing with the house, or at least hire a housekeeper to make sure there are clean sheets and towels. Oh, about Lori and Aaron. Do you know, I'm not sure I've ever seen a more dysfunctional family?"

"You have led a sheltered life, Seth. What bothers me is that apparently the Eastmans tried very hard to present the appearance of success and money, but right under the surface it was a boiling mess. Are we any nearer to knowing what really happened?"

"Do you have any solid reason to doubt that the police got it right?" Seth countered.

"You mean, apart from my gut? No. It's more like what I'm not finding, like more details in the reports. Everybody took the easiest course, picked the obvious solution. Druggy kid with a chip on his shoulder did it, end of story. What do you think of Aaron, Seth?"

Seth had taken off his shoes and dropped down on the bed next to Meg. "I didn't know him then. What I see now is . . . a man who's kind of lost, I guess. The most important event in his life is a blank in his memory. He's been in prison more than half his life, but he seems to have survived. But maybe that means he's bottled up a lot of stuff, and it may come out sometime."

"Are you saying you think he's dangerous?" Meg asked.

Seth contemplated the ceiling. "Maybe only to himself. I know that sounds harsh, but the guy has no family except his siblings, and they aren't exactly supportive, unless Lori is lying about Kevin. He has minimal job skills. He has no roots anywhere. I hate to say it, but I have no idea how he's going to survive. It's a shame." He rolled over to look at Meg. "But that doesn't mean that it's up to us to try to fix him."

"I know," Meg said with a sigh. "I guess the question is, can we answer the simple question he asked us? What really happened that night?"

"Not yet. Maybe never. Can we talk about something else?"

"Sure. Like what?"

"Like when I can dismantle the bathroom—only for a short time, I promise!"

"Yeah, yeah, I've heard that before," Meg replied. Although to be fair, Seth was usually accurate in his estimates. "You said something about this weekend?"

"Well, we've still got some time before the wedding, which gives us a cushion if I run into any snags."

"Oh no, that never happens," Meg said. "If things slip, what are we supposed to do about certain bodily functions?"

Seth grinned. "What they did when the house was built? I think there's an old chamber pot out in the barn, and you can wash in a bucket, right?"

"Must I?"

"Hey, seriously, if things get jammed up we can sleep at my house. All right?"

"I guess. So when does demolition start? I should warn Bree."

"This is Wednesday. I've got some finish work to do on one project, but I could start Friday, and then there'd be the weekend."

"All right. So I need to find tile."

"Quickly. By the way, I forgot to tell you that your mom called my mom, and your folks will be there for Thanksgiving dinner. But they didn't say where they'd stay."

"Oh, goody?" Meg said dubiously. She loved her parents, but that meant they'd be around for a whole week before the wedding. But not in her house, which was a relief.

Seth was watching with suppressed amusement. "If you could see your face . . . Don't worry—your mother said they had plans to visit some other sites between Turkey Day and the wedding. I believe Stockbridge was mentioned."

"Ah," Meg said, relieved. "That does sound more their style. So, point me to someone who sells tile, and let the demolition begin." Unless Lori and Aaron somehow interfered. She doubted that either of them would be much help with picking tiles. "But please ask Art how to find Kevin, will you?"

"I will. I'm going to grab a shower—while it still works." He bounced off the bed and headed down the hall.

23

Seth was already out the door when Meg stumbled down to the kitchen the next morning. Bree was also already there. She looked up and said, "Look what the cat dragged in. Late night?"

Meg poured herself a mug of coffee. "Not so much late as difficult. Aaron's sister showed up out of the blue yesterday."

"Ah," Bree said. "And?"

Meg wrestled with a way to describe Lori without sounding judgmental. "I think she's kind of a drifter. Dropped out of college, got married, had a child. Currently has no husband or partner, and offspring is not living at home. She didn't mention anything about a job. She did say that Aaron had sent her a letter when he knew he was getting out, and mentioned he'd be passing through Granford, so I guess she hopped in her car and just appeared."

"Okay. Did she and Aaron connect?"

"Yup. He showed up while she was here. It was an

interesting evening. They hadn't seen each other since he went to prison."

"She angry?" Bree asked. "I mean, what did she want with him now?"

"No, not angry, really. Curious, I guess. Wouldn't you be?"

"None of my relatives has killed anybody—that I know of. What about Aaron?"

"To tell the truth, Aaron didn't react much at all. I haven't seen him show much emotion about anything. Anyway, Lori's staying at Seth's house, which seems to be turning into a hotel. Aaron had already opted not to stay there, even now that Lori's there, but went back to the alpaca farm. And now we're trying to find the brother, Kevin, so everyone can have a big, happy family reunion."

"Sounds really swell," Bree said sarcastically. "Can I skip that?"

"But wait! There's more!" Meg said sarcastically. "My mother and father will be arriving before Thanksgiving and maybe staying with Lydia at least some of the time around the wedding, with some excursions to fine local establishments. And Seth has decided that this is the weekend he wants to dismantle the only bathroom in the house. He volunteered a chamber pot. You might want to be somewhere else."

"You two do like to keep busy, don't you?"

"It's the metabolism, I think. Seriously, do you have any plans? I can't speak for Lydia, but if she's willing, do you want to come for Thanksgiving dinner? With or without Michael?"

"Let me think about it. Have you talked to Seth about the tiny house idea?"

"Actually I did. He seemed intrigued: he likes exploring new ideas, which is kind of weird if you consider he spends most of his time fixing two-hundred-year-old buildings. But he also likes old materials—we're having some Victorian plumbing fixtures delivered soon. And now I need to go find tile. Do you know anything about tile, Bree?" Meg ended plaintively.

"Nope. Not my thing. You want marble? Granite?"

"I want nonskid, and that's as far as I've gotten. And Seth has already vetoed pink. Everything okay in the orchard?"

"Nice of you to ask, boss. Yes. We're down to our last few trees. All things considered, I think we did pretty well this year."

"That's good to hear." At least one thing in her life was on track. Well, so far the wedding was, too: she had the date, the place, someone to perform the ceremony, and the matron of honor. And guests, although she still didn't know how many. And she had to find something to wear. She'd let Seth worry about licenses and rings. Oh, and she'd like to get this thing with Aaron wrapped up before the big day so she could enjoy her own party. Gail would probably prefer that, too.

Meg was still lost in thought when the phone rang. It was Art. "Hey, Art, what's up?"

"Seth asked me about Aaron's brother, Kevin? I've got a number for him, in Chicago. Seth said he'd make that call. I hear the sister is in town, too—I missed her when she stopped by the station yesterday."

"She is. We had dinner here last night, and she's over at Seth's house right now. She wondered if Seth and I were do-gooders. Are we?"

Art chuckled. "Amateur, I guess. You making any progress on your wild-goose chase?"

"I'm not sure. Let's say for the record that I am 'cautiously optimistic.'"

Bree made a rude noise in the background.

"I heard that," Art said with a laugh. "Let me know if I can help with anything else, as long as it doesn't jeopardize my job or my sanity."

"Of course. Thanks, Art."

As soon as she'd hung up, Seth called. "I got Kevin's number from Art, and I just spoke with him. He wants to come to Granford, but he hasn't decided whether to drive or fly."

"That's wonderful," Meg said glumly. "And the charming Eastman family can all discuss what they don't know, face-to-face."

"Do I detect a lack of enthusiasm?" Seth asked.

"I guess. Thanks for that list of tile places you left for me—and for telling me how much we'd need. I'm headed that way as soon as I finish breakfast."

"All part of the job, ma'am. Happy hunting. I'll talk to you later."

Meg set the phone down—and it rang again immediately. "Rachel? What's up?"

"Meg, thanks for that list of investors you e-mailed me. Have you looked at it?" Rachel sounded breathless.

"I did, but I'm the new kid here, so I didn't recognize a lot of the names, only that the families had been local for a long time."

"Well, there were a couple of interesting ones on the list. One was Jacob Patterson, the insurance agent who sold the Eastmans the policy on the house, not all that long before the fire. He's still in town here, although he's pretty close to retirement age, if there is such a thing for insurance agents. Hang on." Apparently Rachel put her hand over the phone receiver to talk to someone else—her husband? "The other—wait for it—was the judge who presided at Aaron's trial."

"Oh, wow," Meg said, stunned. That might explain the harsh sentence, and the lack of evidence presented at the trial. "Shouldn't the judge have recused himself?"

"*Her*self. You'd think so, wouldn't you? But the list wasn't ever made public, which would make sense if they'd been scammed." Rachel covered the mouthpiece again, but even Meg could hear her. "I'll be right there, Noah! Meg, look, I've got to go, because this baby has decided today is launch day. But I've got a huge favor to ask you."

"Anything, Rachel," Meg said, suddenly on high alert.

"Can you meet the kids at the school bus? Noah's coming with me to the hospital, and Mom's at work in the other direction, and I hate to drag her back again. At least the kids know you."

"Of course I'll meet them, Rachel. What time and where?"

"Between two thirty and three, on the corner two blocks away—away from the center of town, not toward it. You'll see the bus coming. Are you sure it's okay?"

"Of course it is. Which hospital?"

"Dickinson—appropriate, isn't it? Thanks, Meg; you're great. Talk later!" She hung up quickly, leaving Meg holding a mute handset.

"Baby's coming?" Bree asked.

"Apparently. Shoot, it never rains but it pours. I said I'd meet her kids at their school bus in Amherst. If Kevin Eastman shows up here, which would happen only if he finds a flight and figures out where he's going from the airport, tell him where Lori and Aaron may be. And if you have to be somewhere else, Kevin can wing it. I'm going to call Seth, and then I'm going to look for tiles."

"Breathe, Meg!" Bree said, laughing. "And I love your priorities: kid-tending, solve murder, find bathroom accessories. Talk about multitasking! But that's fine. Go do what you gotta do."

Meg raced up the stairs, still clutching her cell phone. In the bedroom, she hit Seth's number as she pulled on a clean pair of jeans. Seth's phone went to voice mail, so she left a message. "Seth, Rachel says the baby's coming, and she and

Noah are headed to the hospital. I'm going to go over and pick up the kids from the bus. Art talked to Kevin Eastman, and Kevin might possibly show up today. And I'm going tile shopping. I'll talk to you later."

Once she'd hung up, she forced herself to stop and think for a moment. Rachel hadn't asked her to call anyone else, so she assumed Lydia knew the score. She herself had told Seth. It was now nine o'clock, and she had plenty of time to get to the bus stop in Amherst by two thirty. Seth had given her a list of several smaller tile stores in the area—he wasn't impressed with what the big-box stores had to offer, so she could probably stop in a few of them and see what they had. She had to admit that her first thought was to stick with neutral colors—that way she could spice things up with towels and accessories. But that seemed too safe—and boring. Maybe she'd fall in love with something spectacular that she couldn't live without. As long as it wasn't pink.

Three stores later Meg had tile shapes and sizes and colors whirling around her head. Who knew there were so many decisions involved? She'd vetoed marble (too soft, and it stained easily) and granite (too hard, and now a fading trend). She didn't want to commit to an artistic design, because that would be time-consuming to install, and to her mind, kind of fussy. All she really wanted was something that was easy to keep clean and not too slippery. Sticking with traditional Victorian-ish tiles was still the most appealing solution. In white. Or off-white. Not too shiny, so water spots wouldn't show. Minimal grout, because grout always looked dirty. The next place that she visited that had this simple list of tiles, she'd commit and buy what she needed. She hoped.

She worked her way toward Amherst, to be sure she'd be on time for the school bus. Somewhere along the way it occurred to her that she didn't have a key to Rachel's house, and with both Rachel and Noah otherwise occupied, she wouldn't be able to get in. Ah well, she'd just have to take the kids home with her—unless, of course, Rachel managed to produce the awaited child before three and the hospital sent her home . . . Didn't they try to do that these days? Still, she didn't mind entertaining the kids for a while, and her house—and her life—couldn't get much more chaotic than it already was.

Tile place number five was the big winner. A fresh-faced young woman greeted her at the door. "Can I help you find something?"

Meg had her spiel memorized by now. "I need tiles for a Victorian-style bathroom with tub, plus one with a shower enclosure, plus a powder room. Here's a list of the measurements." She handed the young woman one of Seth's printouts—good thing she'd made multiple copies.

Her face lit up. "Oh, Seth Chapin! He does great work, and he's usually pretty accurate about calculating what he needs. So he's overhauling your place?"

"He is—two new bathrooms, plus patching the old one after he replaces all the plumbing. He thinks it won't take long, so I guess I need something that's in stock, or that you can get quickly."

"No problem. This is just the showroom—we have a warehouse nearby. What were you thinking?"

Meg recited her list of requirements, and the woman nodded as if in agreement. "That all makes sense to me. But could I make one suggestion?"

"Fire away," Meg said, and realized she was getting a bit punchy.

"How about a decorative border or a top rail? Then you could buy the basic tiles in bulk, but vary each bath just a bit. Let me show you . . ."

In the following half hour, Meg managed to order

everything she needed. It was like buying a puzzle that, when put together, would be a three-dimensional bathroom. It was simple (and the woman promised that setting the tiles would be easy), but as she had been told, the borders added a small touch of elegance. Done!

"So you can deliver all this tomorrow?" Meg asked.

"Sure, no problem. What's the address?" When Meg told her, she said, "But that's Seth's work address." Then her face lit up. "You must be Meg! Congratulations! Did you finally set the date?"

"Uh, thank you, and it's the week after Thanksgiving. Seth tells me he can get the plumbing work done over a weekend. I guess I'm doing the tiling part."

"Oh, sure, no problem. He's good. And it'll be easy, you'll see."

"I hope so!" Meg said fervently. Why was it that so few things in her life turned out to be easy? "Thanks for your help."

Back in the car, Meg checked her watch again. Time to head for Amherst and the school bus. But at least she could check one thing off her list, and it was a big one.

In town she parked down the street from Rachel's house, from which she could see the corner where the bus would arrive. She got out of the car and stood by it, waiting, and the bus arrived at two thirty-seven. She spotted Chloe and Matthew Dickinson as they climbed down the steps of the bus—not together, of course. She went up to greet them.

"Hi, kids. Remember me? Meg Corey? Your Uncle Seth's, uh, fiancée? Your mom asked me to pick you up, because she's having the baby now." At least Meg hoped she was; she hadn't heard anything since that early-morning call.

"Hi, Meg," Chloe said. "Can we go to the hospital to see her?"

"Let's wait until your dad calls us. I don't know how

many people they let in, or what age visitors. Either of you have a key to your house?"

Matthew and Chloe shook their heads.

"Okay, you can come over to my house, and we'll wait there together."

The two children followed her obediently back to the car. Conversation on the way back was strained, and Meg realized how rarely she talked to children. She had no idea what they were doing in school or what their interests outside of school might be. "Do you have any pets?" she ventured out of desperation.

Matthew finally spoke. "Nah. When the B and B is open, Mom worries about the guests and allergies."

"Well, I've got a dog and a cat, and a couple of goats. And there's a new herd of alpacas in the neighborhood."

"What's an alpaca?" Matthew asked. Describing those animals took the entire ride back to Meg's place. When she arrived, there was an unfamiliar car in the driveway.

Bree came out to greet her. "Hi, kids," she said brightly, and then in a quieter voice she added, "No word from Rachel?" Meg shook her head. Bree turned back to the children. "You want to come up and help me pick the last apples?"

"Can we, Meg?" Chloe turned to her to ask, actually looking excited.

"Sure. You can take some home if you want," Meg told them. Then she asked Bree, "What's with the car?"

"Kevin Eastman is in the kitchen." Bree stepped back. "Come on, kids—let's go up the hill."

As the trio made their way up the hill, Meg checked her phone for messages: there were none. Might as well go meet the third Eastman sibling—and hope Seth arrived home soon.

24

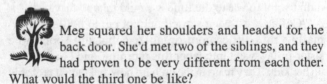 Meg squared her shoulders and headed for the back door. She'd met two of the siblings, and they had proven to be very different from each other. What would the third one be like?

Kevin Eastman was seated at the kitchen table, but sprang to his feet when Meg entered the room. "Hi, I'm Kevin. You must be Meg." He came quickly around the table and offered his hand.

"Yes. Meg Corey, and this is my house. You made good time. How did you find me, once you got to Granford?"

"The chief of police—Preston, was it?—said I'd find you here, and you could tell me where to find Aaron."

"Aaron's nearby, but he doesn't have a phone or a car, so it takes some explaining."

Kevin looked more like Aaron than his sister did. Oddly, he, like Aaron, looked older than his years. He was tall and thin, dressed in nondescript clothes, not particularly new but not obviously shabby. His hair was neatly cut. Mostly he looked worried, and based on the deep creases on his face, that was probably a chronic expression.

"Did Art Preston mention that your sister is here, too?" Meg asked.

"What?" Kevin looked stunned at that news. "I had no idea where to find her. Is she still living in Vermont?"

"I think so. So you don't keep in touch? Didn't Aaron contact you? Because he did send Lori a letter saying he was being released." Meg realized suddenly that they were still standing, on opposite sides of the table. "I'm so sorry—I'm being a lousy hostess. Please sit down. Can I offer you something to drink? You must have left early to catch a plane to arrive here by midafternoon."

"Water's fine. Or coffee, if you have it. I didn't mind; I didn't want to waste the time it would take to drive."

"Coffee it is." Meg started her hot pot to boiling. "Normally I'm a little more organized, but my soon-to-be sister-in-law went into labor this morning, and I had to pick up her kids. They're up in the orchard now, but they'll probably descend on us here as soon as they get bored, and there won't be much chance to talk. Do you have children, Kevin?"

He was quick to answer. "No, I've never been married, and I guess it's getting kind of late for that now. I think about adopting now and then: there are so many needy kids."

"Never say never," Meg said, pouring water over coffee grounds. She wondered if it would be rude to ask if he was in a relationship with anyone, but it really was none of her business. "I might as well go ahead and explain how I came to know Aaron, and we all had dinner together here last night, so I've learned a lot of your family's details in a short time." Once again Meg outlined Aaron's arrival, Gail's overreaction, and Meg's role in tracking Aaron down.

When she had finished, Kevin said, "Lucky guy, I guess. Or maybe he doesn't think so. Did he tell you why he came here, to Granford?"

Meg filled two mugs with coffee, set one in front of Kevin, then sat down with her own across the table from him. "I should let him explain that. We could go look for him now, but I'm responsible for the kids and I can't just dump them on Bree."

"That was the young woman who let me in?"

"Yes. She's my orchard manager, and she shares this house with me. I told her you might arrive today."

"I've read about the itinerant Jamaican pickers around here—I take it she's Jamaican?"

Meg nodded. "Yes, but American-born. Her parents were pickers, but she lived mainly with an aunt here so she could go to school. She graduated from UMass not long ago."

"Good, good," Kevin said almost absently.

"My fiancé should be back soon, and maybe the two of you can go find Lori and Aaron. Lori's staying at Seth's house, and Aaron is staying temporarily at a nearby farm. Seth's house is actually next door, but you can't even see it from here. Do you remember much about Granford?"

"Some," Kevin admitted. "Although I haven't been back for years. I took some time off after I graduated, just to come to terms with . . . the fire and the deaths. I worked odd jobs around here, wherever I could find anything. Let me tell you, the whole thing really hit me hard. And I have to say, Lori and I dealt with it in our own ways. Lori kind of dropped out, while I decided I should dig in and address the problems—like drugs—that can lead to such tragedies. That's why I went into social work."

"Are you a city employee?" Meg asked, curious.

"Yes, although that's not easy these days, in Chicago. Of

course, there's never enough money to do half of what we'd like, but we keep trying. There are a lot of good people who care about kids in difficult situations."

"Why Chicago, rather than Boston?"

Kevin shrugged. "I thought I could be more objective about a city I didn't know. Not that I knew Boston well, but I knew 'of' it, so to speak. I wanted to start over, someplace fresh."

"Did you ever visit Aaron? Write to him?"

"No. I can't say I'm proud of that, but I couldn't believe what had happened. Mom and Dad dead, and Aaron didn't have a scratch on him? That didn't seem right."

Kevin was not the first person to express that opinion, no matter what the underlying reality was. Poor Aaron had been damned because he wasn't hurt? Meg tried to wrap her head around the image of a stoned Aaron sitting on the lawn and watching the house burn, with his family inside. And then passing out? Maybe he'd kept taking drugs while he watched. Had any been found on him? She'd have to check the police report—surely they would have noted that. Had they tested his blood for drugs?

"Meg?" Kevin's voice broke into her thoughts.

Meg snapped back to attention. "Oh, sorry . . . My mind was wandering. I'm worried about Rachel—that's Seth's sister. She went into the hospital this morning, and we haven't heard anything since. I don't mind keeping the kids, but I need to know what to tell them."

"You said Rachel is your fiancé's sister?" Kevin asked. He almost looked as though he cared about the connections between total strangers. "Older or younger?"

"Yes. Younger sister. Their mother lives right over the hill, next to Seth. This house and their two were all built before 1800."

"But you haven't lived here long?"

Meg smiled. "Does it show? Let's put it this way: my family built this house a long time ago, but the last descendant to live in it died over twenty years ago. After that it was a rental; my mother inherited it, but she almost never saw the place. Then I lost my job in Boston, and she thought this would be good . . . therapy, I guess. Working with my hands. And that was before we knew about the orchard. I'm guessing she didn't expect me to stay, but here I am, and Seth and I are getting married in a couple of weeks."

"Are both your parents still alive? And Seth's?"

"Mine are. Seth's father died a few years ago, and he took over the family business—that, you might remember from your time in Granford, if your folks ever had any plumbing done on the house."

Kevin shrugged. "I wouldn't know. Kids don't pay too much attention to stuff like that."

Meg was scrambling for a new topic of conversation when Bree and the children banged their way into the kitchen, followed closely by Seth. Meg felt a surge of relief. She silently mouthed, *Rachel?* to Seth, who shook his head. So no news yet, good or bad?

The children were lugging small baskets of apples. "Look what we collected, Meg!" Chloe said triumphantly. "Are we staying for dinner? Can we make something with them?"

"Let me talk to your uncle Seth a sec, okay?" Meg said.

"I don't want to cook," Matthew said.

Why is the kitchen suddenly so crowded? Meg wondered.

"I've got some stuff to do upstairs," Bree announced. "They're all yours now."

"Okay, got it." First things first. "Seth, this is Kevin Eastman, as you might have guessed already. Kevin, this is my fiancé, Seth Chapin."

"'Fiancé' is a silly word," Chloe announced. "I mean,

why does it have to be French? Aren't there any English words?"

"Honestly, I don't know," Meg told her. "What would you like to use? 'Husband-to-be'? That's kind of long and clunky. 'Future partner'? Too vague. 'Engagee'? That sounds almost as bad as 'fiancé.' Why don't you work on it?"

"I'll think about it. How's Mom?"

"I don't know, sweetie . . . I haven't heard from her or your dad."

Chloe accepted that statement without comment. Meg worried that she was old enough to know something about the problems of having a baby, although there were far fewer now than there would have been a century or two earlier. How many babies had been birthed in this very house?

"Seth, do you know where Aaron and Lori are at the moment? And if they're together? I'm sure Kevin would like to see them."

"I haven't seen either of them since last night," Seth said. "I dropped Lori off at the house. Kevin, Aaron doesn't have a phone, and I don't have Lori's cell number. Want to go hunting for them?"

Kevin stood up. "Sure. It'll feel good to stretch my legs."

"Why don't you bring everyone back here for dinner?" Even as she said it, Meg was wondering what the heck to feed eight people, two of them children, but she could figure something out. Maybe having to be polite in front of the children would keep Kevin, Lori, and Aaron civil, at least for a while. Although Aaron and Lori seemed to have done well the night before, Kevin was a wild card.

"Good idea," Seth said, obviously relieved at having a solution presented to him. "Matthew, can you take care of Max while I'm gone? He could use some exercise. If you take him for a walk, maybe afterward Meg could show you how to feed the goats."

"Cool," Matthew said.

"And Meg and I will make dinner," Chloe announced. "With apples."

"Sounds like a plan," Seth said, smiling. "Kevin, you ready to go?"

"Quick pit stop first, if you don't mind," Kevin said.

"Upstairs," Seth replied. He turned to Matthew. "I'll get you Max's leash, but he knows you, so he won't run too far. Can you handle him?"

Matthew stood up a little straighter. "Sure, no problem."

Meg turned to Chloe. "So, what kind of apple dishes do you like? Pie? Cake? Baked apples?"

"Can we make one of those ones with a weird name? Like grunt or slump? Mom makes those for guests sometimes, and they laugh."

"Of course. Ever since I found out I have an orchard, I've been collecting apple recipes. I'm sure we can find something. You know how to peel apples? With a peeler, I mean?" Meg had a quick vision of turning Chloe loose with a sharp knife—no, not going to happen.

"Sure."

"Then why don't you wash the ones you picked today, and choose the best ones, and start peeling?"

Chloe complied. Matthew was kneeling next to Max, getting reacquainted. Meg approached Seth and said quietly, "Should we be worried?"

"I can't say. Mom should be home from work soon. Rachel told her she didn't need her there, that Noah was enough of a crowd. Maybe she'll call, or you can try her in a bit. You sure you're okay with feeding the crowd?"

"I'm hoping there's something lurking in the freezer that I can expand. Like maybe last Thanksgiving's turkey leftovers, or some of the Christmas ham. We'll manage. At least we'll have dessert!" She leaned forward and kissed him lightly. The children ignored them.

Seth and Kevin had been gone for no more than fifteen minutes when Lydia appeared at the back door. She greeted her granddaughter warmly. Not surprisingly, Chloe's first question was, "How's Mom?"

"I haven't heard any news yet, but I'm sure everything is fine," Lydia told her. "Meg, I passed Matthew and Max on my way over—they were playing a very energetic game of fetch. Matthew said the girls were 'cooking—ick.' That's a quote."

"Chloe and I are making dessert. You want to join us for dinner? I warn you, we may have the whole Eastman family here. Or none of them. Seth took the older brother, Kevin, who showed up this afternoon, to look for the others, and I haven't heard whether he found one or both of them. I'm just going to make a big batch of something and hope for the best."

"Can I help?"

"Go explore the freezer and see what you can find."

Matthew and Max came tumbling in not long after, and Meg listened with a smile as he recounted Max's antics to his grandmother. He and Lydia fed Max; Lolly, who disliked crowds, was hiding somewhere else in the house and would eat later when the chaos subsided. Then Lydia found a couple of packages of mystery meat in the freezer, and she and Meg improvised a huge casserole. Chloe tasted along the way and made suggestions. The slump or grunt came out of the oven after an hour's cooking time, and Meg slid in the casserole and shut the oven door.

"Can we go watch TV now?" Chloe asked.

Meg debated for about two seconds about insisting that

she help wash the dishes she'd helped create, and decided that life lesson could wait for another day. "Sure. You know where it is. Take your brother with you. And don't fight over what show to watch."

"Got it. C'mon, Matthew." The children left the kitchen, followed by Max.

Meg leaned against the kitchen counter. "I'm already exhausted. May I offer you a glass of wine, or would that corrupt the young 'uns?"

"I'm sure they've seen it before."

Meg filled two glasses from the bottle in the refrigerator, and they sat at the table. "Should we be worried?" she asked Lydia quietly.

"I don't know, to be honest. Rachel's first two deliveries were easy enough, but it's been a while. But all her checkups went fine—or at least, that's what she told me. Don't borrow trouble, Meg. Noah will call us as soon as he can."

"I hope so!"

"By the way, I did have one strange conversation with Rachel this morning. About that list of Eastman's clients?"

"Yes, she mentioned that to me, too. Why is that important now?"

"Because she told me Jacob Patterson is on the list. I know the man. Seth's father certainly did, as well. I think if I approached him, he'd talk to me."

"About the fire?"

"Exactly. I can give him a call tomorrow. You want to go with me?"

"Of course. But let's leave the Eastman clan out of it for the moment."

"I agree."

And then Seth returned, followed by a row of Eastmans, and quiet fled.

25

Since dinner was already cooked, Meg could sit at the table and devote some attention to watching the three Eastmans interact. Aaron was still subdued, but Meg was happy to see that Lori was joking with him, and was rewarded with an occasional smile. Kevin, who'd had less time to get comfortable with his brother and sister, was more wary, watching the banter between the others and looking a little lost.

Lydia's phone rang halfway through the meal, and she stood up and walked to the window to answer it. When she turned, she was smiling broadly. "Baby girl, eight pounds ten ounces, mother and daughter are fine. Kids, I guess you're spending the night with me." Chloe and Michael cheered.

Meg felt relief surge through her, and realized how worried she had been about Rachel. "When can she have visitors?"

Lydia resumed her seat. "I didn't think to ask. And I don't

know when they'll send her home—it could be as early as tomorrow, the way health care works these days. So, kids, if you're wondering, yes, you will be going to school tomorrow. Either your mom will be home by the end of the day, when you get out, or I'll take you over to the hospital to visit after school. Got it?" They nodded in unison.

Lydia turned to Meg. "I'll . . . make that call in the morning, once I know what Rachel's schedule will be. If possible, we could do it tomorrow—otherwise it may have to wait for the weekend."

"That's okay, Lydia," Meg told her. "Life has a habit of getting in the way of plans."

No one mentioned anything remotely controversial at the dinner table, which Meg credited to the presence of children, and for which she was grateful. Chloe proudly presented the dessert, which disappeared fast. It was close to eight when Lydia said, "Okay, school day tomorrow. I've got some of your clothes at my house, so we'll be all set. I'll drive you to school in the morning, and one of us will pick you up at school after, so don't get on the bus. Is that clear?"

The children seemed subdued, and only nodded. Lydia stood up. "Aaron, Lori, Kevin—nice to see you all. Meg, thanks for having us. I'll talk to you in the morning."

"Want a ride, Mom?" Seth volunteered.

"No, I think we can use the walk. It's a nice night. Ready, kiddos?"

They were gone in five minutes, after Matthew had made a long farewell to Max. Meg quirked an eyebrow at Seth. "Where's everybody staying tonight?"

"Kevin, you can stay with me at Seth's house," Lori said quickly. "If that's all right with Seth?"

"Sure. I was going to suggest that," Seth said.

"I can drive you over there, Lori, since your car is at his

house." Kevin hesitated a moment. "You want to come, too, Aaron? We haven't really had a chance to talk."

"Maybe tomorrow," Aaron said neutrally. "How long were you planning to stick around?"

"I've got a flight out on Monday. I need to be back next week to help out with the shelter's Thanksgiving dinner."

"There's time, then." He stood up. "Thanks for the meal. I'll be getting back now—I want to finish one long section of fence tomorrow. You know where to find me, Kevin."

Everyone was standing, as they sorted out who was going where and with whom, and made vague plans for the next day. Seeing them all together now, Meg was struck by how quickly they fell into old ways of talking to each other—despite time and distance, she could still see the familial connections. How odd. She waved them all off, then poured herself a last glass of wine and sat down again at the messy table. Seth followed the herd, offering last-minute suggestions.

Lolly crept into the room to see if the coast was clear, then looked piteously at Meg. "Yeah, right, you want food. I've fed all the rest of Granford, so I guess I might as well feed you, too." She dumped half a can of cat food on a plate and set it on the floor in front of Lolly, then resumed her place at the table. Still messy. Let Seth deal with it. Or it'd still be there in the morning. No sound from Bree . . . When had she snuck out? Meg realized she was actually alone in the house. When was the last time that was true?

She sipped her wine, thinking about the Eastman mess. Dad had most likely been a high-end scammer. Lori had dropped out; Kevin had turned into a bleeding-heart social worker; Aaron had spent more than half his life in jail. The fire had been (a) an accident, (b) a murder-suicide perpetrated by Dad, (c) set deliberately by Aaron or started by accident by him, under the influence of who knew what drugs, or (d) started by somebody else altogether. But if (d) was the right answer, who? And why had the fire victims waited too long to get out? Or rather, why had Aaron managed to get out when nobody else did? And why had the police been so quick to point to Aaron, and why had they done such a cursory job of investigating?

Was the solution that everyone had arrived at the correct one? Or was there something else going on that nobody had wanted to look at?

Meg had reached this point in her thinking when Seth returned. "Any more of that?" he asked, pointing toward her glass.

"In the fridge," she answered. "Everybody set for the night?"

"I think so. I can't say I really care. They are adults, after all."

"What do you think is going to happen now? Is this the final farewell for the last of the Eastmans, and they'll all go their separate ways?"

"I have no idea."

"You've spent more time with Aaron over the past few days. Has your opinion changed?"

Seth leaned back in his chair and sipped some wine before answering. "I think he's telling the truth when he says he doesn't remember. I believe he does want to remember, and not for any bad purpose, like revenge. Did he do it? That I can't say. The man I see now, after a quarter century in prison, is pretty passive. I don't know how much prison might have changed him. Maybe he was just a mixed-up kid in high school, and he grew up in prison. As far as I know, he never got into trouble there—I think Art would have told me."

"Then let me ask you, what's the best-case outcome here?" Meg asked.

"That the family comes to terms with what happened and manages to create some sort of relationship going forward."

"They do all seem kind of unattached—I mean, neither Lori nor Kevin seems to have any long-term relationship. Obviously Aaron is a different case. You think that's the result of their upbringing, or the effect of the fire and the deaths?"

Seth shook his head. "I can't say, and I'm not going to guess. Can we table this for now?"

"Sure." Actually, Meg thought, it was kind of a relief not to have to think about it. "I ordered tiles today."

"Great! Will they deliver? That's a lot of weight."

"Tomorrow, they said."

"If we can, we should go see Rachel and the baby tomorrow, before I start on the bathrooms. I'll plan to stick around here and do the demolition work. I've already got all the pipes and blue board and such. And the permits—can't do anything in Massachusetts without the right permits."

"I'd better warn Bree. I told her it was going to happen, and she might want to go over to Michael's. So what're the steps?"

Seth outlined the process for opening up the walls, installing new pipes, fixing whatever wiring might need it, then replacing the walls. "And that's when you come in. We leave the rough attachments for the fixtures until you get the tiles in—after the wiring and plumbing have been officially inspected, of course."

"Of course. And how long do the tiles have to dry or cure or whatever they do?" Meg asked.

"A day, no problem. Then you have to grout them—that's another day. I promise I'll leave at least one toilet operational. If you want to bathe, I've got plenty of buckets."

"You're a prince," Meg muttered. Then more loudly she said, "So we can have everything in place by Sunday?"

"That's my plan. Frame things tomorrow, tile Saturday,

grout Sunday. I guess Monday would be the earliest I can install the fixtures, but that won't take long. Want me to do the dishes?"

"They can wait. You do realize we have the house to ourselves?"

"Ah. I'll do the dishes in the morning."

26

Meg woke early Friday morning to the sound of banging and crashing. It took her a moment to identify the source of the noise: Seth must have started demolition. She lay in bed because she really wasn't ready to face the mess that adding not one but two bathrooms would create. No doubt they'd be as historically correct as indoor plumbing in a colonial house could be, but mess was mess, old or new. She sent a brief prayer to the universe that Seth didn't find anything unexpected when he opened up the walls. Antique pipes and dry rot from years of leaks she could handle. Dead animals, less so. Dead bodies? Please, no! Maybe an old photo or some letters—that would be okay. Or maybe someone had found a convenient hidey-hole for his or her bottle of patent medicine, which had been heavy on the alcohol.

She could hear Bree's voice alternating with Seth's, so Bree had reemerged from wherever she'd gone the night before. Or hidden. Meg reluctantly decided she'd better get up. Seth would have warned her if he'd turned off the water, wouldn't he? Maybe she could grab a quick shower before then.

Downstairs she found Seth looking all too happy, holding a small sledgehammer and already covered with plaster dust. "Oh, good, you're up," he said. "I didn't want to break up the alcove in the bedroom while you were still asleep."

"And you thought I could sleep through this?" Meg asked, waving at some serious holes in the walls. "What is it you're doing here, again?"

"Downstairs powder room, with toilet and sink only. I'm sure you don't want to give up any kitchen space, so I thought I'd carve it out of the front room. I'll continue the line of the chimney, up to the doorway—that would minimize what I'd have to take out and reconstruct. It'll be small but functional. And the plumbing will run up from the basement to that room, and then beyond it up to the new bathroom off the bedroom. We'll tie them all into the existing waste pipe. Make sense to you?"

"I guess. Is there coffee?"

"Of course." Seth waved toward the stove.

Meg poured herself a cup and sat down. "Bree, where'd you disappear to last night?"

"I went to a movie. Looked like you had a real crowd here, and you didn't need me. Seth says the baby came?"

"She did. I hope we'll get to see her today. Lydia took the older kids home with her, and Seth parked the two elder Eastmans at his place. Aaron went back to the alpacas. Is that everybody, or have I forgotten someone?"

"That'll do," Bree said. "I think I'll go hang out with Michael until you get this mess sorted out."

"Seth promises it will all be done by Monday. Right, dear?"

"No problem," Seth replied, between whacks of the

hammer. Meg wasn't sure he had even heard her question, but it was too late to stop him now.

Lydia called shortly after nine. "Kids safely at school. I checked with the hospital—Rachel and the baby are in good shape, so she's going home today. I think it might be better to wait until she gets home to try to see her, don't you? I'll pick up the kids after school and head over there directly. You can join us, or maybe you'd like to wait until she's settled. And what the heck is all that banging and crashing?"

"Seth has begun the great bathroom project. He's still taking out walls, so I thought I'd grab a shower before he dismantles the plumbing. I agree that Rachel probably doesn't need a crowd as soon as she gets back. You go ahead. I can run over tomorrow. So, I've got the day free. Are we on for the insurance agent?"

"Let me give him a call right now. I was waiting to see what Rachel's schedule was before making any other plans. I'll call you as soon as I've talked to him."

"What story are you going to give him?"

"Easy. I'll tell him I'm thinking of changing insurers. Talk to you later!" Lydia hung up.

Meg got up and wandered over to where Seth was staring at what had been a wall, and taking measurements. "Do I have time for a shower?"

"Make it a fast one," he said. "Was that Mom?"

"Yes. She said Rachel and the baby will be home later today. I thought the family needed time to settle in, so I may go over tomorrow. Maybe you can come with me, but only if you get enough done here first."

"Then take your shower so I can get back to work." He grabbed her for a quick kiss. "Good morning."

"Mmm, I love the taste of plaster dust in the morning."

Meg was toweling dry her hair when Lydia called back. "Can you make it at eleven?" Lydia asked.

"Sure. I can't even think here; Seth is destroying things I'd rather not know about. Was he always like that?"

"I'd say yes. He'd make things out of blocks and then smash them with great glee."

"Figures. Let me get dressed. Can you pick me up?"

"Sure. See you about quarter to eleven."

Lydia arrived on time, and Meg hurried out to meet her, relieved to be away from the noise and dust. Seth appeared to be in hog heaven and probably hadn't even noticed that she'd left. "Do you know," Meg said, as she fastened her seat belt, "I don't think I've ever seen walls taken apart? The only construction project I've been part of, up close and personal, was sanding my kitchen floor, and that didn't involve destroying anything."

"I wish I could say I knew what you meant about destruction, but Seth's father was always so busy fixing other people's problems that very little got done around our house. I think that's a large part of how Seth learned: by doing it himself."

"But then he went off to an outstanding school and got a degree in literature, right? That kind of implies that he wanted to get about as far from plumbing as possible. I'm sorry—that sounds rude, given what happened."

"I understand your question. I've always regretted that Seth didn't end up teaching at a university somewhere, but somebody had to keep the business going, and he was the oldest. Do you think he's unhappy with how things turned out?"

"Actually, no, I don't. He likes to fix things, both real, physical things and more abstract problems. I'm not sure his heart was ever in plumbing, but since he's made the transition to restoration and renovation, he's been a lot more cheerful. He's doing something he loves."

"Well, that's good to hear. "

Meg decided it was time to change the subject. "How well do you know Jacob Patterson?"

"Mostly professionally. I'm sure Seth has mentioned that Massachusetts is pretty strict on construction standards and required permitting, so that means all plumbing has to be inspected before you can close up the wall. And the work has to be done by a licensed plumber—no DIY jobs. Without all the right paperwork, no permit, no inspection, no insurance coverage. So my husband and Jacob crossed paths quite often. And it's a small town, so we'd run into each other now and then. But it's not like we were bridge partners or took vacations together."

"How much competition for insurance business is there here? Or was there back when the fire happened?"

"Jacob's the only one who lives in town here. Obviously there are larger firms in other nearby towns. But people in Granford know him, and they like to do business locally, so I think he's done all right. He should be pretty close to retiring now, although it's not a physically demanding job, so I guess he could work as long as he likes."

"And he was on Ken Eastman's list of investors."

"He was."

Lydia pulled into a small paved area in front of a house that looked as though it dated from the 1950s. It had a discreet painted shingle hanging on a post in the front, advertising JACOB PATTERSON, INSURANCE AGENT. "Here we are."

"How do we handle this, Lydia?" Meg asked.

Lydia sighed. "Like I know any more than you do about interrogating people? I'd say start with Aaron returning to town and take it from there."

Jacob greeted them cheerfully at the door. "Lydia, what a treat to see you again! How've you been? And this is Meg

Corey?" He thrust out his hand. "I've heard all sorts of things about you, Meg."

"All good, I hope."

"Well, except for those crimes you keep running into. But that's not your fault, now, is it? Lydia, what can I do for you? You said something about reevaluating your insurance needs?"

"Can we sit down, Jacob?"

"Sure, sure, come on into my office." He led the way into a smaller room toward the back, where there was a desk with two chairs in front of it, and stacks of files. "Please, sit. Sorry about the mess; my receptionist left for lunch—about three years ago." Apparently it was a joke he'd told before, because he waited expectantly for a response from them.

Lydia laughed politely, then turned sober. "Actually, Jacob, there was something else that Meg and I wanted to talk about. You've heard that Aaron Eastman is in town?"

Jacob gave them a long look. "Yes, I have. Sad story, that."

"You set up the insurance policy on the Eastman house, didn't you, Jacob?" Lydia asked.

"I did. Damn good thing, too. It was fully covered, including contents. Life insurance policies for the mister and missus, too."

"And that house coverage included arson?"

"Sure. It was a premium policy, against all contingencies. Even flood, although the Connecticut River never made it anywhere near the house. Course, that was before global warming. Anyway, the policy payouts went into the estate, and from there to the kids."

"And the Eastmans set all that up not too long before they died?" Lydia asked.

Jacob gave her an odd look. "That's right. Ken and Sharon were taking a long look at what coverage they had. The kids were getting older, but they had college costs and such still to come. And the former policies were out-of-date. They were just being responsible. Why do you want to know?"

"Was that your only business dealing with Ken Eastman, Jacob?" Lydia asked softly.

Jacob focused on Lydia with an expression that Meg thought contained equal parts calculation and sorrow. "Now, why would you ask that, Lydia?" he said, clearly stalling.

Lydia glanced at Meg before saying, "Because your name turned up on a list of investors in Kenneth Eastman's investment fund."

Jacob seemed to shrink just a bit. "I see. Where did you find that? It's private. And all of Ken's records went up in flames."

Lydia shook her head. "Not all of them, Jacob. His mother-in-law, maybe with her daughter's help, kept copies of quite a lot of them, and she made sure they were kept in a safe place, not at the house. There are a few boxes' worth, and they make interesting reading. Meg and I have seen them."

"What do you want from me?" Jacob said, in a near-whisper.

"Lydia, let me take this one," Meg said. "Jacob, Aaron Eastman came back to Granford as soon as he was released, because he had some questions about some of the details of the fire that killed his parents." *That's an evasion, Meg!* But she didn't want to give away too much too soon. "Now he wants to stay around until he figures out a few things. By the way, he was the one who took the documents out of the house, and he told us about them." Almost the truth. "Lydia and I have both looked through them, and we decided that there were several things about this Eastman fund that were suspicious. When we learned that you were one of the participants, we came straight to you. We hope you can answer some of our questions."

"So you haven't talked to any of the others?" Jacob asked.

"Not yet," Lydia answered him. "A lot of them have

passed away, but I recognized plenty of the names. What did you know, Jacob?"

Jacob leaned back in his creaking desk chair and looked over their heads. "Then? Not as much as I should have, but I guess you'd have to say I didn't want to know. Ken's fund was paying out good money, and I wasn't going to ask questions. Besides, there were a lot of smart people on that list."

"And when did you finally decide that there was something fishy going on?" Meg asked. "After the fire?"

Jacob shook his head. "No, it was before that. Look, I've always been a pretty honest guy. You have a job like mine, in a small town, you get to know people, and you know things about 'em. Like how much they're worth. What kinds of jewelry or art or cars they've got. How much they want to leave for their children. You know? It's kind of personal, but I didn't run around talking about them, because that would have been wrong. I was real happy when Ken asked me to invest in his fund, because it was like I had arrived socially." Jacob smiled at the memory, but without humor. "It meant I was one of the important folk in Granford. I'd been careful about saving, so I invested a little. And then a little more. Lydia, how well did you know Ken?"

"Hardly at all. My husband, Stephen, wasn't part of Ken's social class. He was one of the ones who worked *for* men like Ken, not with them."

"Well, then you know what I mean. So Ken invited me into his special circle, and I kept investing more and more, and it kept paying out, until it didn't. So I asked him flat out, what's the problem? And that's when Ken told me the fund was underwater, and he'd been juggling the accounts to make the payouts but he just couldn't do it anymore. And then he asked me how much insurance he had on the house, and what would happen if it burned down."

27

 That was something Meg had not expected to hear. "You think Ken Eastman was planning to burn down his own house?" she asked.

Jacob looked down. "Maybe," he said cautiously. "But he didn't come out and say it in so many words." Then he faced Meg and Lydia. "Look, you've got to understand the situation. By the time we had that conversation, I'd sunk just about all the savings I had into his fund. It had been doing really well, so we just kept plowing all the earnings back into it. Or at least, that's what Ken said. But then something went wrong. The statements kept looking real good, but one day I came to him and told him that I needed to take some cash out because I had to put on a new roof, and after he waffled for a while he more or less admitted that the investment fund was in the toilet because of the lousy economy, and the only way I'd get my money out of it was if he could get his hands on a big chunk of change. I guess he had started thinking that collecting the insurance on the house was the easiest way out of the mess he'd gotten himself into."

Jacob shifted uncomfortably in his chair. "He was real careful, you know? He never came out and said, *I'm going to burn down the house for the insurance money.* He just asked if he had good coverage on everything, and that included arson. So I said, that's part of the standard package, and then I made a joke about why he was worried about arson. He kind of shrugged and said something like, you never know. Things happen. And then he went on to say, 'I read somewhere that a water heater could explode without any warning and start a fire.' I told him, sure, it's been known to happen, if you don't vent it properly and there's a spark of some kind to set it off. And then he gave me this weird smile and said, 'I'd better make sure mine's okay.'"

"How long before the fire was that?" Lydia asked.

"Maybe a month? I didn't think anything more about it; I thought he was just joking around. And I never did see the money I asked him for—I had to take out a bank loan for the roof."

"And you didn't remember this conversation when the house did in fact burn to the ground?" Meg demanded.

Jacob turned to look at her. "Why would I? The police said it was the kid's fault, messing around with making drugs or something. No one ever suggested anything different. He was convicted, wasn't he?"

"Yes, he was," Lydia said.

By a judge who had lost a lot of money to Ken Eastman, Meg added silently, although that had never been made public. Maybe that judge hadn't gotten her money back, but it was possible that she'd wanted to shut down the whole investigation before anybody looked too closely at the Eastman finances, fearing there might be a paper trail that led right to her. "Jacob, do you believe that Kenneth Eastman was planning to burn down his own house for the insurance money?" Meg asked, looking him in the eye.

Jacob stared at her for several seconds, then said, "God help me, yes. I didn't ask him directly. Maybe I didn't want to know. I guess I figured, Ken was a smart guy, most of the time, and if he did it, he'd do it in a way that nobody would get hurt. So I went along with it. We bumped up the insurance on his place, which I probably shouldn't have, because there were some issues with it: knob and tube wiring that was still active, no smoke alarms—although those were less common then than they are now. In any event, it was pretty clear to anyone that once a fire got started in that house, the whole place would go up pretty fast. Plus it was well outside of town, and it would take the fire department some time to get trucks out there. By then it would be hard to stop."

"Jacob, as you very well know, three people, including Ken, died in the that fire," Lydia said. "What went wrong?"

Jacob immediately looked defensive. "Why do you think I would know? If you're asking if Ken tried to kill himself, I'd say no."

"So why didn't Ken and Sharon get out? And Sharon's mother?" Meg asked.

"Look, Meg, I don't have any answers," Jacob protested. "I was just sick about it when I heard. And I did get a copy of the fire inspector's report—had to, before I could authorize any insurance payout. The fire happened in the middle of the night, and everybody—except Aaron, it seems—was in bed, asleep. They never left their beds. Had to have been smoke inhalation that got to them."

"Even Virginia?" Meg said. "She was on the ground floor, in a different part of the building. She may have had trouble getting around, but she wasn't crippled. Surely she could have

climbed out a window, under the circumstances." Ideas were
beginning to swirl around in Meg's mind, each one less pleasant than the one before. "What if . . ." she began.

"What, Meg?" Lydia asked. Now both Lydia and Jacob
were looking at her.

"Jacob, do you believe that Ken was planning to use the
water heater to start the fire? Does that fit with the fire report
you saw?"

Jacob held up both hands. "No! I had no reason to think
that. It's possible, in theory, but I couldn't tell you for sure. I
only knew what I'd read about in reports. Ken would have to
have done some digging on how to rig it up, and this was before
the Internet made it all so easy. If I had to guess—and this is
just a guess—I would say he would have rigged it to look like
an electrical fire. I mentioned all that knob and tube stuff. If
you leave it alone, it's safe enough—although a lot of insurers
nowadays won't touch a house that still has it—but when people
start messing around with it, adding new lines and such, that
creates problems. Plus it's easy to access. A lot of it would have
been exposed, running through the joists in the basement—
easier than trying to go through plaster walls. People cut into
it for new circuits, but something jiggles loose and nobody
notices, so it arcs. I don't recall what Ken's looked like, but it
was an old house, right? And a lot of people could have messed
with it over time.

"Bottom line? Ken could've planned to start something
where he could get at it, in the basement—it'd be easy to
loosen a few wires or strip off some of the old insulation.
Loosen the gas feed to the water heater and set up the old
wires to arc, it would all go boom."

"But how would he know when it would start?" Lydia asked.

Jacob shook his head. "I don't know. But isn't it kind of
irrelevant? That part of the basement was where Aaron

started the real fire, which did the job just fine. They found his drug-making equipment there."

"Let's leave Aaron aside for now," Meg said. "Say Ken rigged it so that the wires shorted out and started the fire, and then went back up to bed to wait for the fire to start. Would it have been fast? Or maybe he decided to take a late shower, which would trigger the burner in the water heater? Could that work?"

Lydia looked at her with dismay. "What an awful idea! But assuming that was true—which I'm not ready to do— why didn't he get out? Why didn't Sharon notice smoke or something?"

"Maybe they were waiting until the fire was fully engaged," Meg said. "If they called it in too early, the fire department might have been able to put it out too soon, and good-bye big payout." Which didn't explain how Sharon could have let her own mother die.

Lydia now looked vaguely ill. "What if . . . Oh God, I hate to say this. What if he drugged his wife and his mother-in-law so they couldn't sound the alarm, either? Sharon might not have been in on it, and I seriously doubt her mother was. Virginia was already suspicious of Ken, and maybe she shared that with Sharon. Or maybe Ken wanted them both out of the way." She shook her head as if to clear it. "But something went very wrong, didn't it? Because Ken didn't get out. Was that just stupidity? I mean, he knew there was a fire, but he waited too long to leave? He didn't count on smoke or gasses or whatever knocking him out first?"

"That's a good point, Lydia," Jacob told her. "Most people don't know that it's inhaling the smoke and gasses that kills most people in fires. And it can act fast. Ken might have thought he had more time than he did. And worse—sometimes burning materials like fabric can create cyanide gas, which is definitely poisonous. If they had some fancy curtains in the room below, that might have been a factor."

"What an awful way to die," Lydia whispered.

"Ladies," Jacob said firmly, "these are all guesses. You can't prove any of this. Yes, Ken upped his policy on the house not long before the fire, and on himself and his wife. The investigators knew that; I didn't cover up anything. But I don't think he planned to die. From what I remember of the guy, he was too sure of himself, and he thought he could find a way out of the fix he was in. He probably believed that with the insurance settlement he could make everything right—it's like a gambling addiction, you know? But the point is, we'll never know. I mean, who the heck would've done an autopsy on any of them to see if there were drugs in their system? Or looked through the rubble for an old wire? They had their suspect: Aaron Eastman set the fire, then sat on the lawn and watched the place burn down with his family in it. He was a sick kid."

"But what if he didn't?" Meg protested.

"Is that why you're here? Aaron Eastman comes back from jail claiming that he was innocent?" Now Jacob looked angry. "He was a punk and a druggie. And he loved rubbing his dad's nose in it."

"He was a kid, and he was acting out!" Meg threw back at him. "That doesn't make him a killer."

"Okay, so maybe it was an accident. Maybe he lit up something or was cooking something in the basement and it got out of hand. But that fire happened, and he was the only one who got out, and he wasn't touched by the fire. What else can you think?"

Meg had to admit that what Jacob said made sense. Even if Ken had rigged up some way to start a fire in the base-ment, no one had seen evidence of it at the time, and obviously there was no way to look now. Likewise, even if he had drugged the two women to keep them quiet, it was kind of late to do an autopsy on either of them. "Did the insurer pay out?" she asked finally.

"Yeah, after the fire marshal cleared things. Funny thing is, Eastman was so deep in debt that just paying off the bills ate up most of the money. The kids kind of scraped by on a separate policy that the grandmother left to them, rather than to Ken or Sharon. Of course, the investors, like me, never saw a penny, because Ken had long since cleared out those accounts, and besides, he hadn't left any official records for his fund, or if he did, they went up in flames. It was one big Ponzi scheme, you know? The new money coming in went right back out to pay those great dividends to new investors, and once he had us hooked, he didn't even pay those, except on paper. You'd think we would have known better, but Bernie Madoff got away with it a long time after that. People who are making good money from a fund don't look too hard at it. We were greedy. And most of us never talked about it with one another—we didn't even know who else was taken in. Anyway, it made us look stupid, and there was nothing to be done about it once Ken was dead. Why do you two care? What's it to you?"

Meg and Lydia exchanged a glance. "Jacob, to be honest, Aaron still doesn't remember what happened," Meg said. "He's not looking to blame anyone, and he's done his time. He just wants to know whether he really did what everyone keeps telling him he did."

"Good luck with that!" Jacob said bitterly. "Why can't you just accept the simplest solution? The kid was high on something, and he set a fire, either deliberately or accidentally, and he got out and saved his own skin, without even considering the rest of his family. That's cold. He should pay for that, and he did. And there's no way to prove anything different happened. Sure, his dad was a con artist and cheated a bunch of people out of some money, but that doesn't mean he deserved to die. And his mom and grandmother?"

"But that's the point, Jacob. Aaron can't believe he could have done something like that, or let it happen, and frankly, after spending time with him, I can't, either."

"Prison changes people," Jacob countered.

"Yes, but not usually for the better. He doesn't claim to have found God, but he's clean and sober, and he still doesn't remember. He's just looking for answers." *And if he doesn't find any, what will he do?* Meg wondered, not for the first time.

Jacob stood up. "Ladies, I've said all I have to say. I think you're on a wild-goose chase, but I guess your hearts are in the right place. Now, if you're not looking for insurance, I have work to do."

Lydia and Meg stood up as well. "Thank you for speaking frankly, Jacob," Lydia said. "We'll be on our way now."

Once outside, they went back to the car and sat inside it, but Lydia didn't start the engine. "What have we learned?" she asked Meg.

"We figured out that Ken Eastman was fleecing his neighbors, which might be a motive for someone to kill him. We now know that he took out a whole lot of insurance not long before the fire—that can't have been cheap, and he was already living on the edge. He may or may not have had a hand in starting the fire, but it's unlikely that he planned to die in it. And we have no proof of anything at all. I hate to tell Aaron that we've failed, but I can't think of anything else to ask."

Lydia sighed. "We can look at all the documents again. Maybe we missed something the first time through. Or maybe something will look different, given what we know now. Or maybe we could check out who the executor for the estate was—Lori was old enough, but I can't imagine anyone trusting her to handle it. But I want to go visit Rachel and the baby first. You sure you don't want to come?"

"I don't want to intrude," Meg said.

"Margaret Corey, you're family! Rachel will be happy to see you. Come on, don't you want to meet your new niece by almost-marriage?"

"Oh, all right," Meg replied, smiling. "But we have to wait until school lets out, right? Why don't we have lunch first? And I'd better check in with Seth and make sure the house is still standing."

"That works for me," Lydia said.

Back at the house, when Meg and Lydia walked into the kitchen, Meg was relieved that the pounding had stopped. She picked her way across the floor—which Seth had thoughtfully covered with a drop cloth to protect it from dust and chunks of old plaster—and peered into the space he had assigned to the powder room, which at the moment consisted of a lot of mismatched old boards and yet more holes, both old and new. "Hello in there?" she said loudly.

"Down here," Seth called out from the basement below. "What do you think?"

"I'll reserve judgment for now. Your mom's here. We were going to get some lunch before she has to pick up the kids. You want anything?"

"I ate early. I want to push through on this and at least get the room framed in and the pipes in place. You go ahead."

Lydia was already poking around in the refrigerator, looking for something edible. "I vote for grilled cheese, because it's the only thing you have all the ingredients for."

"Sorry—the pickings are kind of slim for lunch, but I've been feeding the hordes all week. Tomorrow's grocery day. You want to make them, or shall I?"

"I can do it. Why don't you take another look at the fire report, now that we've heard what Jacob had to say?"

"Good idea." As Lydia set a pan on the stove and started slicing cheese, Meg retrieved the file and brought it back to the kitchen table, wiping the dust away first. It seemed so slim. She read through it once, twice, and studied the simple diagrams. Then she decided she needed to consult with someone who knew something about building construction, since she had one on hand.

"Seth?" she called out through the gaps in the floor.

"Yo. You want something?" he replied.

"Yes. I need your construction expertise. It'll only take a minute."

In response, Seth came tromping up the cellar stairs. "What's up? Hi, Mom."

"We talked with the Eastmans' insurance agent this morning," Meg told him. "I'll fill you in later, but one thing we discussed was how the fire might have started. He thinks—very unofficially—that Ken Eastman might have somehow set the fire himself for the insurance money. I know you don't know the house, but if you were going to set a destructive fire in a colonial house that had had electricity added a century or more later, not to mention a couple of changes in heating and plumbing systems, how would you do it?" She handed him the diagram from the fire report.

"Did Jacob talk about the wiring?"

"Yes—still a lot of old knob and tube. Probably a real mishmash with a lot of alterations."

"So that's an obvious choice. Just short it out somewhere and wait."

"But Ken Eastman waited too long. If he knew the fire was going to happen, why didn't he get out?"

"You told me the fire started in the basement, right?" Seth asked.

"Yes, in the furnace room, apparently, or near it. That's where Aaron had his little den, because nobody else ever went down there. If Dad had been there that night tinkering with the wiring, Aaron would have noticed, or Dad would have backed off and waited for another day. Aaron seemed to think that his father didn't know he hung out there."

"Where was the water heater?" Seth asked.

"Uh, I don't know," Meg told him. "Wouldn't it be near the furnace?"

"Not necessarily. Plus they probably were installed at different times. Could have been somewhere else in the basement. You have the plans for the rest of the house?"

"Here." Meg handed him some additional sheets of paper, copies taken from the police and fire reports.

Seth spread them out on the table. "Okay, here's the furnace room in the basement." He pointed. "The parents' bodies were found in their second-floor bedroom. Which happens to be directly above the furnace room."

"Yes, but two stories away. So what?"

"The house had an oil furnace, which had replaced a coal furnace, which wasn't original to the house, which was built with fireplaces only, remember? Like yours. Which means that the heating ducts were added after the fact, probably in the later nineteenth century."

"What's your point?" Lydia said, flipping sandwiches in a skillet.

"Any smoke or gas from a fire in the furnace room or that end of the basement—which was a small, enclosed space—would have risen right up the badly sealed flues to the bedroom. And the parents might not have noticed. Or if they were planning to torch the place, they might have smelled smoke but were going to wait until the building was fully engulfed before exiting. Which only makes sense if the furnace room was not where they set the fire, because that would reach them too quickly right above. They hadn't counted on the fumes, which would have knocked them out."

"Jacob mentioned that the fumes could be deadly. So that gives us a new theory. Aaron started the fire by accident and got himself out, then passed out. We assume he wasn't thinking straight, if he was thinking at all. The parents were either asleep and were overcome by the smoke, or they thought they had more time because Ken thought he knew when the fire was going to start. Only we'll never know because all the evidence was destroyed, except for some bits and pieces of Aaron's meth lab or whatever scattered around."

"You know you've just claimed that there were two separate fires—Ken's and Aaron's—in the same part of the house, at the same time?" Seth said, his voice skeptical. "Isn't that a pretty huge coincidence?"

Lydia set a plate with the grilled sandwiches cut into halves on the table and sat down. "What if Aaron's fire was small and he thought he'd put it out, so he went outside to get some air? But the fire wasn't out, so it triggered Dad's little booby trap, and Dad wasn't expecting it then? He really was asleep, and then the fumes got to him?"

Seth sighed. "Ladies, I know you mean well and you're trying to help Aaron, but you're spinning this out well past ridiculous. I'll buy that Kenneth Eastman may have wanted to destroy his house, but I find it hard to believe that he would have wanted anyone to die, including himself. He could have rigged it for a time when no one was home. Well, maybe his mother-in-law, because it sounds like there was no love lost there."

Meg slumped in her chair. "I know, you're right. But Dad

wasn't an arson expert or even an electrician. Maybe he messed up on the timing. Or maybe something Aaron did set it off too soon, when Dad wasn't expecting it. And there's no way to prove any of this."

"Exactly," Seth said. "Sorry, Meg."

Lydia added, "At least we've increased the probability that the fire was an accident, and Aaron didn't mean to kill anyone. We can't fault the fire investigators, because if the fire started in the basement, there would have been nothing left to look at, apart from some fragments of Aaron's glassware or whatever. This fire happened in October, right?" When Meg nodded, she said, "So Dad would have known that the two older children were safely off at school, and he probably assumed Aaron would be in his room. Maybe he even checked, and Aaron sneaked out later. But Ken had no reason to think that Aaron was in the basement. And if Ken had reacted normally to the fire, he would have roused his wife and son and his mother-in-law and tried to get everyone out, wouldn't he? So we can deduce that he didn't react because he was already incapacitated by the fumes. Aaron was arrested and tried, the insurance company paid out, and that was the end of the story."

"So why was Aaron convicted on such inconclusive evidence?" Seth demanded.

"Mainly because he got himself out," Meg said quickly. "And he never showed any emotion during the trial. If he'd acted devastated, maybe the jury would have been more sympathetic. Plus the judge might have been biased, because she'd been part of Ken's investment scheme—something that never came out."

Several moments passed until Seth said, "I think you've done all you can." Then he changed the subject. "What's next for you?"

"We're going to see the baby," Lydia said.

28

Lydia drove the two of them to Rachel's house in Amherst. "You're quiet," she said to Meg.

"I'm angry," Meg told her. "I'd like to throttle Jacob for never saying anything about any of this back then. Maybe there wasn't any proof, but his information might have introduced reasonable doubt. Or if the jury bought into the accident theory, Aaron might have gotten a shorter sentence. It's all wrong."

"What are we going to tell Aaron?" Lydia asked.

"I don't know. I'm trying to avoid thinking about that conversation. Are we planning to stay long at Rachel's?"

"I'll see how it goes; it's up to her. Are you in a hurry?"

"No, not really. If I go home too soon, I'll just get in Seth's way, and I want him to finish his project quickly."

"So that's his wedding present? Bathrooms?"

"It is. Unique, isn't it?"

"That it is. What are you planning to give him?"

"Besides me?" Meg smiled in spite of her grumpy mood. "Actually . . . you remember his friend Eric, who deals in architectural salvage out of a barn in Hadley?"

"The name sounds vaguely familiar. Why?"

"When we were at his place looking at plumbing fixtures, Eric mentioned that he'd just acquired a bunch of antique carpenter tools and equipment, and he wondered if Seth would like them. Seth passed, because I guess he didn't want to indulge a hobby, what with everything else that's going on. But I went back to tell Eric to set them aside for me. Everyone needs a few indulgences in their life, don't they?"

"That sounds perfect. If a bit hard to wrap. But then, so is a bathroom." Lydia smiled. "Your parents will be arriving soon. Are you ready for them?"

"Heck, I don't know. I love my parents, but I don't have the time to entertain them at the moment. Not that I'm suggesting that you should! They're here to see me, but I've still got to figure out what's going on with this wedding stuff. At least they didn't show up in the middle of the harvest, like last time."

"Your mom can help with the wedding part."

"Maybe," Meg said dubiously. "But there's really not much that needs to be done. And holding it in a restaurant with a university professor handling the vows is definitely outside her comfort zone. Plus, most of the decisions have been made. Sorry, I'm just whining. Too much happening right now."

"I can set her to making Thanksgiving food. That'd keep her busy. Don't stress too much about it, Meg: it'll all work out."

Meg hoped that Lydia was right. They joined a long line of waiting parents at the school that Chloe and Matthew attended, and once they had collected the two children and installed them in the car, seat belts fastened, Lydia headed toward Rachel's house. "Are you looking forward to meeting your sister?" Lydia asked over her shoulder.

"I guess," Chloe said, with little enthusiasm.

"I wanted it to be a boy," Matthew muttered. "Now Dad and me, we'll be outnumbered."

"You'll survive," Lydia said. "And be nice to your mom— she's going to get tired a lot for a while." She pulled into Rachel's driveway three minutes later. The kids piled out first and ran to the front door, which Rachel opened quickly. She grabbed up her children with one large hug, but then cautioned them. "Careful, loves—things are still a bit sore. Go on in; your dad's inside. Hi, Mom, Meg. Come meet her—I assume it's the baby you want to see, not me."

"Rachel, you amaze me," Meg said. "You had a baby yesterday. What are you doing home so soon?"

"I guess you haven't spent much time in hospitals—it's not like a hotel, and there's no way to get any rest. It was an easy delivery, and I know the ropes. I'd rather be here. Noah can help out for a couple of days, and Chloe's old enough to help, too. Get inside! It's chilly out there."

In the front parlor, Rachel's usually tidy room was chaotic, with assorted blankets and piles of diapers and a very small cradle taking up the space. "Noah?" Rachel called out. "We've got company."

Noah came into the room, drying his hands on a dish towel. "Hey, Lydia. Hi, Meg. You guys want some tea or something?"

"Don't worry about us," Lydia said. "We just popped in to meet the baby."

"She's asleep at the moment. But then, they're usually at their cutest when they're asleep, at least for a few years. Take a peek!" Rachel said.

Lydia and Meg tiptoed over to the cradle and looked down at the sleeping infant. She looked like . . . a very young baby. A bit scrunched up—but then, she was less than twenty-four hours old. Meg tried to remember the last time she'd seen a baby that young, and came up with . . . never. She was wearing a tiny knit cap, so Meg couldn't see her hair, but her hands were bare, with teeny-tiny fingernails. The baby flexed her fingers in her sleep, and Meg suddenly realized that she was looking at a person, not a thing. A human, who was going to go on to lead a whole life, and things would never be so simple again. At that moment, the baby opened her eyes, which turned out to be an almost slatey blue, and which looked preternaturally wise. She shut them again quickly.

Rachel came up to stand beside her. "Wow," Meg said. "She's adorable."

"She looks like a baby, Meg. All babies are adorable," Rachel said, albeit fondly, looking down on her new daughter.

"What are you going to name her?" Lydia asked. "Have you decided?"

"We've decided on Margaret, but it'll probably be Maggie for short. Or Mags."

Meg felt tears pricking behind her eyes. "I'm honored. That is, if there aren't seven other Margarets up your family tree?"

"Nope, you can take the blame. Although nobody has ever called you Maggie, right?"

"Maybe Meggie, but Maggie's good for her."

"Well, there we go. You want to sit for a bit?"

"As long as you aren't exhausted," Lydia said. "If you are, just say so and we'll go."

Somehow they drifted toward the dining room and sat at the table there. "Not with all these great hormones perking. Of course, the downside is that I might burst into tears at the drop of a hat. But it passes. So talk to me. What's new with your arson investigation?"

"Oh, right!" Meg had to shake herself to switch to a new subject. "Your noticing that the insurance agent was on the investors list was a big help. We talked to him this morning and learned some very interesting stuff." Meg outlined the gist of the conversation, with a few prompts from Lydia.

Rachel appeared to be following, although every now and then her eyelids drooped. When Meg had wrapped up her explanation, Rachel roused herself to say, "So there really was something fishy going on?"

"It looks like it. But it seems a little late to do anything about it. If Kenneth Eastman did set that fire, something went terribly wrong, but there's no way to prove anything. I hope what crumbs of comfort we can give Aaron will help him."

"He'll know you cared enough to try, and that's something," Rachel said. "Listen, guys, I think it's time for my nap, so I'm going to throw you out. But come again!"

"Of course we will," Lydia said warmly. "You take care of yourself, and let either of us know if you need anything."

"Will do. Bye, you two. Great to see you." Rachel bestowed hugs on each of them, and Meg could swear there were tears in her eyes.

Back on the road, Lydia said, "Where to now?"

"Home, I guess. If Seth's made as much progress as he hoped, he may need my help to wrestle fixtures. Or something. And I'm the designated tiler—something I've never done before."

"Ah, it's easy," Lydia said. "Take it from me. I used to help Seth's dad in a pinch, and I got pretty good at it. It's even simpler now than it was then. Give me a shout if you need help."

"I will, believe me. I don't want to live with crooked lines or lumps and bumps for the next however many years. I want to get it right."

Lydia dropped Meg off at her back door, and Meg walked into the house feeling some trepidation. It was quiet: was that good or bad? She went through the kitchen, into the dining room, then turned right. "Behold, it's a room! A teeny-tiny room!" she crowed.

Seth emerged from the cellar stairs behind her. "That it is. With pipes and wiring. Once the inspector signs off on it, I can put up the walls. If you're very good, you might get a door sometime soon."

"I am so excited!" Meg said. Seth just raised an eyebrow at her, so she amended her statement. "Great progress. I'm impressed. Have you moved on to the upstairs yet?"

"Sort of. I've framed in the closet and moved the door, and I've opened up the wall between what will be the two bathrooms. If you shower, it may be a bit drafty. How's the baby?"

"Small and babylike. I didn't see her awake, although she has amazing eyes, which she opened for about two seconds. Did Rachel tell you what she wants to call her?"

"No, we haven't had much time for chitchat lately. What?"

"Margaret, aka Maggie," Meg said—and was once again surprised by how moved she felt by Rachel's choice of name.

"Nice. Did you come away wanting one of your own?"

"Not yet. But ask me again later. Can we get the wedding out of the way first?"

"That was the plan," Seth replied. "The tile was delivered . . . Looks nice."

"I got so overwhelmed by all the choices that I picked the simplest patterns that they had in stock. But I thought they went with the house."

"I agree. There's nothing wrong with simple."

"So when do I get to tile?" Meg asked, not sure whether she wanted to start sooner or later.

"Let me finish the rough-in upstairs. The timing may be tricky—you'll have to get the tiling done before we move the new old tub up there, and that's definitely a two-man job, so I'll need help."

"I am not going to volunteer! And don't you try to handle it all by yourself, either. All we need is for one or the other of us to throw our back out before the wedding."

"I hear you."

"You about ready to quit for the day?"

"Just a couple more pipes," Seth said. "Pizza for dinner?"

"Sounds good to me. I'll go pick it up."

By six Seth had scrubbed off most of the plaster and other ancient dust, and he and Meg were seated at the kitchen table, where a large pizza occupied the center. "Where's Bree?" Seth asked, before digging in.

"Michael's, I think. If you're asking if we can eat this whole thing, the answer is yes."

Seth grinned and helped himself to a couple of slices, and Meg followed suit. After finishing her first slice, Meg said, "I think we've gone about as far as we can go looking at this arson problem for Aaron. There's just not enough evidence to prove anything."

"I think you've done a great job. Well, that is if Aaron doesn't mind hearing that his father was probably a con artist who cheated half the rich folk of Granford."

"But the important point is that Dad may have had a hand in starting that fire, even though he ended up getting caught in it. That part still doesn't make sense to me. If he knew there was going to be a fire, why wasn't he able to get out?"

Seth finished his second slice and reached for another

before answering. "People make a lot of assumptions about fires, most of them wrong. Fact: if you have a smoke alarm and it goes off, you have two minutes to get out of the building. Don't stop to collect the family jewels or your photo albums, because then you won't get out at all."

"That's depressing. Any more fun facts?" Meg asked.

"Yes. A very high percentage of fire deaths are caused by smoke inhalation. Not burns. But a lot of people take a look around and say to themselves, *Gee, it's not here yet—I've got plenty of time*. Not true. And that's the most likely scenario here. Ken Eastman didn't want to get out too soon—he wanted to make sure the house would be a total loss so he could collect the full insurance. But he waited too long, and he paid the price."

"That's what Jacob said, too. But there's no way to prove it. How long does it take to die from smoke inhalation?"

"To inhale enough fumes to kill you? Or if the fumes are contaminated with something other than smoke? Could be as short as two minutes."

"So it's possible that Dad set the fire then went back upstairs to wait for a bit, but he miscalculated. Could Aaron in the basement have come to, recognized that he was in danger, and made his way outside, and then realized that nobody else had made it out? And then passed out again?"

"Maybe. He could have been exposed to the same fumes, which would make him even woozier than whatever he had been smoking or sniffing before that. And that could have been long enough to kill the other family members. Fumes would spread fast in leaky old houses. In which case, there was nothing he could have done to save them."

"That may be the best we can do for him," she said softly. "He couldn't have done anything to help his family. But that's not the same as causing their deaths."

"So we should tell him that."

"You have any idea how long the other Eastmans plan to hang around?"

"Didn't Kevin say something about leaving Monday? I don't think Lori plans too far ahead. And Aaron? Hard to say. He's doing good work on the fence, but that's not a long-term solution to anything. You want to ask them over tomorrow night and get it over with?"

"That's probably the best idea. And then we can get back to our lives, right?"

"Sounds like a plan."

29

Meg refused to entertain the Eastman tribe at every meal. The evening before she had called the three siblings and invited them to come to dinner the following night, Saturday, pointedly saying nothing about that night. They were grown-ups, if a motley crew of them, and they had at least two cars among themselves plus a working kitchen at Seth's house: let them figure out where to eat. She and Seth had far too much on their respective plates to deal with everyone at once. Meg's parents were due to arrive sometime early the following week—they were being uncharacteristically vague about their plans, but maybe that just meant they were mellowing with age. Her father, Phillip, had always been almost aggressively driven professionally, and had thrived on it, but maybe he had finally realized that it was time to slow down and smell the roses. Or, given the time of year, the apples.

Her mother had had a rather odd experience the last

occasion she had spent time in Granford, and since it had involved a death and a murder accusation, maybe she was dragging her feet about coming back, consciously or unconsciously, despite having accepted the invitation to Thanksgiving dinner at Lydia's. It was kind of Lydia to have invited them to stay at her house for Thanksgiving, but Meg suspected that her parents would prefer the comforts of a fine hotel. She hadn't heard the final arrangements. Meg admitted to herself that she felt she was acting childish, putting her own needs and wants ahead of her parents', but hers were definitely legitimate: planning a wedding, finishing a bathroom or two, and fixing Aaron's life. She still wasn't sure how that last had crept in. At least the bathroom construction did not involve dealing with the stew of personalities of the unfamiliar people who were wandering in and out of their house, but rather focusing on putting sticky stuff on surfaces and laying out tiles. Lots of tiles. Why was it she had decided to go with tiny tiles? She could have chosen big ones, a foot or more per side. But no, she wanted authentic, or sort of authentic. To be consistent with the eighteenth-century nature of her home she would have to have chosen chamber pots and an outhouse. No thank you.

Over breakfast she asked Seth, "So, where are we in the construction project?"

"All pipes roughed in, and the inspector will stop by any minute now," he replied confidently. "I'll need you to tile the bathroom walls and floors, in that order, before I can set the fixtures in place."

"Can I do it in a day?" she asked.

"We'll see. I have every faith in your innate abilities," Seth said with a wicked gleam in his eye.

"Gee, thanks," Meg muttered. "Have you found anyone to haul the bathtub in?"

"Aaron might be able to help out. Kevin probably wouldn't be able to handle it with me, and there's no way to fit three adult males and a bathtub in the stairwell, not without taking the balustrade apart, and I assume you don't want to do that."

"I don't want to undo anything in the house. Keep things moving forward, please," Meg said emphatically. "You sure everything will fit?"

"I've measured everything more than once. Don't you trust me?" Seth asked, helping himself to jam for his bagel.

"Of course. I'm just deflecting my anxiety."

"Onto a bathtub? Why are you anxious?"

Men are so clueless, Meg thought. "Plenty of things. That unfinished list of tasks for the wedding—I don't even know what I'm wearing yet. My parents' looming arrival. Having to face the dysfunctional Eastman clan with less-than-stellar news. Take your pick."

Seth's expression softened. "Hey, you know I'll back you up. And you've done your best for Aaron. Better than he had any right to expect, given how long ago all this happened."

Meg finished her toast and took her dishes to the sink. "Actually, right now I'm looking forward to doing something manual, so I don't have to think. Will we be able to talk to each other through the floor? Or walls?"

"Sure."

Meg drained her coffee mug. "Okay, I'm good to go."

A knock at the back door signaled the arrival of the town inspector, whom Seth greeted like the old friend that he was. He said a quick hello to Meg, then the two men disappeared upstairs to look at the changes there. They ended up downstairs again to check out the powder room. "Looks good, Seth," the man said. "Like there was ever any doubt. I'll be on my way. Congrats, you two, by the way."

"Thanks for stopping by so quickly," Seth replied.

"Wow, that was fast," Meg said, when the inspector had left.

"We work together a lot. Besides, I got it right."

"What happens now?"

"You start tiling." Seth grinned at her as he ticked the steps off on his fingers. "The walls are prepped, and I've cleaned all the construction dirt off the floor. In case you don't know, there's a plywood subflooring, then a layer of cement backer board glued to the plywood with construction adhesive. I'll put in an antifracture membrane, since old houses tend to shift and you don't want anything to crack. You're going to check your layout for the tiles, and line things up so they're square. Remember, the level is your friend—keep checking to make sure things aren't sliding downhill. Then we mix up some thin-set mortar and away you go. Don't worry: I'll be around to give you pointers."

"So, mortar and set, then repeat 'til the walls and floor are covered? How long does it take to set up?"

"You'll have to let it set overnight, then clean up the joints. Then you can grout. That doesn't take as long to set as the mortar."

"So at least one bathroom could be done by the end of tomorrow?"

"If all goes as planned."

"Does that ever happen?" Meg asked, smiling.

"Now and then." Seth smiled back.

"But I still have to deal with dinner for the crowd this evening. I suppose I could have suggested tomorrow night instead, but I really want to get this over with and move on."

"I can understand that, Meg. Aaron has waited a long time for some answers. You may not have them all, but he doesn't need to wait any longer. He should get on with his life, too."

"Exactly," Meg said. The problem was, she didn't see any clear path ahead for Aaron, whether or not he could accept his reduced guilt in the death of his parents. He'd been so young when he'd been sent to prison, and whatever skills—professional and social—he had learned had come from inside prison walls. How would he cope in the "real" world?

Upstairs, Seth patiently explained once again the steps in laying out the tiles. Meg knew she wasn't stupid, but this was a whole new skill, and since she was going to have to live with the results, she wanted to get things right. Finally Seth said, "Okay, now fly, little bird. I'm going to go downstairs and work on the powder room." He left, and Meg wavered, unsure.

"I can do this," she said. And so she began, picking a starting point and calculating out from that. Seth had mixed the mortar for her, to a soupy consistency, and with her heart in her throat, Meg spread a small amount on one wall, carefully distributed it with her notched trowel, took a deep breath, and started. Spread, set, space, repeat. The larger wall tiles went up easily and had built-in spacers; the smaller tiles she'd chosen for the floor came in manageable sheets. In a fit of daring she had decided to add decorative border moldings at the tops of the half-high wall tiles. But even that turned out to be no problem.

Why had she been so worried? Or was tiling really just the object of her transferred anxieties? It didn't matter. The work was happily mindless, and Meg was pleased as the floor grew quickly. She remembered putting together jigsaw puzzles with her mother, when she was a child. She wondered briefly if her mother had kept those. Maybe she should ask her mother to bring a few along with her when she visited. She tried to envision sitting with Seth in front of a crackling fire and putting together little pieces of cardboard and wood, and almost laughed out loud. They were always so busy, and most of the time their activities had to have a tangible product, like a building or a barn full of apples, not just a pretty picture that would be broken down again shortly. But it had been fun . . .

Solving the puzzle of the Eastman fire was less easy. No one had looked very hard at the time of the fire, and too many years had passed to find much tangible evidence now. Aaron had paid his debt to society, as the saying went, and no doubt he'd paid a psychological price as well. But he'd been little more than a child then, and a stoned one at that; was he a different person now? A better one? Hard to say. Meg's heart ached for him: the man she knew now had no violence or hatred in him, or so she thought. Or wanted to believe.

After a couple of hours, the walls and floor of the largest bathroom were finished, and Meg stood in the doorway admiring her handiwork. The lines were straight, and she hadn't slopped too much mortar on the tiles. It looked good: simultaneously Victorian and modern. She felt a spurt of pride.

Seth came up behind her. "Nice," he said, and sounded as though he meant it. "You up for starting the master bath and shower? I've installed everything essential."

Giddy with her success, Meg said, "Sure, why not? It's smaller than the other bath, right? Oh, but does that mean we'll be taking sponge baths in the kitchen sink?"

"It is smaller, and yes to the latter. But only for a day or two. Just grit your teeth and think of our forebears."

"Uh-huh," Meg replied, unconvinced. "I'm not convinced they bathed at all."

After another hour, including some jiggering with fitting

corners and edges, aided by Seth, the shower walls and floor were done as well. Meg checked her watch. "Shoot, I'd better start cooking. I told the Eastmans to arrive around seven. Is the house clean enough for company?"

"Don't worry about it," Seth said. "Blame everything on construction dust."

"Right, including the clumps of dog and cat hair creeping around the floor."

"I don't think our company will complain. You want a bucket of hot water to clean up with? You, not the bathroom. Mortar is definitely not your color, and you're wearing quite a bit of it."

"Thanks a lot."

Once more or less relieved of mortar spatters, Meg went downstairs to start a hearty chicken stew for dinner; luckily Bree had volunteered to refill the bare pantry and fridge. As she chopped, she wondered what they all could talk about without walking through any minefields. *Aaron, what are your plans for the future?* No, that wouldn't work. Maybe they could talk about the alpacas, which were cute and funny—and safe. *Will the three of you keep in touch now?* Equally perilous as a topic of conversation. Lori had barely managed to keep Aaron informed of her address; Kevin had apparently not made any effort at all to reach out to him. But they were family—didn't that count for something? Hadn't Robert Frost said, "Home is the place where, when you have to go there, they have to take you in"? But where was home for the fractured Eastmans?

Aaron was the first to arrive, walking across the fields from the alpaca farm. "Meg, Seth," he greeted them as he walked into the kitchen. "Smells good in here."

"I hope it tastes good, too," Meg told him. "How are the alpacas?" Oops, she'd already blown that topic.

"I'm getting kind of fond of them. The way they look at you, it's like they think you're acting silly, no matter what you do."

"Are they friendly?"

"I'd say they're not unfriendly, if you know what I mean. But they keep a distance. Works out fine."

Meg had run out of easy questions, so she looked at Seth in mute appeal. He fell back on the tried-and-true male option: "Want to see how the construction's coming along?"

The two men went upstairs, and Meg gave a small sigh of relief. Then Lori knocked at the back door, and Kevin followed her in, having apparently offered her a ride over. "Come in and get warm," Meg said. "Just hang your coats on the pegs there. Can I get you something to drink? I've got cider, hard and soft, wine, beer . . ."

"Cider's good for me," Lori said. "Is it from your own trees?"

"No, but it's from Granford—this year's crop."

Lori nodded. "This is a terrific room here, especially after dark. So welcoming. I love all the wood."

"I refinished the floor myself. It was the first thing I did to the house, after I moved in."

"Looks great."

Meg handed Lori a glass of fresh cider. "Kevin?"

"A beer sounds good. You've got a lot of history with this place?"

Meg handed him a bottle of beer. "You can have a glass if you want. Yes, this place was built by my seventh great-grandfather. At least I think it was seventh—I always get confused with the numbering. Anyway, a direct ancestor. It stayed in the family, but not my line. My mother inherited it from two maiden sisters a couple of decades ago. I moved in going on two years ago. And I've probably learned more about the people who lived here since then than my mother ever knew."

"Must be nice, having that kind of roots," Kevin said, taking a large swallow of his beer. "I mean, our house was about the same age, but Dad liked it mostly because it was big and showy and in the right part of town, not because we had any real history with it."

Minefield alert, Meg thought, even though it was Kevin who had brought it up. "What's it like where you live now?"

Kevin shrugged. "Nothing special. I don't have a family, so I live in a small apartment. I don't spend much time there anyway. Mind if I have another beer?"

He'd finished the first one fast. Was he nervous? "Help yourself, Kevin," Meg told him. "Lori, where are you living now?"

"I rent a floor in a house in a small town—well, bigger than Granford, maybe, but hardly a city. Hey, you guys, I've got a futon if either one of you wants to come and visit." Lori looked at each of her brothers in turn, with mute appeal in her eyes. Both men avoided her glance. *Yes, a warm and connected family*, Meg thought to herself. *Not.* When had it all gone wrong? Or had it ever been right?

Dinner lurched along with conversation in fits and starts. At least Meg hadn't assumed it was a purely social occasion, because in that case it would have to be called a failure. Maybe it was the pending discussion of What Really Happened that had put a damper on the evening. Aaron was mostly silent but watchful. Kevin kept drinking, becoming increasingly morose. Lori tried to fill the silences with cheerful babble, for which Meg was grateful. But she had to admit she was anxious herself. As she had told Seth, she just wanted this to be over so they could all move on.

When the bowls were all empty after the main course,

Meg decided it was time to act. Seth cleared the table, and they exchanged a glance; he nodded, then sat down again. "Aaron, Lori, Kevin, I'm sure you know I, we, wanted to talk to you about what we've learned about the fire that destroyed your home."

Meg took a moment to survey the siblings' responses. Aaron looked briefly hopeful; Kevin looked upset; Lori looked something like eager. It was Lori who spoke first. "Have you found something new?"

"Possibly, although it doesn't answer all the questions," Meg said. "And what we've uncovered isn't always pleasant to hear, I'm afraid."

"Just go ahead and spit it out, will you?" Aaron said, although not rudely.

"All right," Meg began. "From documents we've seen, the ones that Aaron came looking for, and from people we've talked to, it looks like your father was a con man. I can't speak to his official job, but he created a shell investment fund that was mainly a Ponzi scheme." When Lori looked blank, Meg explained what that was, until Lori nodded. "He managed to convince a lot of the wealthier people in Granford to invest with him, but the reality was, there actually wasn't much money there. When it looked like the whole thing was about to fall apart, we're guessing that he decided that torching the house to claim the insurance on it was the best or fastest way out of the hole."

Aaron had been staring at her intently as she spoke. Now he said, "You mean, he set the fire?"

"We have no physical evidence of that, but it looks like a strong possibility," Meg told him gently.

"Then how did he and Mom end up dead? And Gramma? Did he want to kill me, too?"

Seth spoke up. "Aaron, we don't have all the answers.

There's little evidence to work with. If we accept this motive, I think we have to assume that he planned to get out, with your mother and grandmother, and he would have checked your room, too. Did he know about your little den in the basement?"

"I don't think so. He wasn't the type to prowl around and kick the furnace. He called in other people to do that. So you're saying he didn't know I was down there? Maybe he and our mother died trying to find me?"

That was a thought that Meg hadn't considered. It might temper Aaron's legal guilt, but it would still leave him with a personal wound, that they might have died trying to save him. "Aaron, we don't know that," Meg said gently. "From what I've read, it looks like they died in their bedroom, which was directly above the furnace room. Seth thinks it might have been due to smoke inhalation, so they never had a chance to get out."

"Their bedroom was directly above the furnace room, and they found what was little more than my old chemistry set in that room, and that was one reason they looked at me," Aaron said stubbornly. "They figured I caused the fire and cleared out, which is why I was found outside. So even if it was the smoke or fumes or whatever, it was still my fault."

Suddenly Kevin spoke. "No, it wasn't." Everyone turned to look at him. "I know because I was there."

30

 Aaron looked at his brother with something like wonder. "You were there that night, in the house?"

Kevin nodded. "I was there with you in the basement."

Lori looked shell-shocked. "What the hell? How come you never told anybody?"

"Because I thought I was the one who started the fire." That silenced his siblings momentarily.

"Kevin, I think you're going to have to explain yourself," Seth finally said.

"I kind of have to start from the beginning, okay?" Everyone nodded. "Okay, remember, I was eighteen, a senior at Dad's snobby alma mater. Lori was off messing up at college, so there was a lot of pressure on me to do better. My grades were okay and I was on the right track to get into an Ivy school. But I wasn't happy. I didn't have a lot of friends at school—most people figured I was kind of a nerd. So one night I decided to do something about it, and it was a whole lot easier to find drugs than to find a girl around there. So I called Aaron. You really don't remember any of this, baby brother?"

Aaron shook his head. "I never have, and believe me, I've tried. In prison I read that the combination of shock and the drugs I was playing with can kind of wipe the slate clean. The memories just aren't there. Sorry."

"What are you apologizing for?" Kevin said. "That's what let me get away with it all these years."

"Kevin, you said you were going to explain," Lori said impatiently. "What the hell happened?"

"Look, I knew what Aaron was doing in the basement. I wasn't totally clueless, and I did a little snooping because he kept disappearing down there, even when I was around, but we never talked about it. I was so squeaky-clean back then! I thought I needed to loosen up a little, experiment, like, and I figured Aaron would know where to get the stuff I'd heard about and how to use it. Even if he was younger, I guess I kind of trusted him to look out for me. I couldn't ask the guys at school."

"Thanks a lot, Kevin," Aaron said. Kevin shot him a quick look to see if he was being sarcastic, but it was hard to tell.

"Yeah, well . . . So I called Aaron and I said some kind of vague things about getting some stuff, and somehow he figured out what I meant and he said, sure, no problem. I drove down late one night without telling anybody. I parked before I got too near the house so nobody could see the car from there, and walked over, and Aaron let me in through the basement door. As far as I know, Mom and Dad never knew I was there. And Aaron was really cool about the whole thing. He didn't make fun of me, and he told me that he thought as a first-timer I should stick to weed. He had some good stuff, he said, and he showed me what to do. God, this sounds so stupid now, but I'd never smoked

anything, although it was around at school. I couldn't say if
Aaron had taken anything else, but at the beginning he
didn't seem too out of it. He just sat there with this kind of
half smile on his face and watched me get wasted."

"Wow," Aaron said. "I did that?"

"Yeah, you did," Kevin said with a humorless smile. "I
can't tell you how long this went on. What time did the fire
department think the fire started?"

"Maybe around one a.m.," Meg said.

Kevin nodded. "Okay, so I would have arrived around
eleven, maybe—I know it was pretty dark. We would have
been smoking down there for maybe two hours? And then . . ."

"The fire started?" Meg prompted.

Kevin nodded. "The basement was kind of a pit, because
nobody went down there. I was really wasted, you know? And
that stuff you gave me, Aaron, it made me kind of paranoid."

Aaron shrugged. "It happens. You never know until you
try. As I remember it, at least, I hear things have changed."

"Can you get on with it?" Lori demanded. "So the two
of you are stoned out of your minds on the floor in the basement. What about the fire?"

Kevin looked down at his feet. "I might have tossed a
butt in the wrong place—there was a lot of random trash
down there."

"That would be a roach, brother of mine," Aaron said.

"Yeah, whatever. And suddenly there was this kind of
'whoosh' and what looked like a fireball, and the walls kind
of shook, and I didn't know if I was hallucinating or what.
But it got hot pretty fast. Aaron, you were just sitting there
admiring the pretty flames, so I grabbed you and hauled you
out the back door and dumped you on the lawn. By the time
I turned around, there was fire everywhere, and I couldn't get
back in. But what was so weird was that I didn't see anybody

moving around inside the building, or hear anybody shouting. I really didn't think I could do anything, and I guess I panicked because I thought everybody would blame me. Aaron was no help by then: he was more or less passed out."

Kevin paused, and shut his eyes for a moment. Then he opened them and looked around the table, and when he spoke, his voice was bitter. "So I left. I goddamn went back to my little dorm room at school, and lay there staring at the ceiling until somebody came to my room a few hours later to tell me that my parents were dead and my home had burned to the ground." By then Kevin had tears running down his face. "And I never told anybody. I'm so sorry, Aaron. I was a chickenshit kid, and I let you take the blame. Oh, and one more thing: you weren't cooking anything that night. I didn't see any equipment or chemical-type stuff. You had a lighter, and that was it."

Kevin's confession had stunned everyone. Seth was the first to speak, after a long silence, and Meg was happy to let him take the lead. "Let me see if I've got this straight, Kevin. You sneaked away from school, without anyone noticing, and drove to your family's house so you could experiment with drugs with Aaron's help."

Kevin nodded. "I was a senior, so I didn't have to sign in or out. I didn't tell anyone what I was going to do; I just went. So no witnesses, right? I was going to be back before morning anyway, although maybe I didn't think that part through very well. I thought I'd take a few puffs or whatever, just to see what it was all about, and then leave."

Seth nodded. "The two of you were smoking Aaron's weed in the basement, and you believed that you inadvertently started a fire there."

"Right."

Seth went on, "So you got Aaron out, and by then the fire had spread fast."

"Yeah. So?"

"Did it ever occur to you that if in fact you did set a fire in the basement with a discarded roach, it couldn't possibly have spread that fast? At least not without some sort of accelerant?"

"You mean, it wasn't me? It was Dad's fire?"

"Maybe. We don't know how he might have planned to start a fire, but we know he was asking about water heaters blowing up before that. We're guessing that whenever or however it started, he didn't rush to get out because he wanted to be sure that the house was destroyed so he could claim the maximum insurance value. So he waited—too long, apparently. Look, Kevin, there's no way to tell now whether you started a fire or not. But if you did, and that was the only one, there should have been time for your parents to get out, and to get your grandmother out, too . . . unless there were other factors involved."

"Oh, wow," Kevin said, almost to himself.

"And you let Aaron take the rap for it, you asshole?" Lori burst out. "How could you do that? You let him go to jail for what you did! Or thought you did. Whatever."

"And I'm sorry about that! You think that hasn't been eating at me all these years?" Kevin protested. "But by the time I got home, everybody had already decided how it happened, and Aaron had been arrested. And he didn't remember!"

Seth looked levelly at Kevin. "It took months to bring the case to trial, Kevin. You could have stepped up at any time. Or since."

Meg sneaked a glance at Aaron's face, and his expression almost broke her heart. There was something so innocent about it, like he was having trouble believing what he was hearing. There was no anger, no hate, just a deep bewilderment. His brother's selfish choices had shaped his entire adult life, and he was struggling to understand what had happened. Meg fought down the absurd thought that now would be a good time to offer dessert, but she was pretty sure that cake wasn't going to do much to make up for all the wasted years shared by the Eastmans.

They were all startled when Aaron shoved back his chair and stood up. "I need to think about this. I've got to get out of here."

Lori stood up, too. "Aaron, walk me back to the other house, will you? I don't want to be in the same car with him right now." She nodded toward Kevin.

Aaron hesitated, then shrugged. "Okay. Let's go, then."

Lori looked back briefly at Meg and mouthed, *We'll talk*, then took Aaron's arm and went out the door with him.

That left Kevin sitting like a lump at the table, avoiding everyone's eyes. "What happens now?" he said to no one in particular.

Meg said, almost sharply, "Before you ask, we haven't involved any law enforcement authorities, although Art Preston did give us the original police files on the fire. Seth and I have no idea what legal impact what you've just told us may have on anyone or anything. I think right now you all need to digest what we've just dumped on you. Go back to the house now and try to get used to it. We can talk tomorrow."

"Sure, that's worked for twenty-five years now," Kevin muttered. He finally looked up at Meg and Seth. "I'm sorry. Look, I appreciate what the two of you have done, trying to help Aaron, and that you shared it with us. I don't know what we're going to do next, but we'll let you know. We can't just hide our heads in the sand anymore—well, I can't. If that means talking to the cops, I'll do it. It's time I stepped up. Good night." And Kevin went quickly out the back door, leaving Meg and Seth alone in the kitchen.

"Well," Meg began, "that wasn't what I expected."

"I didn't, either," Seth said. "Now what?"

"I have no idea. Do we need to tell law enforcement? Do we start a drive to exonerate Aaron Eastman, at the expense of his brother? You think Aaron would want that?"

Seth shook his head. "I don't know, Meg. I think the first thing to do is to talk unofficially to Art . . . tomorrow. All we can say now is that Aaron looks somewhat less guilty than he did, and Kevin somewhat more, but there's no way to prove anything. I have no clue what Kevin's confession changes, if anything. But we owe it to them to let them decide what they want to do, because they have to live with the outcome."

"I agree." Meg reached out and took his hand. "Seth, why is it our lives are never simple? I mean, really— you're a builder, I grow apples. How do we keep finding ourselves in the middle of these difficult ethical and legal dilemmas? Issues that have a real impact on other people's lives?"

"Just lucky?" Seth smiled at her, then his expression sobered again. "Frankly, I don't know what the best outcome would be here, either legally or ethically. Aaron has paid a heavy price for something he wasn't responsible for. Kevin hasn't paid for something he might or might not have done. None of the three of them has led what we would call a happy life, but that's not our problem to fix. I'm guessing that law enforcement is going to throw up their hands at this one."

"But that doesn't help Aaron!" Meg protested quickly. "He's still going to have a record, unless somebody acknowledges it was all a mistake."

"Meg, I don't have a clue how the official exoneration process works, or if it's even possible for Aaron. Why don't we talk to Art? As a friend? Maybe that smacks of passing the buck, but we aren't qualified to deal with this. Maybe he can tell us what the options are."

"That makes sense, if he's willing. But it all makes me sad." She stood up and started clearing dishes from the table. Seth stood as well, turned her around, and wrapped his arms around her. They stood silently for a few moments, leaning against each other. Finally Meg pushed back far enough to see Seth's face, and to say, "Well, at least I still have grouting to look forward to."

He smiled. "That you do. But let me say this: you did the right thing in trying to help Aaron."

"You believe that?" Meg looked up at him.

"Yes, I do. You are a good person, and that's why I love you. Well, one of the reasons."

"Like seeks like, sir," Meg replied. "Neither of us seems to pick the easy way out of anything. But at least we do it together."

Seth called Art as early as it seemed respectable for a Sunday morning. He came back to the kitchen to tell Meg, "He'll be over after breakfast. I told him it wouldn't take long."

They ate their own breakfast in near silence, waiting. *For what?* Meg wondered. *Closure?* Art arrived quickly, and Seth let him in. "Coffee?" he asked, as they came into the kitchen together.

"Sure, why not? Hi, Meg. Your man here was being kind of cryptic over the phone. I assume this isn't about what I'm wearing to the wedding?"

"Nothing so simple," Meg said. "Please, sit."

Once Art was supplied with coffee, he said, "Okay, shoot. Seth, what's up?"

"Can we keep this off the record, just between us, for now?" Seth asked.

Art looked bewildered, but he nodded.

Seth took a breath and launched into the story that Kevin

had told them the night before, supplemented by what they had learned from the insurance agent. By the time Seth was finished, Art's expression was grave. "You two are so much fun to hang out with," he said. "I never know what you're going to come up with next. What is it you want me to do?"

"I don't know, Art," Meg answered him. "Tell us if there is anything to be done, or if this is the end of it."

"I assume you're thinking of official exoneration for Aaron? Not criminal charges against his brother or Patterson, for concealing evidence?"

"Is exoneration possible?"

Art rubbed his hands over his face. "I'm no expert, but my semieducated guess is no. It's a complicated process, and most of the cases don't work out. You may have some new evidence, but there's not a lot here that would be useful in court. Most of the cases that do succeed are based on conclusive new evidence, like DNA tests that weren't available at the original trial. Look, I don't want to burst your bubble, guys. I think Aaron Eastman has had a lousy deal all the way, but that doesn't mean the original trial was flawed."

"What about Kevin Eastman?" Seth asked.

"What about him? Aaron was tried and convicted of the crime. Even if he could be exonerated, I don't know that anyone is going to want to try to prosecute Kevin, and I'm pretty sure the statute of limitations for arson ran out a long time ago. There's no physical evidence that Kevin was responsible for the fire, just the suspicion . . . and neither Kevin nor Aaron was thinking straight at the time. Heck, maybe dear old Dad had taken a fatal dose of something or other, and figured the insurance would provide for the kids if he and Mom were gone. Nobody looked for any kind of drugs in their systems. I'm sorry, but I think this is over. I know that's not what you want to hear. How did Aaron take the news?"

"Hard to say," Seth said. "He seemed kind of numb when he left. At least his sister was with him."

"What're you going to do now?" Art asked.

"Tell him that we've done all we can," Meg said sadly. "He can pursue exoneration legally if he wants, but that's up to him, and he'll probably hear what you just told us. And I doubt he'd want to throw his brother under the bus at this late date. Nobody wins. But thanks for listening, Art."

"Always glad to help. By the way, I thought I'd wash my best blue jeans for the big event. Will that do?"

"You're ahead of me, at least," Meg said, summoning up a smile. "I haven't even figured out what I'm wearing. My mother's going to pitch a fit when she shows up and then probably drag me off to the nearest mall—I don't think the local boutiques will be up to her standards, but there's no time for serious shopping."

"I'll be seeing you, then," Art said. "Please don't dredge up any other crimes between now and the wedding, okay?"

"Deal," said Seth.

Meg and Seth stood in the doorway as Art pulled away, then turned back to the kitchen. "So that's that," Meg said, helping herself to the last of the coffee. "Poor Aaron. How's he supposed to find a job with this hanging over him?"

"I won't tell you it will be easy," Seth said.

Then Meg went still. "I might have an idea . . ."

"What?"

She looked at Seth. "Rick Sainsbury. He owes us, right? I think this might be a good time to call in that favor."

"Think he's even around, or still off celebrating his election win?"

"One way to find out. We have his home number, remember?"

31

Meg tracked down Rick Sainsbury's home number and made the call. She was surprised when he actually answered; she had expected him to be in Washington, reveling in his status as newly elected congressman, and where she'd have to wade through multiple layers of people who were trained to deflect people like her.

"Meg, how nice to hear from you!" he said with a measure of sincerity. "You haven't stumbled onto another crime, have you? That seems to be the usual way we come into contact."

"No, or rather yes, but I think there's some good to come from it. Can we talk, face-to-face? I promise I won't take up much of your time."

"Let me check my schedule." There was a pause but without words, and Meg guessed that he was scrolling through his phone calendar. "I've got an appointment in Amherst at four. Could I swing by, say, three?"

"Perfect. Thank you, Rick." Meg hung up to find Seth staring at her with an amused expression. "What?"

"I never thought I'd see you trading favors with a congressman," Seth said. "You have hidden depths."

"It's not for me, it's for Aaron, remember?" Meg reminded him. "And this should help balance the debt between us."

"What do you plan to ask him?"

"I'm really not sure. We've already more or less decided that none of the legal channels would work, but maybe Rick will come up with some ideas. Especially if they make him look good."

"Cynic," Seth said, smiling. "But it's worth a try. Just remember, he can't unilaterally pardon Aaron, and I don't think he has close ties to the governor, who may be the only one who could. Do you want me there?"

"Much as I'd love to have your moral support, I guess I feel like this is my crusade. Do you mind sitting this one out?" Meg asked.

"Not really. I don't think my presence would help your chances. If you're sure it's okay."

"It is, and thank you. Anyway, he won't be here until three, so do I have time to grout the bathroom? And clean up? I'd like to look respectable to greet my elected representative, or at least get the grout out of my hair."

"I think we can manage that. I'll give you a quick and dirty grout lesson, and then I'll get to work on the powder room."

Grouting proved less demanding than tiling, although no less messy, and Meg was downstairs, cleaned up, with a pot of coffee waiting, when Congressman Rick rang her doorbell in the front. She opened the door quickly. "Thanks for coming on such short notice, Rick. I can still call you Rick, right?"

"Of course. You've done a lot for me and my family, and if there's some way I can repay that, I'm listening."

"Come on back to the kitchen, then, and I'll explain."

Rick declined coffee, but listened attentively as Meg outlined the history of the Eastman fire and the subsequent trial, and what had come to light since. He didn't interrupt, but waited until Meg had finished before commenting.

"Good summary, Meg. I remember the fire, vaguely, and Aaron's arrest—he was only a few years older than me. But it took a while to come to trial, so I lost sight of what happened. I didn't realize that Aaron was out, or back in town, but I've only just come back myself. I hate to admit it, but I think Art Preston is right: there's not enough to reopen the trial. I can look into how Massachusetts handles pardons, or ask my staff to do it, but I wouldn't pin too many hopes on that."

"I'd appreciate it if you could get the details, but I realize that any legal avenues are going to be complicated and slow. What I'm most concerned about now is what Aaron is supposed to do tomorrow, and next week, and next year. I mean, the man is past forty, and he's been in prison since he was a teenager. He has no money, no home, and his surviving family members can't offer much in the way of support. His only real asset at the moment is the computer skills he's learned in prison. To put it bluntly, he needs a job. Can you help with that?"

Rick smiled. "Maybe I can. Look, can I meet the guy, talk to him? You said he's working near here at the moment?"

"Yes," Meg said. "If you're sticking around Granford over the Thanksgiving holiday, do you think you can squeeze in some time to get together with him?"

"I'll try, Meg, and I mean that—I'm not just blowing you off. You're trying to do a good thing here. But then, it's not the first time, is it?" An oblique reference to the occasions she'd done a good turn for him—because it was the right thing to do, not because she was trying to curry favor.

She didn't respond directly to his comment. Instead she said, "Aaron needs help, and if you can provide that, he'll be grateful, and so will I. And if you can get some good press out of it, all the better." She grinned wickedly at him.

"Point taken." Rick glanced at his watch. "I'd better be going. I don't want to be late for my next appointment. But I will be in touch, I promise." He stood up.

Meg did as well. "Is that a Rick promise, or a Congressman Sainsbury promise?" she asked.

"Both."

As they turned toward the front door, the doorbell rang. "Now what?" Meg muttered to herself. She led the way to the door, and opened it to find her mother and father standing on the front stoop. "Mother? Dad? Was I expecting you today?"

"No, darling," her mother answered, "And we're not staying long. Are we invited in?"

"Well, sure, of course."

Once the Coreys were in the hall, they saw Rick, and Meg rushed to make introductions. "This is—" she began.

"Congressman Sainsbury," her father interrupted. "I followed your campaign with interest, and not just because my daughter lives in your district. Which we do not, so we'll let you be on your way."

"It's a pleasure to meet both of you, Mr. and Mrs. Corey. Your daughter and I share an interesting history, as she may have told you. But I am running late for a meeting, so I have to leave."

"No problem," Phillip Corey said, while Meg and her mother watched in amusement.

"I'll be in touch, Meg," Rick said as he went out the door.

"Thanks, Rick," Meg called out after him.

When the door shut behind him, Elizabeth Corey turned to Meg. "Well, that was interesting. How did you come to be on first-name terms with your new congressman?"

"I'll explain later," Meg said. "Not to be rude, but what are you doing here? I thought you weren't arriving until Tuesday."

"We aren't, officially. But your father is treating me to a couple of days at a very nice resort north of here, and there was something I wanted to drop off for you."

"Please, not wedding presents! I don't want any stuff, and that's why I didn't invite every family friend in the universe . . . although I hope you explained why."

"I know, I know, dear, and no, it's nothing like that." She turned to her husband. "Phillip, could you go get it?"

"Of course."

When her father went out to retrieve the mysterious "it" from the car, Meg asked, "What are you talking about?"

"You told me you hadn't decided what you wanted to wear for the wedding, right?"

"Yes. Please don't tell me you've brought your wedding dress." Meg quailed at the memory of that garment, which she'd seen now and then when she was growing up. She remembered lace and a lot of buttons.

"No, because I know quite well that's not your style. But did you know I saved my mother's outfit?"

Meg drew a blank. "Uh, no. Why?"

"I'm not sure you remember the story, but she and your grandfather married toward the end of World War Two. It was wartime, so they didn't have a big formal wedding. It was much more along the lines of what you're planning—a small event for family and close friends, in her parents' home. And she wore a very nice suit—it wasn't a traditional white dress, but it was something of a splurge for her. I thought it might fit you."

"Are we anywhere near the same size?" Meg asked.

Elizabeth smiled. "That's hard to say, but I brought it so we could find out. Ah, here's Phillip."

Meg's father appeared, carrying a full-length garment bag that looked vintage. "Safe and sound, my dear." He handed the bag to Meg.

Meg realized they were still standing in the front hall. "Good grief, I know you taught me better manners than this. Please, come all the way in. Can I get you anything? Coffee? Tea? Food?"

"Don't worry about us," her father told her. "We've got another hour's drive ahead of us. Come on. I want to see this thing on you before we go."

"Well, at least come to the dining room, where the light's better." She led the way, holding high the garment bag. Elizabeth and Phillip sat, watching expectantly, so Meg had no choice but to go ahead and unveil the contents of the bag. She hung the hook of the hanger over a door and unzipped the bag.

Once revealed, Meg knew she had never seen it before. It was a dove-gray suit, clearly belonging to the 1940s, with a cinched waist. The slender skirt fell to midknee. It was made of a lovely light wool, and it appeared to be in pristine condition. "This is really nice," Meg said, and meant it.

"Try on the jacket, will you?" her mother said. "We might as well know now whether it fits."

Meg slipped the jacket off the hanger and slid her arms into it. She pulled the halves of the front together and found that the buttons met easily. The sleeves were long enough. But most important, it felt right. Not too fussy, but still nice—not to mention historical, from her own family.

"It's perfect," her mother said quietly. "My mother would be happy if you'd wear it."

"Thank you," Meg said, fighting tears.

She looked up to see Seth standing in the kitchen doorway. "Sorry to interrupt. Hello, Elizabeth, Phillip—I didn't know you'd be here." He turned to Meg. "All's well with Rick?"

"I think so."

"You look great in that," Seth added.

"Good enough for the wedding?" Meg asked.

"Definitely."

Elizabeth stood up quickly. "Hello and good-bye, Seth— we've accomplished our mission here. We'll see you both next week." She stepped in to give Meg a quick hug, and ran her hand fondly over the suit jacket Meg was still wearing. "It does become you, sweetheart." Then she turned to her husband. "Come on, Phillip, we've miles to go before we sleep."

Phillip, smiling, raised a farewell hand and followed Elizabeth out the door.

"Okay, what just happened here?" Seth asked.

"My mother swooped in and gave me my grandmother's wedding dress—er, suit. I wish all my problems could be resolved so easily. But I think Rick will help, and I asked him to see if he could find Aaron a job, at least for a while. Something a cut above fencing in alpacas."

"Can you take off that jacket now?"

"Why? Do you hate it?"

"No, I think it's great. But I don't want to mess it up when I kiss you properly."

"Oh." Meg carefully removed the jacket, hung it back on its hanger, and turned and wrapped her arms around Seth's neck. "You mean, like this?"

32

Nicky and Brian had transformed the restaurant for the wedding and the party. Darkness fell early in December, so they had distributed candles everywhere possible (that was safe), and where there was a fire hazard, battery-run tea lights. The space inside glowed, sending golden light into the night and drawing the guests in.

Inside it was crowded, though short of packed. Nicky had known the capacity of the restaurant and had used it wisely. She wouldn't have gotten hung up on the legal limit, but she knew her business well enough to know what people's comfort level was. They wanted to be able to circulate easily; to stop and chat with friends and neighbors without feeling like they were clogging up the flow of traffic; to reach Nicky's wonderful food and walk away with a delightful sampling of bite-sized goodies without worrying about dropping them either on the floor or down the front of someone's shirt. Nicky had found the right balance.

Meg leaned back against Seth and admired the scene from their relatively quiet corner. This is what a wedding should be: happy people gathered together to celebrate. They'd let people come find them if they chose, and many of them did. Meg could see her parents deep in conversation with a pair of couples about their own age, on the opposite side of the room; Lydia and Christopher were standing close to each other, their heads together, and Meg wondered idly if there were any sparks there. They seemed to enjoy each other's company, but if they were seeing each other, they'd been very quiet about it. No matter. As if sensing her thoughts, Christopher excused himself to Lydia and came over to talk to them.

"That was a lovely ceremony, Christopher," Meg said. "I'm glad we stuck to the traditional text, with only a few small changes." Like discarding any reference to "obey."

"Ah, my dear, the old ways have survived this long for a good reason. I hope you both will be very happy. You certainly look happy."

"I am," Meg said simply. She had been in Granford two years short a month now, and was amazed at how her life had changed, in ways she never could have foreseen. Two years before she'd been jobless, all but homeless, and, yes, depressed. And that was before she had found a body in her yard. And back then, when Seth had first met her, he had thought she was either delusional or just annoying. Worse, his opinion had darkened even more when she had managed to involve his own family in solving that murder. How and when had that turned around? It was hard to remember now.

If she had realized she would end up working in agriculture, she might have managed her education differently, but becoming a farmer had just kind of happened, not that she regretted it. It was honest work, if demanding, and she took pride in her apple harvest. She was glad Bree had signed on with her to manage the orchard, and stuck with her this far. They'd turned a decent profit this year, despite some major obstacles, and Meg hoped next year would be better still, especially if they managed to install that automated irrigation system she coveted. Another year or two beyond that, the new trees that she and Seth owned together would begin bearing fruit. *Meg, what are you doing at your own wedding thinking about business?* She swallowed a laugh.

"Penny for your thoughts?" Seth's breath was warm on her neck as he leaned close to whisper in her ear.

"Irrigation plans. Oh, and that was a great shower this morning." And it had been ready just in time for the wedding—only a few days later than scheduled.

Seth burst out laughing. "You are the very soul of romance, Mrs. Chapin."

"Am I Mrs. Chapin? That's one more thing we never really settled. Ms. Chapin? Ms. Corey-Chapin? Or is that too much my mother's generation's kind of thing?"

"Whatever you want, Meg. My ego does not depend on what name you choose. Although I'm sure all those generations of ancestors around here might have other ideas."

"I'll think about it. At least I wouldn't have to change all my monograms."

"You have anything that's monogrammed?" Seth asked in mock horror.

"Nope. See? Easy."

"I'm glad Rachel came. Maggie seems not to mind the fuss."

"Babies are tough—they can sleep through anything. Like cats. Your mother and Christopher seem to be getting along well," Meg observed.

"No, she hasn't told me anything, if that's what you're asking."

"Maybe. It would be nice, wouldn't it? Christopher's one of the most interesting older men I've met."

Nicky bustled over. "How is everything? Do you like the food? I kind of mingled old favorites with some new experiments. Do you need your champagne topped up? The crowd doesn't look like it's going anywhere soon."

Meg laughed. "Nicky, take a breath. Do they have to leave at any particular time? Because we're happy to keep the party going as long as there's food and drink and people, not necessarily in that order."

"We're good on all of those, I think—I wouldn't skimp for you two, since this place probably wouldn't exist if it weren't for you. If there's anything left over, it will go to a local shelter."

"Good idea. Thank you."

As soon as Nicky had left, Rachel made her way over. "Maggie-lamb here needs feeding, so we should go. This has been so lovely! Just the right size, and all the people we wanted to see. And Christopher was great, wasn't he? I could listen to him say anything with that accent of his—British with just a dash of Aussie."

Meg smiled. "Obviously that's why we chose him. Patrick Stewart had a prior commitment, and Liam Neeson is filming on some other continent."

Rachel looked bewildered, then laughed. "Okay, you're kidding."

"Of course I am," Meg told her.

Rachel looked at the two of them with tears in her eyes. She dashed them away impatiently. "Leftover baby hormones. But let me say this: I am so happy that you two found each other, and I am sure that you will lead long and productive and contented lives, with just enough speed bumps to make things interesting. And on that note I will go home and give Maggie dinner and take my shoes off."

"I'm glad you all could come—even Maggie, although she won't remember her first wedding. We'll talk later."

"Bye, Rachel. Hey"—Seth nudged Meg—"over there."

Meg followed his gaze to see Aaron Eastman sidle in. He was wearing new clothes and had gotten a decent haircut, but that wasn't the biggest change. He stood straighter now, and actually smiled more. Rick had found him a job on his staff working in data management and had good things to say about him, and he'd promised to pursue the pardon angle, sooner or later. Meg figured it was the best possible outcome, at least for now.

Aaron looked up to see Meg watching him, so he moved through the crowd until he was standing in front of them. "Congratulations to you both."

"Thank you, Aaron. Hey, we haven't seen any alpacas lately. Did you finish the fencing?"

"I did. I'm trying to learn to follow through and finish what I start, and the Gardners are nice people, and I figured I owed them. Anyway, thanks for inviting me to the wedding—you and Seth deserve to be happy."

"So do you, Aaron," Meg said.

He ducked his head, but he was smiling. "Well, I'm definitely happier now than I was a month ago. By the way, I need to tell you that I'm glad you found me. Back then I wasn't sure I was going to make it, or wanted to, but things are looking up. Thank you both."

He moved away before Meg or Seth could respond. Meg felt Seth's arms tighten around her.

"You know, you might have said something a lot like that when I first met you," he said.

Meg turned to face him. "If you recall, my original plan was to fix up the house and sell it as fast as I could and get out of town. Things didn't quite work out that way, did they?"

Seth smiled at her. "Not exactly, but I reap the rewards. And I'm glad you think it's important to help people like Aaron."

"Some things are worth fighting for, Seth. I'm very glad I stayed."

"So am I."

Recipes

Spicy Fish

Wrapping up the apple harvest plus planning a wedding and solving a decades-old crime doesn't leave much time for cooking, so Meg looks for quick and easy recipes. Spicy Fish is a tasty solution. Most markets offer quick-frozen fish. Make sure you choose a firm-fleshed one (a more delicate fish like flounder or trout might not stand up to this recipe).

> 4 tablespoon olive oil
> 1 clove garlic, crushed or minced
> 1 cup flour
> 1 teaspoon ground cumin
> 1 tablespoon dry mustard
> 1 tablespoon ground turmeric
> 1 teaspoon ground white pepper

  1 teaspoon ground coriander
  1 teaspoon curry powder
  2 tablespoons cooking oil
  1 pound fish fillets (skinned)
  Salt and pepper to taste
  2 tablespoons lemon juice

In a small saucepan, heat the olive oil and garlic over medium heat until the garlic just begins to brown (about 3 minutes—do not burn!). Place in a small bowl and set aside to cool for an hour.

Combine the flour and spices in a large bowl.

In a cast-iron skillet, heat the cooking oil over medium-high.

Dredge the fish fillets in the flour-spice mixture and shake off the excess. Season with salt and black pepper. Place the fillets in the heated pan and cook until they begin to brown lightly (1–2 minutes). Turn the fillets in the pan, then immediately remove the pan from the heat and let the fish rest in the pan for about a minute.

Retrieve the garlic-flavored oil and whisk it with the lemon juice to make a kind of vinaigrette. Spoon it over the fish when you serve—it really brightens up the flavor.

Serve with rice, orzo, or couscous on the side.

Toffee Crunch Blondies

People who are working hard in the orchard all day need more than healthy meals, so Meg whips up these delectable Toffee Crunch Blondies that should please anyone with a sweet tooth.

½ cup butter, softened
1 cup brown sugar, packed
2 eggs, at room temperature
1 teaspoon vanilla
2 cups all-purpose flour
1 teaspoon baking powder
½ teaspoon baking soda
¼ teaspoon salt
2 tablespoons milk
1 cup toffee bits or chunks
1 cup chocolate chips or chunks
1 cup white chocolate chips

Preheat the oven to 350 degrees. Grease a 9"x13" pan.

In a large bowl, beat the butter and brown sugar until they are fluffy. Beat in the eggs and continue to beat until the mixture is creamy. Add the vanilla and blend.

Sift together the flour, baking powder, baking soda, and salt. Then stir it into the batter along with the milk.

By hand, stir in the two kinds of chocolate and the toffee chunks. (Use whatever form you like, but make sure the proportions are equal.)

Spread the dough evenly in the baking pan. Bake 25–30 minutes until the top is golden brown. Let cool, then cut into bars. Try not to eat them all at once!

Apple Cider Cake

Brian and Nicky Czarnecki are hosting Meg and Seth's wedding in their Granford restaurant, Gran's. Nicky is doing the cooking, and of course there will be cake—but not too fancy.

In honor of the bride who grows apples and the groom who rebuilds old houses, Nicky has found an antique recipe for apple cider cake that dates to 1827 (modernized just a bit for current use).

> 2 pounds flour (about 6 cups)
> 1 pound sugar (about 2 cups)
> 1 tablespoon baking powder
> 1–2 teaspoons cinnamon
> ½ teaspoon cloves (or more if you like)
> ½ pound butter, softened
> 2 cups cider
> One pound raisins or currants (soak these for a few
>   minutes in boiling water to soften them)

Preheat the oven to 350 degrees F.

In a *large* bowl, place the dry ingredients and whisk them together. Add the soft butter and work it in until it's evenly distributed (mixture will be crumbly).

Add the cider (fresh and local if you have it) and mix until you have a stiff batter. Add the raisins last and mix again.

Butter and flour a 9"x13" baking pan. Spoon the batter into the pan and smooth out the top. Place in the preheated oven and bake until the top is lightly browned and the edges begin to pull away from the pan—probably around an hour. Cool in the pan.

This is a hearty cake that tastes fine without dressing it up. But for a wedding, it would go well with maple frosting, maybe with a drizzle of caramel sauce. Watch it disappear!

"Another winner of a series."
—The Maine Suspect

FROM *NEW YORK TIMES* BESTSELLING AUTHOR
SHEILA CONNOLLY

The County Cork Mysteries

An Early Wake

Scandal in Skibbereen

Buried in a Bog

PRAISE FOR THE COUNTY CORK MYSTERIES

"Connolly invests this leisurely series opener with a
wealth of Irish color and background."
—*Richmond Times-Dispatch*

"[A] well-set and nicely paced cozy."
—*Library Journal*

sheilaconnolly.com
facebook.com/SheilaConnollyWriter
penguin.com

M1629T0115

P.O. 0005512812 202